STRANGE HAUNTS

STRANGE HAUNTS

STORIES BY
F. MARION CRAWFORD
&
H. B. MARRIOTT WATSON

COACHWHIP PUBLICATIONS
Landisville, Pennsylvania

Strange Haunts: Stories by F. Marion Crawford and H. B. Marriott Watson.
Copyright © 2011 Coachwhip Publications
No claim made on public domain material.

F. Marion Crawford (1854-1909)
H. B. Marriott Watson (1863-1921)

ISBN 1-61646-091-1
ISBN-13 978-1-61646-091-4

Cover Image: Trees (Hog Island Rec. Area, Florida) © Martha Dodd

CoachwhipBooks.com

CONTENTS

STORIES BY F. MARION CRAWFORD

STORIES BY H. B. MARRIOTT WATSON

Stories by
F. Marion Crawford

THE UPPER BERTH

I

Somebody asked for the cigars. We had talked long, and the conversation as beginning to languish; the tobacco smoke had got into the heavy curtains, he wine had got into those brains which were liable to become heavy, and it was already perfectly evident that, unless somebody did something to rouse our oppressed spirits, the meeting would soon come to its natural conclusion, and we, the guests, would speedily go home to bed, and most certainly to sleep. No one had said anything very remarkable; it may be that no one had anything very remarkable to say. Jones had given us every particular of his last hunting adventure in Yorkshire. Mr. Tompkins, of Boston, had explained at elaborate length those working principles, by the due and careful maintenance of which the Atchison, Topeka, and Santa Fé Railroad not only extended its territory, increased its departmental influence, and transported live stock without starving them to death before the day of actual delivery, but, also, had for years succeeded in deceiving those passengers who bought its tickets into the fallacious belief that the corporation aforesaid was really able to transport human life without destroying it. Signor Tombola had endeavoured to persuade us, by arguments which we took no trouble to oppose, that the unity of his country in no way resembled the average modern torpedo, carefully planned, constructed with all the skill of the greatest European arsenals, but, when constructed, destined to be directed by feeble hands into a region where it must undoubtedly explode,

unseen, unfeared, and unheard, into the illimitable wastes of
political chaos.

It is unnecessary to go into further details. The conversation
had assumed proportions which would have bored Prometheus on
his rock, which would have driven Tantalus to distraction, and
which would have impelled Ixion to seek relaxation in the simple
but instructive dialogues of Herr Ollendorff, rather than submit
to the greater evil of listening to our talk. We had sat at table for
hours; we were bored, we were tired, and nobody showed signs of
moving.

Somebody called for cigars. We all instinctively looked towards
the speaker. Brisbane was a man of five-and-thirty years of age,
and remarkable for those gifts which chiefly attract the attention
of men. He was a strong man. The external proportions of his figure presented nothing extraordinary to the common eye, though
his size was above the average. He was a little over six feet in height,
and moderately broad in the shoulder; he did not appear to be
stout, but, on the other hand, he was certainly not thin; his small
head was supported by a strong and sinewy neck; his broad, mus-
cular hands appeared to possess a peculiar skill in breaking wal-
nuts without the assistance of the ordinary cracker, and, seeing
him in profile, one could not help remarking the extraordinary
breadth of his sleeves, and the unusual thickness of his chest. He
was one of those men who are commonly spoken of among men as
deceptive; that is to say, that though he looked exceedingly strong
he was in reality very much stronger than he looked. Of his features I need say little. His head was small, his hair is thin, his eyes
are blue, his nose is large, he has a small moustache, and a square
jaw. Everybody knows Brisbane, and when he asked for a cigar
everybody looked at him.

"It is a very singular thing," said Brisbane.

Everybody stopped talking. Brisbane's voice was not loud, but
possessed a peculiar quality of penetrating general conversation,
and cutting it like a knife. Everybody listened. Brisbane, perceiv-
ing that he had attracted their general attention, lit his cigar with
great equanimity.

"It is very singular," he continued, "that thing about ghosts. People are always asking whether anybody has seen a ghost. I have."

"Bosh! What, you? You don't mean to say so, Brisbane? Well, for a man of his intelligence!"

A chorus of exclamations greeted Brisbane's remarkable statement. Everybody called for cigars, and Stubbs, the butler, suddenly appeared from the depths of nowhere with a fresh bottle of dry champagne. The situation was saved; Brisbane was going to tell a story.

I am an old sailor, said Brisbane, and as I have to cross the Atlantic pretty often, I have my favourites. Most men have their favourites. I have seen a man wait in a Broadway bar for three-quarters of an hour for a particular car which he liked. I believe the bar-keeper made at least one-third of his living by that man's preference. I have a habit of waiting for certain ships when I am obliged to cross that duck-pond. It may be a prejudice, but I was never cheated out of a good passage but once in my life. I remember it very well; it was a warm morning in June, and the Custom House officials, who were hanging about waiting for a steamer already on her way up from the Quarantine, presented a peculiarly hazy and thoughtful appearance. I had not much luggage—I never have. I mingled with the crowd of passengers, porters, and officious individuals in blue coats and brass buttons, who seemed to spring up like mushrooms from the deck of a moored steamer to obtrude their unnecessary services upon the independent passenger. I have often noticed with a certain interest the spontaneous evolution of these fellows. They are not there when you arrive; five minutes after the pilot has called 'Go ahead!' they, or at least their blue coats and brass buttons, have disappeared from deck and gangway as completely as though they had been consigned to that locker which tradition ascribes to Davy Jones. But, at the moment of starting, they are there, clean shaved, blue coated, and ravenous for fees. I hastened on board. The *Kamtschatka* was one of my favourite ships. I saw was, because she emphatically no longer is. I cannot conceive of any inducement which could entice me to make another voyage in her. Yes, I know what you are going to say. She is uncommonly clean in the run aft, she has enough bluffing off in the bows to keep her dry, and the lower berths are most of them double. She has a lot of advantages, but I won't cross in her again. Excuse the digression. I got on board. I hailed a steward, whose red nose and redder whiskers were equally familiar to me.

"One hundred and five, lower berth," said I, in the business-like tone peculiar to men who think no more of crossing the Atlantic than taking a whisky cocktail at down-town Delmonico's.

The steward took my portmanteau, greatcoat, and rug. I shall never forget the expression on his face. Not that he turned pale. It is maintained by the most eminent divines that even miracles cannot change the course of nature. I have no hesitation in saying that he did not turn pale; but, from his expression, I judged that he was either about to shed tears, to sneeze, or to drop my portmanteau. As the latter contained two bottles of particularly fine old sherry presented to me for my voyage by my old friend Snigginson van Pickyns, I felt extremely nervous. But the steward did none of these things.

"Well, I'm d—d!" said he in a low voice, and led the way.

I supposed my Hermes, as he led me to the lower regions, had had a little grog, but I said nothing, and followed him. One hundred and five was on the port side, well aft. There was nothing remarkable about the state-room. The lower berth, like most of those upon the *Kamtschatka*, was double. There was plenty of room; there was the usual washing apparatus, calculated to convey an idea of luxury to the mind of a North American Indian; there were the usual inefficient racks of brown wood, in which it is more easy to hand a large-sized umbrella than the common tooth-brush of commerce. Upon the uninviting mattresses were carefully bolded together those blankets which a great modern humorist has aptly compared to cold buckwheat cakes. The question of towels was left entirely to the imagination. The glass decanters were filled with a transparent liquid faintly tinged with brown, but from which an odour less faint, but not more pleasing, ascended to the nostrils, like a far-off sea-sick reminiscence of oily machinery. Sad-coloured curtains half-closed the upper berth. The hazy June daylight shed a faint illumination upon the desolate little scene. Ugh! how I hate that state-room!

The steward deposited my traps and looked at me, as though he wanted to get away—probably in search of more passengers and more fees. It is always a good plan to start in favour with those functionaries, and I accordingly gave him certain coins there and then.

"I'll try and make yer comfortable all I can," he remarked, as he put the coins in his pocket. Nevertheless, there was a doubtful intonation in his voice which surprised me. Possibly his scale of fees had gone up, and he was not satisfied; but on the whole I was inclined to think that, as he himself would have expressed it, he was "the better for a glass." I was wrong, however, and did the man injustice.

II

Nothing especially worthy of mention occurred during that day. We left the pier punctually, and it was very pleasant to be fairly under way, for the weather was warm and sultry, and the motion of the steamer produced a refreshing breeze. Everybody knows what the first day at sea is like. People pace the decks and stare at each other, and occasionally meet acquaintances whom they did not know to be on board. There is the usual uncertainty as to whether the food will be good, bad, or indifferent, until the first two meals have put the matter beyond a doubt; there is the usual uncertainty about the weather, until the ship is fairly off Fire Island. The tables are crowded at first, and then suddenly thinned. Pale-faced people spring from their seats and precipitate themselves towards the door, and each old sailor breathes more freely as his sea-sick neighbour rushes from his side, leaving him plenty of elbow-room and an unlimited command over the mustard.

One passage across the Atlantic is very much like another, and we who cross very often do not make the voyage for the sake of novelty. Whales and icebergs are indeed always objects of interest, but, after all, one whale is very much like another whale, and one rarely sees an iceberg at close quarters. To the majority of us the most delightful moment of the day on board an ocean steamer is when we have taken our last turn on deck, have smoked our last cigar, and having succeeded in tiring ourselves, feel at liberty to turn in with a clear conscience. On that first night of the voyage I felt particularly lazy, and went to bed in one hundred and five rather earlier than I usually do. As I turned in, I was amazed to see that I was to have a companion. A portmanteau, very like my own, lay in the opposite corner, and in the upper berth had been deposited a neatly-folded rug, with a stick and umbrella. I had hoped to be alone, and I was disappointed; but I wondered who my roommate was to be, and I determined to have a look at him.

Before I had been long in bed he entered. He was, as far as I could see, a very tall man, very thin, very pale, with sandy hair and whiskers and colourless grey eyes. He had about him, I thought, an air of rather dubious fashion; the short of man you might see in Wall Street, without being able precisely to say what he was doing there—the sort of man who frequents the Café Anglais, who always seems to be alone and who drinks champagne; you might meet him on a racecourse, but he would never appear to be doing anything there either. A little over-dressed—a little odd. There are three or four of his kind on every ocean steamer. I made up my mind that I did not care to make his acquaintance, and I went to sleep saying to myself that I would study his habits in order to avoid him. If he rose early, I would rise late; if he went to bed late, I would go to bed early. I did not care to know him. If you once know people of that kind they are always turning up. Poor fellow! I need not have taken the trouble to come to so many decisions about him, for I never saw him again after that first night in one hundred and five.

I was sleeping soundly when I was suddenly waked by a loud noise. To judge from the sound, my room-mate must have sprung with a single leap from the upper berth to the floor. I heard him fumbling with the latch and bolt of the door, which opened almost immediately, and then I heard his footsteps as he ran at full speed down the passage, leaving the door open behind him. The ship was rolling a little, and I expected to hear him stumble or fall, but he ran as though he were running for his life. The door swung on its hinges with the motion of the vessel, and the sound annoyed me. I got up and shut it, and groped my way back to my berth in the darkness. I went to sleep again; but I have no idea how long I slept.

When I awoke it was still quite dark, but I felt a disagreeable sensation of cold, and it seemed to me that the air was damp. You know the peculiar smell of a cabin which has been wet with sea-water. I covered myself up as well as I could and dozed off again, framing complaints to be made the next day, and selecting the most powerful epithets in the language. I could hear my room-mate turn over in the upper berth. He had probably returned while I was asleep. Once I thought I heard him groan, and I argued that he was sea-sick. That is particularly unpleasant when one is below. Nevertheless I dozed off and slept till early daylight.

The ship was rolling heavily, much more than on the previous evening, and the grey light which came in through the porthole changed in tint with every movement according as the angle of the vessel's side turned the glass seawards or skywards. It was very cold—unaccountably so for the month of June. I turned my head and looked at the porthole, and saw to my surprise that it was wide open and hooked back. I believe I swore audibly. Then I got up and shut it. As I turned back I glanced at the upper berth. The curtains were drawn close together; my companion had probably felt cold as well as I. It struck me that I had slept enough. The stateroom was uncomfortable, though, strange to say, I could not smell the dampness which had annoyed me in the night. My room-mate was still asleep—excellent opportunity for avoiding him, so I dressed at once and went on deck. The day was warm and cloudy, with an oily smell on the water. It was seven o'clock as I came out—much later than I had imagined. I came across the doctor, who was taking his first sniff of the morning air. He was a young man from the West of Ireland—a tremendous fellow, with black hair and blue eyes, already inclined to be stout; he had a happy-go-lucky, healthy look about him which was rather attractive.

"Fine morning," I remarked, by way of introduction.

"Well," said he, eyeing me with an air of ready interest, "it's a fine morning and it's not a fine morning. I don't think it's much of a morning."

"Well, no—it is not so very fine," said I.

"It's just what I call fuggly weather," replied the doctor.

"It was very cold last night, I thought," I remarked. "However, when I looked about, I found that the porthole was wide open. I had not noticed it when I went to bed. And the state-room was damp, too."

"Damp!" said he. "Whereabouts are you?"

"One hundred and five—"

To my surprise the doctor started visibly, and stared at me.

"What is the matter?" I asked.

"Oh—nothing," he answered; "only everybody has complained of that state-room for the last three trips."

"I shall complain too," I said. "It has certainly not been properly aired. It is a shame!"

"I don't believe it can be helped," answered the doctor. "I believe there is something—well, it is not my business to frighten passengers."

"You need not be afraid of frightening me," I replied. "I can stand any amount of damp. If I should get a bad cold I will come to you."

I offered the doctor a cigar, which he took and examined very critically.

"It is not so much the damp," he remarked. "However, I dare say you will get on very well. Have you a room-mate?"

"Yes; a deuce of a fellow, who bolts out in the middle of the night, and leaves the door open."

Again the doctor glanced curiously at me. Then he lit the cigar and looked grave.

"Did he come back?" he asked presently.

"Yes. I was asleep, but I waked up, and heard him moving. Then I felt cold and went to sleep again. This morning I found the porthole open."

"Look here," said the doctor quietly, "I don't care much for this ship. I don't care a rap for her reputation. I tell you what I will do. I have a good-sized place up here. I will share it with you, though I don't know you from Adam."

I was very much surprised at the proposition. I could not imagine why he should take such a sudden interest in my welfare. However, his manner as he spoke of the ship was peculiar.

"You are very good, doctor," I said. "But, really, I believe even now the cabin could be aired, or cleaned out, or something. Why do you not care for the ship?"

"We are not superstitious in our profession, sir," replied the doctor, "but the sea makes people so. I don't want to prejudice you, and I don't want to frighten you, but if you will take my advice you will move in here. I would as soon see you overboard," he added earnestly, "as know that you or any other man was to sleep in one hundred and five."

"Good gracious! Why?" I asked.

"Just because on the last three trips the people who have slept there actually have gone overboard," he answered gravely.

The intelligence was startling and exceedingly unpleasant, I confess. I looked hard at the doctor to see whether he was making game of me, but he looked perfectly serious. I thanked him warmly for his offer, but told him I intended to be the exception to the rule by which every one who slept in that particular state-room went overboard. He did not say much, but looked as grave as ever, and hinted that, before we got across, I should probably reconsider his proposal. In the course of time we went to breakfast, at which only an inconsiderable number of passengers assembled. I noticed that one or two of the officers who breakfasted with us looked grave. After breakfast I went into my state-room in order to get a book. The curtains of the upper berth were still closely drawn. Not a word was to be heard. My room-mate was probably still asleep.

As I came out I met the steward whose business it was to look after me. He whispered that the captain wanted to see me, and then scuttled away down the passage as if very anxious to avoid any

questions. I went toward the captain's cabin, and found him waiting for me.

"Sir," said he, "I want to ask a favour of you."

I answered that I would do anything to oblige him.

"Your room-mate had disappeared," he said. "He is known to
have turned in early last night. Did you notice anything extraordinary in his manner?"

The question coming, as it did, in exact confirmation of the
fears the doctor had expressed half an hour earlier, staggered me.

"You don't mean to say he has gone overboard?" I asked.

"I fear he has," answered the captain.

"This is the most extraordinary thing—" I began.

"Why?" he asked.

"He is the fourth, then?" I exclaimed. In answer to another
question from the captain, I explained, without mentioning the
doctor, that I had heard the story concerning one hundred and five.
He seemed very much annoyed at hearing that I knew of it. I told
him what had occurred in the night.

"What you say," he replied, "coincides almost exactly with what
was told me by the room-mates of two of the other three. They bolt
out of bed and run down the passage. Two of them were seen to go
overboard by the watch; we stopped and lowered boats, but they
were not found. Nobody, however, saw or heard the man who was
lost last night—if he is really lost. The steward, who is a superstitious fellow, perhaps, and expected something to go wrong, went
to look for him, this morning, and found his berth empty, but his
clothes lying about, just as he had left them. The steward was the
only man on board who knew him by sight, and he has been searching everywhere for him. He has disappeared! Now, sir, I want to
beg you not to mention the circumstance to any of the passengers;
I don't want the ship to get a bad name, and nothing hangs about
an ocean-goer like stories of suicides. You shall have your choice
of any one of the officers' cabins you like, including my own, for
the rest of the passage. Is that a fair bargain?"

"Very," said I; "and I am much obliged to you. But since I am
alone, and have the state-room to myself, I would rather not move.

If the steward will take out that unfortunate man's things, I would as leave stay where I am. I will not say anything about the matter, and I think I can promise you that I will not follow my room-mate."

The captain tried to dissuade me from my intention, but I preferred having a state-room alone to being the chum of any officer on board. I do not know whether I aced foolishly, but if I had taken his advice I should have had nothing more to tell. There would have remained the disagreeable coincidence of several suicides occurring among men who had slept in the same cabin, but that would have been all.

That was not the end of the matter, however, by any means. I obstinately made up my mind that I would not be disturbed by such tales, and I even went so far as to argue the question with the captain. There was something wrong about the state-room, I said. It was rather damp. The porthole had been left open last night. My room-mate might have been ill when he came on board, and he might have become delirious after he went to bed. He might even now be hiding somewhere on board, and might be found later. The place ought to be aired and the fastening on the port looked to. If the captain would give me leave, I would see that what I thought necessary were done immediately.

"Of course you have a right to stay where you are if you please," he replied, rather petulantly; "but I wish you would turn out and let me lock the place up, and be done with it."

I did not see it in the same light, and left the captain, after promising to be silent concerning the disappearance of my companion. The latter had had no acquaintances on board, and was not missed in the course of the day. Towards evening I met the doctor again, and he asked me whether I had changed my mind. I told him I had not.

"Then you will before long," he said, very gravely.

III

We played whist in the evening, and I went to bed late. I will confess now that I felt a disagreeable sensation when I entered my state-room. I could not help thinking of the tall man I had seen on the previous night, who was now dead, drowned, tossing about in the long swell, two or three hundred miles astern. His face rose very distinctly before me as I undressed, and I even went so far as to draw back the curtains of the upper berth, as though to persuade myself that he was actually gone. I also bolted the door of the state-room. Suddenly I became aware that the porthole was open, and fastened back. This was more than I could stand. I hastily threw on my dressing-gown and went in search of Robert, the steward of my passage. I was very angry, I remember, and when I found him I dragged him roughly to the door of one hundred and five, and pushed him towards the open porthole.

"What the deuce do you mean, you scoundrel, by leaving that port open every night? Don't you know it is against the regulations? Don't you know that if the ship heeled and the water began to come in, ten men could not shut it? I will report you to the captain, you blackguard, for endangering the ship!"

I was exceedingly wroth. The man trembled and turned pale, and then began to shut the round glass plate with the heavy brass fittings.

"Why don't you answer me?" I said roughly.

"If you please, sir," faltered Robert, "there's nobody on board as can keep this 'ere port shut at night. You can try it yourself, sir. I ain't a-going to stop hany longer on board o' this vessel, sir; I ain't, indeed. But if I was you, sir, I'd just clear out and go and sleep with the surgeon, or something, I would. Look 'ere, sir, is that fastened what you may call securely, or not, sir? Try it, sir, see if it will move a hinch."

I tried the port, and found it perfectly tight.

"Well, sir," continued Robert triumphantly, "I wager my reputation as a A1 steward that in 'arf an hour it will be open again; fastened back, too, sir, that's the horful thing—fastened back!"

I examined the great screw and the looped nut that ran on it.

"If I find it open in the night, Robert, I will give you a sovereign. It is not possible. You may go."

"Soverin' did you say, sir? Very good, sir. Thank ye, sir. Good-night, sir. Pleasant reepose, sir, and all manner of hinchantin' dreams, sir."

Robert scuttled away, delighted at being released. Of course, I thought he was trying to account for his negligence by a silly story, intended to frighten me, and I disbelieved him. The consequence was that he got his sovereign, and I spent a very peculiarly unpleasant night.

I went to bed, and five minutes after I had rolled myself up in my blankets the inexorable Robert extinguished the light that burned steadily behind the ground-glass pane near the door. I lay quite still in the dark trying to go to sleep, but I soon found that impossible. It had been some satisfaction to be angry with the steward, and the diversion had banished that unpleasant sensation I had at first experienced when I thought of the drowned man who had been my chum; but I was no longer sleepy, and I lay awake for some time, occasionally glancing at the porthole, which I could just see from where I lay, and which, in the darkness, looked like a faintly-luminous soup-plate suspended in blackness. I believe I must have lain there for an hour, and, as I remember, I was just dozing into sleep when I was roused by a draught of cold air, and by distinctly feeling the spray of the sea blown upon my face. I started to my feet, and not having allowed in the dark for the motion of the ship, I was instantly thrown violently across the stateroom upon the couch which was placed beneath the port-hole. I recovered myself immediately, however, and climbed upon my knees. The port-hole was again wide open and fastened back!

Now these things are facts. I was wide awake when I got up, and I should certainly have been waked by the fall had I still been dozing. Moreover, I bruised my elbows and knees badly, and the bruises were there on the following morning to testify to the fact, if I myself had doubted it. The porthole was wide open and fastened back—a thing so unaccountable that I remember very well feeling astonishment rather that fear when I discovered it. I at once closed the plate again, and screwed down the loop nut with all my strength. It was very dark in the state-room. I reflected that the port had certainly been opened within an hour after Robert had at first shut it in my presence, and I determined to watch it, and see whether it would open again. Those brass fittings are very heavy and by no means easy to move; I could not believe that the clamp had been turned by the shaking of the screw. I stood peering out through the thick glass at the alternate white and grey streaks of the sea that foamed beneath the ship's side. I must have remained there a quarter of an hour.

Suddenly, as I stood, I distinctly heard something moving behind me in one of the berths, and a moment afterwards, just as I turned instinctively to look—though I could, of course, see nothing in the darkness—I heard a very faint groan. I sprang across the state-room, and tore the curtains of the upper berth aside, thrusting in my hands to discover if there were any one there. There was some one.

I remember that the sensation as I put my hands forward was as though I were plunging them into the air of a damp cellar, and from behind the curtains came a gust of wind that smelled horribly of stagnant sea-water. I laid hold of something that had the shape of a man's arm, but was smooth, and wet, and icy cold. But suddenly, as I pulled, the creature sprang violently forward against me, a clammy oozy mass, as it seemed to me, heavy and wet, yet endowed with a sort of supernatural strength. I reeled across the state-room, and in an instant the door opened and the thing rushed out. I had not had time to be frightened, and quickly recovering myself, I sprang through the door and gave chase at the top of my speed, but I was too late. Ten yards before me I could see—I am sure I saw it—a dark shadow moving in the dimly lighted passage, quickly as the shadow of a fast horse thrown before a dog-cart by the lamp on a dark night. But in a moment it had disappeared, and I found myself holding on to the polished rail that ran along the bulkhead where the passage turned towards the companion. My hair stood on end, and the cold perspiration rolled down my face. I am not ashamed of it in the least: I was very badly frightened.

Still I doubted my senses, and pulled myself together. It was absurd, I thought. The Welsh rare-bit I had eaten had disagreed with me. I had been in a nightmare. I made my way back to my state-room, and entered it with an effort. The whole place smelled of stagnant sea-water, as it had when I had waked on the previous evening. It required my utmost strength to go in, and grope among my things for a box of wax lights. As I lighted a railway reading lantern which I always carry in case I want to read after the lamps are out, I perceived that the porthole was again open, and a sort of creeping horror began to take possession of me which I never felt before, nor wish to feel again. But I got a light and proceeded to examine the upper berth, expecting to find it drenched with sea-water.

But I was disappointed. The bed had been slept in, and the smell of the sea was strong; but the bedding was as dry as a bone. I fancied that Robert had not had the courage to make the bed after the accident of the previous night—it had all been a hideous dream. I drew the curtains back as far as I could and examined the place very carefully. It was perfectly dry. But the porthole was open again. With a sort of dull bewilderment of horror I closed it and screwed it down, and thrusting my heavy stick through the brass loop, wrenched it with all my might, till the thick metal began to bend under the pressure. Then I hooked my reading lantern into the red velvet at the head of the couch, and sat down to recover my senses if I could. I sat there all night, unable to think of rest—hardly able to think at all. But the porthole remained closed, and I did not believe it would now open again without the application of a considerable force.

The morning dawned at last, and I dressed myself slowly, thinking over all that had happened in the night. It was a beautiful day and I went on deck, glad to get out into the early, pure sunshine, and to smell the breeze from the blue water, so different from the noisome, stagnant odour of my state-room. Instinctively I turned aft, towards the surgeon's cabin. There he stood, with a pipe in his mouth, taking his morning airing precisely as on the preceding day.

"Good-morning," said he quietly, but looking at me with evident curiosity.

"Doctor, you were quite right," said I. "There is something wrong about that place."

"I thought you would change your mind," he answered, rather triumphantly. "You have had a bad night, eh? Shall I make you a pick-me-up? I have a capital recipe."

"No, thanks," I cried. "But I would like to tell you what happened."

I then tried to explain as clearly as possible precisely what had occurred, not omitting to state that I had been scared as I had never been scared in my whole life before. I dwelt particularly on the phenomenon of the porthole, which was a fact to which I could testify, even if the rest had been an illusion. I had closed it twice in the night, and the second time I had actually bent the brass in wrenching it with my stick. I believe I insisted a good deal on this point.

"You seem to think I am likely to doubt the story," said the doctor, smiling at my detailed account of the state of the porthole. "I do not doubt in the least. I renew my invitation to you. Bring your traps here, and take half my cabin."

"Come and take half of mine for one night," I said. "Help me to get at the bottom of this thing."

"You will get to the bottom of something else if you try," answered the doctor.

"What?" I asked.

"The bottom of the sea. I am going to leave this ship. It is not canny."

"Then you will not help me to find out—"

"Not I," said the doctor quickly. "It is my business to keep my wits about me—not to go fiddling about with ghosts and things."

"Do you really believe it is a ghost?" I enquired, rather contemptuously. But as I spoke I remembered very well the horrible sensation of the supernatural which had got possession of me during the night. The doctor turned sharply on me—

"Have you any reasonable explanation of these things to offer?" he asked. "No; you have not. Well, you say you will find an explanation. I say that you won't, sir, simply because there is not any."

"But, my dear sir," I retorted, "do you, a man of science, mean to tell me that such things cannot be explained?"

"I do," he answered stoutly. "And, if they could, I would not be concerned in the explanation."

I did not care to spend another night alone in the state-room, and yet I was obstinately determined to get at the root of the disturbances. I do not believe there are many men who would have slept there alone, after passing two such nights. But I made up my mind to try it, if I could not get any one to share a watch with me. The doctor was evidently not inclined for such an experiment. He said he was a surgeon, and that in case any accident occurred on board he must be always in readiness. He could not afford to have his nerves unsettled. Perhaps he was quite right, but I am inclined to think that his precaution was prompted by his inclination. On enquiry, he informed me that there was no one on board who would be likely to join me in my investigations, and after a little more conversation I left him. A little later I met the captain, and told him my story. I said that, if no one would spend the night with me, I would ask leave to have the light burning all night, and would try it alone.

"Look here," said he, "I will tell you what I will do. I will share your watch myself, and we will see what happens. It is my belief that we can find out between us. There may be some fellow skulking on board, who steals a passage by frightening the passengers. It is just possible that there may be something queer in the carpentering of that berth."

I suggested taking the ship's carpenter below and examining the place; but I was overjoyed at the captain's offer to spend the night with me. He accordingly sent for the workman and ordered him to do anything I required. We went below at once. I had all the bedding cleared out of the upper berth, and we examined the place thoroughly to see if there was a board loose anywhere, or a panel which could be opened or pushed aside. We tried the planks everywhere, tapped the flooring, unscrewed the fittings of the lower berth and took it to pieces—in short, there was not a square inch of the state-room which was not searched and tested. Everything was in perfect order, and we put everything back in its place. As we were finishing our work, Robert came to the door and looked in.

"Well, sir—find anything, sir?" he asked, with a ghastly grin.

"You were right about the porthole, Robert," I said, and I gave him the promised sovereign. The carpenter did his work silently and skilfully, following my directions. When he had done he spoke.

"I'm a plain man, sir," he said. "But it's my belief you had better just turn out your things, and let me run half a dozen four-inch screws through the door of this cabin. There's no good never came o' this cabin yet, sir, and that's all about it. There's been four lives lost out o' here to my own remembrance, and that is four trips. Better give it up, sir—better give it up!"

"I will try it for one night more," I said.

"Better give it up, sir—better give it up! It's a precious bad job," repeated the workman, putting his tools in his bag and leaving the cabin.

But my spirits had risen considerably at the prospect of having the captain's company, and I made up my mind not to be prevented from going to the end of this strange business. I abstained from Welsh rare-bits and grog that evening, and did not even join in the customary game of whist. I wanted to be quite sure of my nerves, and my vanity made me anxious to make a good figure in the captain's eyes.

IV

The captain was one of those splendidly tough and cheerful specimens of seafaring humanity whose combined courage, hardihood, and calmness in difficulty leads them naturally into high positions of trust. He was not the man to be led away by an idle tale, and the mere fact that he was willing to join me in the investigation was proof that he thought there was something seriously wrong, which could not be accounted for on ordinary theories, nor laughed down as a common superstition. To some extent, too, his reputation was at stake, as well as the reputation of the ship. It is no light thing to lose passengers overboard, and he knew it.

About ten o'clock that evening, as I was smoking a last cigar, he came up to me, and drew me aside from the beat of the other passengers who were patrolling the deck in the warm darkness.

"This is a serious matter, Mr. Brisbane," he said. "We must make up our minds either way—to be disappointed or to have a pretty rough time of it. You see I cannot afford to laugh at the affair, and I will ask you to sign your name to a statement of whatever occurs. If nothing happens tonight we will try it again tomorrow and next day. Are you ready?"

So we went below, and entered the state-room. As we went in I could see Robert the steward, who stood a little further down the passage, watching us, with his usual grin, as though certain that something dreadful was about to happen. The captain closed the door behind us and bolted it.

"Supposing we put your portmanteau before the door," he suggested. "One of us can sit on it. Nothing can get out then. Is the port screwed down?"

I found it as I had left it in the morning. Indeed, without using a lever, as I had done, no one could have opened it. I drew back the curtains of the upper berth so that I could see well into it. By the captain's advice I lighted my reading lantern, and placed it so that it shone upon the white sheets above. He insisted upon sitting on the portmanteau, declaring that he wished to be able to swear that he had sat before the door.

Then he requested me to search the state-room thoroughly, an operation very soon accomplished, as it consisted merely in looking beneath the lower berth and under the couch below the porthole. The spaces were quite empty.

"It is impossible for any human being to get in," I said, "or for any human being to open the port."

"Very good," said the captain calmly. "If we see anything now, it must be either imagination or something supernatural."

I sat down on the edge of the lower berth.

"The first time it happened," said the captain, crossing his legs and leaning back against the door, "was in March. The passenger who slept here, in the upper berth, turned out have been a lunatic—at all events, he was known to have been a little touched, and he had taken his passage without the knowledge of his friends. He rushed out in the middle of the night, and threw himself overboard, before the officer who had the watch could stop him. We stopped and lowered a boat; it was a quiet night, just before that heavy weather came on; but we could not find him. Of course his suicide was afterwards accounted for on the ground of his insanity."

"I suppose that often happens?" I remarked, rather absently.

"Not often—no," said the captain; "never before in my experience, though I have heard of it happening on board of other ships. Well, as I was saying, that occurred in March. On the very next trip— What are you looking at?" he asked, stopping suddenly in his narration.

I believe I gave no answer. My eyes were riveted upon the port-hole. It seemed to me that the brass loop-nut was beginning to turn very slowly upon the screw—so slowly, however, that I was not sure it moved at all. I watched it intently, fixing its position in my mind, and trying to ascertain whether it changed. Seeing where I was looking, the captain looked too.

"It moves!" he exclaimed, in a tone of conviction. "No, it does not," he added, after a minute.

"If it were the jarring of the screw," said I, "it would have opened during the day; but I found it this evening jammed tight as I left it this morning."

I rose and tried the nut. It was certainly loosened, for by an effort I could move it with my hands.

"The queer thing," said the captain, "is that the second man who was lost is supposed to have got through that very port. We had a terrible time over it. It was in the middle of the night, and the weather was very heavy; there was an alarm that one of the ports was open and the sea running in. I came below and found everything flooded, the water pouring in every time she rolled, and the whole port swinging from the top bolts—not the porthole in the middle. Well, we managed to shut it, but the water did some damage. Ever since that the place smells of sea-water from time to time. We supposed the passenger had thrown himself out, though the Lord only knows how he did it. The steward kept telling me that he cannot keep anything shut here. Upon my word—I can smell it now, cannot you?" he enquired, sniffing the air suspiciously.

"Yes—distinctly," I said, and I shuddered as that same odour of stagnant sea-water grew stronger in the cabin. "Now, to smell like this, the place must be damp," I continued, "and yet when I examined it with the carpenter this morning everything was perfectly dry. It is most extraordinary—hallo!"

My reading lantern, which had been placed in the upper berth, was suddenly extinguished. There was still a good deal of light from the pane of ground glass near the door, behind which loomed the regulation lamp. The ship rolled heavily, and the curtain of the upper berth swung far out into the state-room and back again. I rose quickly from my seat on the edge of the bed, and the captain at the same moment started to his feet with a loud cry of surprise. I had turned with the intention of taking down the lantern to examine it, when I heard his exclamation, and immediately afterwards his call for help. I sprang towards him. He was wrestling with all his might with the brass loop of the port. It seemed to turn against his hands in spite of all his efforts. I caught up my cane, a heavy oak stick I always used to carry, and thrust it through the ring and bore on it with all my strength. But the strong wood snapped suddenly and I fell upon the couch. When I rose again the port was wide open, and the captain was standing with his back against the door, pale to the lips.

"There is something in that berth!" he cried, in a strange voice, his eyes almost starting from his head. "Hold the door, while I look—it shall not escape us, whatever it is!"

But instead of taking his place, I sprang upon the lower bed, and seized something which lay in the upper berth.

It was something ghostly, horrible beyond words, and it moved in my grip. It was like the body of a man long drowned, and yet it moved, and had the strength of ten men living; but I gripped it with all my might—the slippery, oozy, horrible thing—the dead white eyes seemed to stare at me out of the dusk; the putrid odour of rank sea-water was about it, and its shiny hair hung in foul wet curls over its dead face. I wrestled with the dead thing; it thrust itself upon me and forced me back and nearly broke my arms; it wound its corpse's arms about my neck, the living death, and over-powered me, so that I, at last, cried aloud and fell, and left my hold.

As I fell the thing sprang across me, and seemed to throw itself upon the captain. When I last saw him on his feet his face was white and his lips set. It seemed to me that he struck a violent blow at the dead being, and then he, too, fell forward upon his face, with an inarticulate cry of horror.

The thing paused an instant, seeming to hover over his pros-trate body, and I could have screamed again for very fright, but I had no voice left. The thing vanished suddenly, and it seemed to my disturbed senses that it made its exit through the open port, though how that was possible, considering the smallness of the aperture, is more than any one can tell. I lay a long time on the floor, and the captain lay beside me. At last I partially recovered my senses and moved, and instantly I knew that my arm was bro-ken—the small bone of my left forearm near the wrist.

I got upon my feet somehow, and with my remaining hand I tried to raise the captain. He groaned and moved, and at last came to himself. He was not hurt, but he seemed badly stunned.

Well, do you want to hear any more? There is nothing more. That is the end of my story. The carpenter carried out his scheme of running half a dozen four-inch screws through the door of one hundred and five; and if ever you take a passage in the *Kam-tschatka*, you may ask for a berth in that state-room. You will be told that it is engaged—yes—it is engaged by that dead thing.

I finished the trip in the surgeon's cabin. He doctored my bro-ken arm, and advised me not to "fiddle about with ghosts and things" any more. The captain was very silent, and never sailed again in that ship, though it is still running. And I will not sail in her either. It was a very disagreeable experience, and I was very badly frightened, which is a thing I do not like. That is all. That is how I saw a ghost—if it was a ghost. It was dead, anyhow.

By the Waters of Paradise

I

I remember my childhood very distinctly. I do not think that the fact argues a good memory, for I have never been clever at learning words by heart, in prose or rhyme; so that I believe my remembrance of events depends much more upon the events themselves than upon my possessing any special facility for recalling them. Perhaps I am too imaginative, and the earliest impressions I received were of a kind to stimulate the imagination abnormally. A long series of little misfortunes, connected with each other so as to suggest a sort of weird fatality, so worked upon my melancholy temperament when I was a boy that, before I was of age, I sincerely believed myself to be under a curse, and not only myself, but my whole family, and every individual who bore my name.

I was born in the old place where my father, and his father, and all his predecessors had been born, beyond the memory of man. It is a very old house, and the greater part of it was originally a castle, strongly fortified, and surrounded by a deep moat supplied with abundant water from the hills by a hidden aqueduct. Many of the fortifications have been destroyed, and the moat has been filled up. The water from the aqueduct supplies great fountains, and runs down into huge oblong basins in the terraced gardens, one below the other, each surrounded by a broad pavement of marble between the water and the flower-beds. The waste surplus finally escapes through an artificial grotto, some thirty yards long, into a stream, flowing down through the park to the meadows beyond, and thence to the distant river. The buildings were extended a little and greatly altered more than two hundred years ago, in the time of Charles II., but since then little has been done to improve them, though they have been kept in fairly good repair, according to our fortunes.

In the gardens there are terraces and huge hedges of box and evergreen, some of which used to be clipped into shapes of animals, in the Italian style. I can remember when I was a lad how I used to try to make out what the trees were cut to represent, and how I used to appeal for explanations to Judith, my Welsh nurse. She dealt in a strange mythology of her own, and peopled the gardens with griffins, dragons, good genii and bad, and filled my mind with them at the same time. My nursery window afforded a view of the great fountains at the head of the upper basin, and on moonlight nights the Welshwoman would hold me up to the glass, and bid me look at the mist and spray rising into mysterious shapes, moving mystically in the white light like living things.

"It's the Woman of the Water," she used to say; and sometimes she would threaten that, if I did not go to sleep, the Woman of the Water would steal up to the high window and carry me away in her wet arms.

The place was gloomy. The broad basins of water and the tall evergreen hedges gave it a funereal look, and the damp-stained marble causeways by the pools might have been made of tombstones. The grey and weather-beaten walls and towers without, the dark and massively furnished rooms within, the deep, mysterious recesses and the heavy curtains, all affected my spirits. I was silent and sad from my childhood. There was a great clock-tower above, from which the hours rang dismally during the day and tolled like a knell in the dead of night. There was no light nor life in the house, for my mother was a helpless invalid, and my father had grown melancholy in his long task of caring for her. He was a thin, dark man, with sad eyes; kind, I think, but silent and unhappy. Next to my mother, I believe he loved me better than anything on earth, for he took immense pains and trouble in teaching me, and what he taught me I have never forgotten.

Perhaps it was his only amusement, and that may be the reason why I had no nursery governess or teacher of any kind while he lived.

I used to be taken to see my mother every day, and sometimes twice a day, for an hour at a time. Then I sat upon a little stool near her feet, and she would ask me what I had been doing, and what I wanted to do. I dare say she saw already the seeds of a profound melancholy in my nature, for she looked at me always with a sad smile, and kissed me with a sigh when I was taken away.

One night, when I was just six years old, I lay awake in the nursery. The door was not quite shut, and the Welsh nurse was sitting sewing in the next room. Suddenly I heard her groan, and say in a strange voice, "One—two—one—two!" I was frightened, and I jumped up and ran to the door, barefooted as I was.

"What is it, Judith?" I cried, clinging to her skirts. I can remember the look in her strange dark eyes as she answered.

"One—two leaden coffins, fallen from the ceiling!" she crooned, working herself in her chair.

"One—two—a light coffin and a heavy coffin, failing to the floor!"

Then she seemed to notice me, and she took me back to bed and sang me to sleep with a queer old Welsh song.

I do not know how it was, but the impression got hold of me that she had meant that my father and mother were going to die very soon. They died in the very room where she had been sitting that night. It was a great room, my day nursery, full of sun when there was any; and when the days were dark it was the most cheerful place in the house. My mother grew rapidly worse, and I was transferred to another part of the building to make place for her. They thought my nursery was gayer for her, I suppose; but she could not live. She was beautiful when she was dead, and I cried bitterly.

"The light one, the light one—the heavy one to come," crooned the Welshwoman. And she was right. My father took the room after my mother was gone, and day by day he grew thinner and paler and sadder.

"The heavy one, the heavy one—all of lead," moaned my nurse, one night in December, standing still, just as she was going to take away the light after putting me to bed. Then she took me up again, and wrapped me in a little gown, and led me away to my father's room. She knocked, but no one answered. She opened the door, and we found him in his easy-chair before the fire, very white, quite dead.

So I was alone with the Welshwoman till strange people came, and relations, whom I had never seen; and then I heard them saying that I must be taken away to some more cheerful place. They were kind people, and I will not believe that they were kind only because I was to be very rich when I grew to be a man. The world never seemed to be a very bad place to me, nor all the people to be miserable sinners, even when I was most melancholy. I do not remember that any one ever did me any great injustice, nor that I was ever oppressed or ill-treated in any way, even by the boys at school. I was sad, I suppose, because my childhood was so gloomy, and, later, because I was unlucky in everything I undertook, till I finally believed I was pursued by fate, and I used to dream that the old Welsh nurse and the Woman of the Waters between them had vowed to pursue me to my end. But my natural disposition should have been cheerful, as I have often thought.

Among lads of my age I was never last, or even among the last, in anything; but I was never first.

If I trained for a race, I was sure to sprain my ankle on the day when I was to run. If I pulled an oar with others, my oar was sure to break. If I competed for a prize, some unforeseen accident prevented my winning it at the last moment. Nothing to which I put my hand succeeded, and I got the reputation of being unlucky, until my companions felt it was always safe to bet against me, no matter what the appearances might be. I became discouraged and listless in everything. I gave up the idea of competing for any distinction at the University, comforting myself with the thought that I could not fail in the examination for the ordinary degree. The day before the examination began I fell ill; and when at last I recovered, after a narrow escape from death, I turned my back upon Oxford, and went down alone to visit the old place where I had been born, feeble in health and profoundly disgusted and discouraged. I was twenty-one years of age, master of myself and of my fortune; but so deeply had the long chain of small unlucky circumstances affected me, that I thought seriously of shutting myself up from the world to live the life of a hermit, and to die as soon as possible. Death seemed the only cheerful possibility in my existence, and my thoughts soon dwelt upon it altogether.

I had never shown any wish to return to my own home since I had been taken away as a little boy, and no one had ever pressed me to do so. The place had been kept in order after a fashion, and did not seem to have suffered during the fifteen years or more of my absence. Nothing earthly could affect those odd grey walls that had fought the elements for so many centuries. The garden was more wild than I remembered it; the marble causeways about the pools looked more yellow and damp than of old, and the whole place at first looked smaller. It was not until I had wandered about the house and grounds for many hours that I realised the huge size of the home where I was to live in solitude. Then I began to delight in it, and my resolution to live alone grew stronger.

The people had turned out to welcome me, of course, and I tried to recognise the changed faces of the old gardener and the old housekeeper, and to call them by name. My old nurse I knew at once. She had grown very grey since she heard the coffin fall in the nursery fifteen years before, but her strange eyes were the same, and the look in them woke all my old memories. She went over the house with me.

"And how is the Woman of the Water?" I asked, trying to laugh a little. "Does she still play in the moonlight?"

"She is hungry," answered the Welshwoman, in a low voice.

"Hungry? Then we will feed her." I laughed. But old Judith turned very pale, and looked at me strangely.

"Feed her? Ay—you will feed her well," she muttered, glancing behind her at the ancient housekeeper, who tottered after us with feeble steps through the halls and passages.

I did not think much of her words. She had always talked oddly, as Welshwomen will, and though I was very melancholy I am sure I was not superstitious, and I was certainly not timid. Only, as in a far-off dream, I seemed to see her standing with the light in her hand and muttering, "The heavy one—all of lead," and then leading a little boy through the long corridors to see his father lying dead in a great easy-chair before a smouldering fire. So we went over the house, and I chose the rooms where I would live; and the servants I had brought with me ordered and arranged everything, and I had no more trouble. I did not care what they did, provided I was left in peace, and was not expected to give directions; for I was more listless than ever, owing to the effects of my illness at college.

I dined in solitary state, and the melancholy grandeur of the vast old dining-room pleased me. Then I went to the room I had selected for my study, and sat down in a deep chair, under a bright light, to think, or to let my thoughts meander through labyrinths of their own choosing, utterly indifferent to the course they might take.

The tall windows of the room opened to the level of the ground upon the terrace at the head of the garden. It was in the end of July, and everything was open, for the weather was warm. As I sat alone I heard the unceasing plash of the great fountains, and I fell to thinking of the Woman of the Water. I rose, and went out into the still night and sat down upon a seat on the terrace, between two gigantic Italian flower-pots. The air was deliciously soft and sweet with the smell of the flowers, and the garden was more congenial to me than the house. Sad people always like running water and the sound of it at night, though I cannot tell why. I sat and listened in the gloom, for it was dark below, and the pale moon had not yet climbed over the hills in front of me, though all the air above was light with her rising beams. Slowly the white halo in the eastern sky ascended in an arch above the wooded crests, making the outline of the mountains more intensely black by contrast, as though the head of some great white saint were rising from behind a screen in a vast cathedral, throwing misty glories from below. I longed to see the moon herself, and I tried to reckon the seconds before she must appear. Then she sprang up quickly, and in a moment more hung round and perfect in the sky. I gazed at her, and then at the floating spray of the tall fountains, and down at the pools, where the water-lilies were rocking softly in their sleep on the velvet surface of the moonlit water. Just then a great swan floated out silently into the midst of the basin, and wreathed his long neck, catching the water in his broad bill, and scattering showers of diamonds around him.

Suddenly, as I gazed, something came between me and the light. I looked up instantly. Between me and the round disc of the moon rose a luminous face of a woman, with great strange eyes, and a woman's mouth, full and soft, but not smiling, hooded in black, staring at me as I sat still upon my bench. She was close to me—so close that I could have touched her with my hand. But I was transfixed and helpless. She stood still for a moment, but her expression did not change. Then she passed swiftly away, and my hair stood up on my head, while the cold breeze from her white dress was wafted to my temples as she moved. The moonlight, shining through the tossing spray of the fountain, made traceries of shadow on the gleaming folds of her garments. In an instant she was gone, and I was alone.

I was strangely shaken by the vision, and some time passed before I could rise to my feet, for I was still weak from my illness, and the sight I had seen would have startled any one. I did not reason with myself, for I was certain that I had looked on the unearthly, and no argument could have destroyed that belief. At last I got up and stood unsteadily, gazing in the direction in which I thought the face had gone; but there was nothing to be seen—nothing but the broad paths, the tall, dark evergreen hedges, the tossing water of the fountains and the smooth pool below. I fell back upon the seat and recalled the face I had seen. Strange to say, now that the first impression had passed, there was nothing startling in the recollection; on the contrary, I felt that I was fascinated by the face, and would give anything to see it again. I could retrace the beautiful straight features, the long dark eyes and the wonderful mouth, most exactly in my mind, and, when I had reconstructed every detail from memory, I knew that the whole was beautiful, and that I should love a woman with such a face.

"I wonder whether she is the Woman of the Water!" I said to myself. Then rising once more I wandered down the garden, descending one short flight of steps after another, from terrace to terrace by the edge of the marble basins, through the shadow and through the moonlight; and I crossed the water by the rustic bridge above the artificial grotto, and climbed slowly up again to the highest terrace by the other side. The air seemed sweeter, and I was very calm, so that I think I smiled to myself as I walked, as though a new happiness had come to me. The woman's face seemed always before me, and the thought of it gave me an unwonted thrill of pleasure, unlike anything I had ever felt before.

I turned, as I reached the house, and looked back upon the scene. It had certainly changed in the short hour since I had come out, and my mood had changed with it. Just like my luck, I thought, to fall in love with a ghost! But in old times I would have sighed, and gone to bed more sad than ever, at such a melancholy conclusion. Tonight I felt happy, almost for the first time in my life. The gloomy old study seemed cheerful when I went in. The old pictures on the walls smiled at me, and I sat down in my deep chair with a new and delightful sensation that I was not alone. The idea of having seen a ghost, and of feeling much the better for it, was so absurd that I laughed softly, as I took up one of the books I had brought with me and began to read.

That impression did not wear off. I slept peacefully, and in the morning I threw open my windows to the summer air, and looked down at the garden, at the stretches of green and at the coloured flowerbeds, at the circling swallows, and at the bright water.

"A man might make a paradise of this place," I exclaimed. "A man and a woman together!"

From that day the old castle no longer seemed gloomy, and I think I ceased to be sad; for some time, too, I began to take an interest in the place, and to try and make it more alive. I avoided

my old Welsh nurse, lest she should damp my humour with some
dismal prophecy, and recall my old self by bringing back memories of my dismal childhood. But what I thought of most was the
ghostly figure I had seen in the garden that first night after my
arrival. I went out every evening and wandered through the walks
and paths; but, try as I might, I did not see my vision again. At
last, after many days, the memory grew more faint, and my old
moody nature gradually overcame the temporary sense of lightness I had experienced.

The summer turned to autumn, and I grew restless. It began to
rain. The dampness pervaded the gardens, and the outer halls
smelted musty, like tombs; the grey sky oppressed me intolerably.
I left the place as it was and went abroad, determined to try anything which might possibly make a second break in the monoto-
nous melancholy from which I suffered.

II

Most people would be struck by the utter insignificance of the
small events which, after the death of my parents, influenced my
life and made me unhappy. The gruesome forebodings of a Welsh
nurse, which chanced to be realised by an odd coincidence of
events, should not seem enough to change the nature of a child,
and to direct the bent of his character in after years. The little disappointments of schoolboy life, and the somewhat less childish
ones of an uneventful and undistinguished academic career, should
not have sufficed to turn me out at one-and-twenty years of age a
melancholic, listless idler. Some weakness of my own character may
have contributed to the result, but in a greater degree it was due
to my having a reputation for bad luck. However, I will not try to
analyse the causes of my state, for I should satisfy nobody, least of
all myself. Still less will I attempt to explain why I felt a temporary revival of my spirits after my adventure in the garden. It is
certain that I was in love with the face I had seen, and that I longed
to see it again; that I gave up all hope of a second visitation, grew
more sad than ever, packed up my traps, and finally went abroad.
But in my dreams I went back to my home, and it always appeared

to me sunny and bright, as it had looked on that summer's morning after I had seen the woman by the fountain.

I went to Paris. I went further, and wandered about Germany. I tried to amuse myself, and I failed miserably. With the aimless whims of an idle and useless man, came all sorts of suggestions for good resolutions. One day I made up my mind that I would go and bury myself in a German university for a time, and live simply like a poor student. I started with the intention of going to Leipzic, determined to stay there until some event should direct my life or change my humour, or make an end of me altogether. The express train stopped at some station of which I did not know the name. It was dusk on a winter's afternoon, and I peered through the thick glass from my seat.

Suddenly another train came gliding in from the opposite direction, and stopped alongside of ours. I looked at the carriage which chanced to be abreast of mine, and idly read the black letters painted on a white board swinging from the brass handrail: "Berlin—Cologne—Paris." Then I looked up at the window above. I started violently and the cold perspiration broke out upon my forehead, In the dim light, not six feet from where I sat, I saw the face of a woman, the face I loved, the straight, fine features, the strange eyes, the wonderful mouth, the pale skin. Her head-dress was a dark veil which seemed to be tied about her head and passed over the shoulders under her chin. As I threw down the window and knelt on the cushioned seat, leaning far out to get a better view, a long whistle screamed through the station, followed by a quick series of dull, clanking sounds; then there was a slight jerk, and my train moved on. Luckily the window was narrow, being the one over the seat, beside the door, or I believe I would have jumped out of it then and there. In an instant the speed increased, and I was being carried swiftly away in the opposite direction from the thing I loved.

For a quarter of an hour I lay back in my place, stunned by the suddenness of the apparition. At last one of the two other passengers, a large and gorgeous captain of the White Königsberg Cuirassiers, civilly but firmly suggested that I might shut my window, as the evening was cold. I did so, with an apology, and relapsed into silence. The train ran swiftly on for a long time, and it was already beginning to slacken speed before entering another station when I roused myself, and made a sudden resolution. As the carriage stopped before the brilliantly lighted platform, I seized my belongings, saluted my fellow passengers, and got out, determined to take the first express back to Paris.

This time the circumstances of the vision had been so natural that it did not strike me that there was anything unreal about the face, or about the woman to whom it belonged. I did not try to explain to myself how the face, and the woman, could be travelling by a fast train from Berlin to Paris on a winter's afternoon, when both were in my mind indelibly associated with the moonlight and the fountains in my own English home. I certainly would not have admitted that I had been mistaken in the dusk, attributing to what I had seen a resemblance to my former vision which did not really exist. There was not the slightest doubt in my mind, and I was positively sure that I had again seen the face I loved. I did not hesitate, and in a few hours I was on my way back to Paris. I could not help reflecting on my ill-luck. Wandering as I had been for many months, it might as easily have chanced that I should be travelling in the same train with that woman, instead of going the other way. But my luck was destined to turn for a time.

I searched Paris for several days. I dined at the principal hotels; I went to the theatres; I rode in the Bois de Boulogne in the morning, and picked up an acquaintance, whom I forced to drive with me in the afternoon. I went to mass at the Madeleine, and I attended the services at the English Church. I hung about the Louvre and Notre Dame. I went to Versailles. I spent hours in parading the Rue de Rivoli, in the neighbourhood of Meurice's corner, where foreigners pass and repass from morning till night. At last I received an invitation to a reception at the English Embassy. I went, and I found what I had sought so long.

There she was, sitting by an odd lady in grey satin and diamonds, who had a wrinkled but kindly face and keen grey eyes that seemed to take in everything they saw, with very little inclination to give much in return. But I did not notice the chaperon. I saw only the face that had haunted me for months, and in the excitement of the moment I walked quickly towards the pair, forgetting such a trifle as the necessity for an introduction.

She was far more beautiful than I had thought, but I never doubted that it was she herself and no other. Vision or no vision before, this was the reality, and I knew it. Twice her hair had been covered, now at last I saw it, and the added beauty of its magnificence glorified the whole woman. It was rich hair, fine and abundant, golden, with deep ruddy tints in it like red bronze spun fine. There was no ornament in it, not a rose, not a thread of gold, and I felt that it needed nothing to enhance its splendour; no thing but her pale face, her dark strange eyes, and her heavy eyebrows. I could see that she was slender, too, but strong withal, as she sat there quietly gazing at the moving scene in the midst of the brilliant lights and the hum of perpetual conversation.

I recollected the detail of introduction in time, and turned aside to look for my host. I found him at last. I begged him to present me to the two ladies, pointing them out to him at the same time.

"Yes—uh—by all means—uh—" replied his Excellency, with a pleasant smile. He evidently had no idea of my name, which was not to be wondered at.

"I am Lord Cairngorm," I observed.

"Oh—by all means," answered the Ambassador, with the same hospitable smile. "Yes—uh—the fact is, I must try and find out who they are; such lots of people, you know."

"Oh, if you will present me, I will try and find out for you," said I, laughing.

"Ah, yes—so kind of you—come along," said my host.

We threaded the crowd, and in a few minutes we stood before the two ladies.

"'Lowmintrduce L'd Cairngorm," he said; then, adding quickly to me, "come and dine tomorrow, won't you?" he glided away with his pleasant smile, and disappeared in the crowd.

I sat down beside the beautiful girl, conscious that the eyes of the duenna were upon me.

"I think we have been very near meeting before," I remarked, by way of opening the conversation.

My companion turned her eyes full upon me with an air of enquiry. She evidently did not recall my face, if she had ever seen me.

"Really—I cannot remember," she observed, in a low and musical voice. "When?"

"In the first place, you came down from Berlin by the express, ten days ago. I was going the other way, and our carriages stopped opposite each other. I saw you at the window."

"Yes—we came that way, but I do not remember—" She hesitated.

"Secondly," I continued, "I was sitting alone in my garden last summer—near the end of July—do you remember? You must have wandered in there through the park; you came up to the house and looked at me—"

"Was that you?" she asked, in evident surprise. Then she broke into a laugh. "I told everybody I had seen a ghost; there had never been any Cairngorms in the place since the memory of man. We left the next day, and never heard that you had come there; indeed, I did not know the castle belonged to you."

"Where were you staying?" I asked.

"Where? Why, with my aunt, where I always stay. She is your neighbour, since it is you."

"I—beg your pardon—but then—is your aunt Lady Bluebell? I did not quite catch—"

"Don't be afraid. She is amazingly deaf. Yes. She is the relict of my beloved uncle, the sixteenth or seventeenth Baron Bluebell—I forget exactly how many of them there have been. And I—do you know who I am?" She laughed, well knowing that I did not.

"No," I answered frankly. "I have not the least idea. I asked to be introduced because I recognised you. Perhaps—perhaps you are a Miss Bluebell?"

"Considering that you are a neighbour, I will tell you who I am," she answered. "No; I am of the tribe of Bluebells, but my name is

Lammas, and I have been given to understand that I was christened Margaret. Being a floral family, they call me Daisy. A dreadful American man once told me that my aunt was a Bluebell and that I was a Harebell—with two l's and an e—because my hair is so thick. I warn you, so that you may avoid making such a bad pun."

"Do I look like a man who makes puns?" I asked, being very conscious of my melancholy face and sad looks.

Miss Lammas eyed me critically.

"No; you have a mournful temperament. I think I can trust you," she answered. "Do you think you could communicate to my aunt the fact that you are a Cairngorm and a neighbour? I am sure she would like to know."

I leaned towards the old lady, inflating my lungs for a yell. But Miss Lammas stopped me.

"That is not of the slightest use," she remarked. "You can write it on a bit of paper. She is utterly deaf."

"I have a pencil," I answered, "but I have no paper. Would my cuff do, do you think?"

"Oh yes!" replied Miss Lacunas, with alacrity; "men often do that."

I wrote on my cuff: "Miss Lammas wishes me to explain that I am your neighbour, Cairngorm." Then I held out my arm before the old lady's nose. She seemed perfectly accustomed to the proceeding, put up her glasses, read the words, smiled, nodded, and addressed me in the unearthly voice peculiar to people who hear nothing.

"I knew your grandfather very well," she said. Then she smiled and nodded to me again, and to her niece, and relapsed into silence.

"It is all right," remarked Miss Lammas.

"Aunt Bluebell knows she is deaf, and does not say much, like the parrot. You see, she knew your grandfather. How odd, that we should be neighbours! Why have we never met before?"

"If you had told me you knew my grandfather when you appeared in the garden, I should not have been in the least surprised,"

I answered rather irrelevantly. "I really thought you were the ghost of the old fountain. How in the world did you come there at that hour?"

"We were a large party, and we went out for a walk. Then we thought we should like to see what your park was like in the moonlight, and so we trespassed. I got separated from the rest, and came upon you by accident, just as I was admiring the extremely ghostly look of your house, and wondering whether anybody would ever come and live there again. It looks like the castle of Macbeth, or a scene from the opera. Do you know anybody here?"

"Hardly a soul. Do you?"

"No. Aunt Bluebell said it was our duty to come. It is easy for her to go out; she does not bear the burden of the conversation."

"I am sorry you find it a burden," said I. "Shall I go away?"

Miss Lammas looked at me with a sudden gravity in her beautiful eyes, and there was a sort of hesitation about the lines of her full, soft mouth.

"No," she said at last, quite simply, "don't go away. We may like each other, if you stay a little longer—and we ought to because we are neighbours in the country."

I suppose I ought to have thought Miss Lammas a very odd girl. There is, indeed, a sort of freemasonry between people who discover that they live near each other, and that they ought to have known each other before. But there was a sort of unexpected frankness and simplicity in the girl's amusing manner which would have struck any one else as being singular, to say the least of it. To me, however, it all seemed natural enough. I had dreamed of her face too long not to be utterly happy when I met her at last, and could talk to her as much as I pleased. To me, the man of ill luck in everything, the whole meeting seemed too good to be true. I felt again that strange sensation of lightness which I had experienced after I had seen her face in the garden. The great rooms seemed brighter, life seemed worth living; my sluggish, melancholy blood ran faster, and filled me with a new sense of strength. I said to myself that without this woman I was but an imperfect being, but that with her I could accomplish everything to which I should set my hand. Like the great Doctor, when he thought he had cheated Mephistopheles at last, I could have cried aloud to the fleeting moment, *Verweile doch du bist so schön!*

"Are you always gay?" I asked suddenly. "How happy you must be!"

"The days would sometimes seem very long if I were gloomy," she answered thoughtfully. "Yes, I think I find life very pleasant, and I tell it so."

"How can you 'tell life' anything?" I enquired. "If I could catch my life and talk to it, I would abuse it prodigiously, I assure you."

"I dare say. You have a melancholy temper. You ought to live out of doors, dig potatoes, make hay, shoot, hunt, tumble into ditches, and come home muddy and hungry for dinner. It would be much better for you than moping in your rook tower, and hating everything."

"It is rather lonely down there," I murmured apologetically, feeling that Miss Lammas was quite right.

"Then marry, and quarrel with your wife," she laughed. "Anything is better than being alone."

"I am a very peaceable person. I never quarrel with anybody. You can try it. You will find it quite impossible."

"Will you let me try?" she asked, still smiling.

"By all means—especially if it is to be only a preliminary canter," I answered rashly.

"What do you mean?" she enquired, turning quickly upon me.

"Oh—nothing. You might try my paces with a view to quarrelling in the future. I cannot imagine how you are going to do it. You will have to resort to immediate and direct abuse."

"No. I will only say that if you do not like your life, it is your own fault. How can a man of your age talk of being melancholy, or of the hollowness of existence? Are you consumptive? Are you subject to hereditary insanity? Are you deaf, like Aunt Bluebell? Are you poor, like—lots of people? Have you been crossed in love? Have you lost the world for a woman, or any particular woman for the sake of the world? Are you feeble-minded, a cripple, an outcast? Are you—repulsively ugly?" She laughed again. "Is there any reason in the world why you should not enjoy all you have got in life?"

"No. There is no reason whatever, except that I am dreadfully unlucky, especially in small things."

"Then try big things, just for a change," suggested Miss Lammas. "Try and get married, for instance, and see how it turns out."

"If it turned out badly, it would be rather serious."

"Not half so serious as it is to abuse everything unreasonably. If abuse is your particular talent, abuse something that ought to be abused. Abuse the Conservatives—or the Liberals—it does not matter which, since they are always abusing each other. Make yourself felt by other people. You will like it, if they don't. It will make a man of you. Fill your mouth with pebbles, and howl at the sea, if you cannot do anything else. It did Demosthenes no end of good, you know. You will have the satisfaction of imitating a great man."

"Really, Miss Lammas, I think the list of innocent exercises you propose—"

"Very well—if you don't care for that sort of thing, care for some other sort of thing. Care for something, or hate something. Don't be idle. Life is short, and though art may be long, plenty of noise answers nearly as well."

"I do care for something—I mean somebody," I said.

"A woman? Then marry her. Don't hesitate."

"I do not know whether she would marry me," I replied. "I have never asked her."

"Then ask her at once," answered Miss Lammas. "I shall die happy if I feel I have persuaded a melancholy fellow-creature to rouse himself to action. Ask her, by all means, and see what she says. If she does not accept you at once, she may take you the next time. Meanwhile, you will have entered for the race. If you lose, there are the 'All-aged Trial Stakes,' and the 'Consolation Race.'"

"And plenty of selling races into the bargain. Shall I take you at your word, Miss Lammas?"

"I hope you will," she answered.

"Since you yourself advise me, I will. Miss Lammas, will you do me the honour to marry me?"

For the first time in my life the blood rushed to my head and my sight swam. I cannot tell why I said it. It would be useless to try to explain the extraordinary fascination the girl exercised over me, or the still more extraordinary feeling of intimacy with her which had grown in me during that half-hour. Lonely, sad, unlucky as I had been all my life, I was certainly not timid, nor even shy. But to propose to marry a woman after half an hour's acquaintance was a piece of madness of which I never believed myself capable, and of which I should never be capable again, could I be placed in the same situation. It was as though my whole being had been changed in a moment by magic—by the white magic of her nature brought into contact with mine. The blood sank back to my heart, and a moment later I found myself staring at her with anxious eyes. To my amazement she was as calm as ever, but her beautiful mouth smiled, and there was a mischievous light in her dark-brown eyes.

"Fairly caught," she answered. "For an individual who pretends to be listless and sad you are not lacking in humour. I had really not the least idea what you were going to say. Wouldn't it be singularly awkward for you if I had said 'Yes'? I never saw anybody begin to practice so sharply what was preached to him—with so very little loss of time!"

"You probably never met a man who had dreamed of you for seven months before being introduced."

"No, I never did," she answered gaily. "It smacks of the romantic. Perhaps you are a romantic character after all. I should think you were, if I believed you. Very well; you have taken my advice, entered for a Stranger's Race and lost it. Try the All-aged Trial Stakes. You have another cuff, and a pencil. Propose to Aunt Bluebell; she would dance with astonishment, and she might recover her hearing."

III

That was how I first asked Margaret Lammas to be my wife, and I will agree with any one who says I behaved very foolishly. But I have not repented of it, and I never shall. I have long ago understood that I was out of my mind that evening, but I think my temporary insanity on that occasion has had the effect of making me a saner man ever since. Her manner turned my head, for it was so different from what I had expected. To hear this lovely creature, who, in my imagination, was a heroine of romance, if not of tragedy, talking familiarly and laughing readily was more than my equanimity could bear, and I lost my head as well as my heart. But when I went back to England in the spring, I went to make certain arrangements at the Castle—certain changes and improvements which would be absolutely necessary. I had won the race for which I had entered myself so rashly, and we were to be married in June.

Whether the change was due to the orders I had left with the gardener and the rest of the servants, or to my own state of mind, I cannot tell. At all events, the old place did not look the same to me when I opened my window on the morning after my arrival. There were the grey walls below me, and the grey turrets flanking the huge building; there were the fountains, the marble causeways, the smooth basins, the tall box hedges, the water-lilies and the swans, just as of old. But there was something else there, too—something in the air, in the water, and in the greenness that I did not recognise—a light over everything by which everything was transfigured. The clock in the tower struck seven, and the strokes of the ancient bell sounded like a wedding chime. The air sang with the thrilling treble of the songbirds, with the silvery music of the Flashing water, and the softer harmony of the leaves stirred by the fresh morning wind. There was a smell of new-mown hay from the distant meadows, and of blooming roses from the beds below, wafted up together to my window. I stood in the pure sunshine and drank the air and all the sounds and the odours that were in it; and I looked down at my garden and said, "It is Paradise, after all. I think the men of old were right when they called heaven a garden, and Eden a garden inhabited by one man and one woman, the Earthly Paradise."

I turned away, wondering what had become of the gloomy memories I had always associated with my home. I tried to recall the impression of my nurse's horrible prophecy before the death of my parents—an impression which hitherto had been vivid enough. I tried to remember my own self, my dejection, my listlessness, my bad luck, and my petty disappointments. I endeavoured to force myself to think as I used to think, if only to satisfy myself that I had not lost my individuality. But I succeeded in none of these efforts. I was a different man, a changed being, incapable of sorrow, of ill-luck, or of sadness. My life had been a dream, not evil, but infinitely gloomy and hopeless. It was now a reality, full of hope, gladness, and all manner of good. My home had been like a tomb; to-day it was Paradise. My heart had been as though it had not existed; to-day it beat with strength and youth, and the certainty of realised happiness. I revelled in the beauty of the world, and called loveliness out of the future to enjoy it before time should bring it to me, as a traveller in the plains looks up to the mountains, and already tastes the cool air through the dust of the road.

Here, I thought, we will live and live for years. There we will sit by the fountain towards evening and in the deep moonlight. Down those paths we will wander together. On those benches we will rest and talk. Among those eastern hills we will ride through the soft twilight, and in the old house we will tell tales on winter nights, when the logs burn high, and the holly berries are red, and the old clock tolls out the dying year. On these old steps, in these dark passages and stately rooms, there will one day be the sound of little pattering feet, and laughing child-voices will ring up to the vaults of the ancient hall. Those tiny footsteps shall not be slow and sad as mine were, nor shall the childish words be spoken in an awed whisper. No gloomy Welshwoman shall people the dusty corners with weird horrors, nor utter horrid prophecies of death and ghastly things. All shall be young, and fresh, and joyful, and happy, and we will turn the old luck again, and forget that there was ever any sadness.

So I thought, as I looked out of my window that morning and for many mornings after that, and every day it all seemed more real than ever before, and much nearer. But the old nurse looked at me askance, and muttered odd sayings about the Woman of the Water. I cared little what she said, for I was far too happy.

At last the time came near for the wedding. Lady Bluebell and all the tribe of Bluebells, as Margaret called them, were at Bluebell Grange, for we had determined to be married in the country, and to come straight to the Castle afterwards. We cared little for travelling, and not at all for a crowded ceremony at St. George's in Hanover Square, with all the tiresome formalities afterwards. I used to ride over to the Grange every day, and very often Margaret would come with her aunt and some of her cousins to the Castle. I was suspicious of my own taste, and was only too glad to let her have her way about the alterations and improvements in our home.

We were to be married on the thirtieth of July, and on the evening of the twenty-eighth Margaret drove over with some of the Bluebell party. In the long summer twilight we all went out into the garden. Naturally enough, Margaret and I were left to ourselves, and we wandered down by the marble basins.

"It is an odd coincidence," I said; "it was on this very night last year that I first saw you."

"Considering that it is the month of July," answered Margaret, with a laugh, "and that we have been here almost every day, I don't think the coincidence is so extraordinary, after all."

"No, dear," said I, "I suppose not. I don't know why it struck me. We shall very likely be here a year from to-day, and a year from that. The odd thing, when I think of it, is that you should be here at all. But my luck has turned. I ought not to think anything odd that happens now that I have you. It is all sure to be good."

"A slight change in your ideas since that remarkable performance of yours in Paris," said Margaret. "Do you know, I thought you were the most extraordinary man I had ever met."

"I thought you were the most charming woman I have ever seen. I naturally did not want to lose any time in frivolities. I took you at your word, I followed your advice, I asked you to marry me, and this is the delightful result—what's the matter?"

Margaret had started suddenly, and her hand tightened on my arm. An old woman was coming up the path, and was close to us before we saw her, for the moon had risen, and was shining full in our faces. The woman turned out to be my old nurse.

"It's only old Judith, dear, don't be frightened," I said. Then I spoke to the Welshwoman: "What are you about, Judith? Have you been feeding the Woman of the Water?"

"Ay—when the clock strikes, Willie—my lord, I mean," muttered the odd creature, drawing aside to let us pass, and fixing her strange eyes on Margaret's face.

"What does she mean?" asked Margaret, when we had gone by.

"Nothing, darling. The old thing is mildly crazy, but she is a good soul."

We went on in silence for a few moments, and came to the rustic bridge just above the artificial grotto through which the water ran out into the park, dark and swift in its narrow channel. We stopped, and leaned on the wooden rail. The moon was now behind us, and shone full upon the long vista of basins and on the huge walls and towers of the Castle above.

"How proud you ought to be of such a grand old place!" said Margaret, softly.

"It is yours now, darling," I answered. "You have as good a right to love it as I—but I only love it because you are to live in it, dear."

Her hand stole out and lay on mine, and we were both silent. Just then the clock began to strike far off in the tower. I counted the strokes—eight-nine ten—eleven—I looked at my watch—twelve—thirteen—I laughed. The bell went on striking.

"The old clock has gone crazy, like Judith," I exclaimed. Still it went on, note after note ringing out monotonously through the still air. We leaned over the rail, instinctively looking in the direction whence the sound came. On and on it went. I counted nearly a hundred, out of sheer curiosity, for I understood that something had broken and that the thing was running itself down.

Suddenly there was a crack as of breaking wood, a cry and a heavy splash, and I was alone, clinging to the broken end of the rail of the rustic bridge.

I do not think I hesitated while my pulse beat twice. I sprang clear of the bridge into the black rushing water, dived to the bottom, came up again with empty hands, turned and swam downwards through the grotto in the thick darkness, plunging and diving at every stroke, striking my head and hands against jagged stones and sharp corners, clutching at last something in my fingers, and dragging it up with all my might. I spoke, I cried aloud, but there was no answer. I was alone in the pitchy blackness with my burden, and the house was five hundred yards away. Struggling still, I felt the ground beneath my feet, I saw a ray of moonlight—the grotto widened, and the deep water became a broad and shallow brook as I stumbled over the stones and at last laid Margaret's body on the bank in the park beyond.

"Ay, Willie, as the clock struck!" said the voice of Judith, the Welsh nurse, as she bent down and looked at the white face. The old woman must have turned back and followed us, seen the accident, and slipped out by the lower gate of the garden. "Ay," she groaned, "you have fed the Woman of the Water this night, Willie, while the clock was striking."

I scarcely heard her as I knelt beside the lifeless body of the woman I loved, chafing the wet white temples, and gazing wildly into the wide-staring eyes. I remember only the first returning look of consciousness, the first heaving breath, the first movement of those dear hands stretching out towards me.

That is not much of a story, you say. It is the story of my life. That is all. It does not pretend to be anything else. Old Judith says my luck turned on that summer's night, when I was struggling in the water to save all that was worth living for. A month later there was a stone bridge above the grotto, and Margaret and I stood on it, and looked up at the moonlit Castle, as we had done once before, and as we have done many times since. For all those things happened ten years ago last summer, and this is the tenth Christmas Eve we have spent together by the roaring logs in the old hall, talking of old times; and every year there are more old times to talk of. There are curly-headed boys, too, with red-gold hair and dark-brown eyes like their mother's, and a little Margaret, with solemn black eyes like mine. Why could she not look like her mother, too, as well as the rest of them?

The world is very bright at this glorious Christmas time, and perhaps there is little use in calling up the sadness of long ago, unless it be to make the jolly firelight seem more cheerful, the good wife's face look gladder, and to give the children's laughter a merrier ring, by contrast with all that is gone. Perhaps, too, some sad-faced, listless, melancholy youth, who feels that the world is very hollow, and that life is like a perpetual funeral service, just as I used to feel myself, may take courage from my example, and having found the woman of his heart, ask her to marry him after half an hour's acquaintance. But, on the whole, I would not advise any man to marry, for the simple reason that no man will ever find a wife like mine, and being obliged to go further, he will necessarily fare worse. My wife has done miracles, but I will not assert that any other woman is able to follow her example.

Margaret always said that the old place was beautiful, and that I ought to be proud of it. I dare say she is right. She has even more imagination than I. But I have a good answer and a plain one, which is this—that all the beauty of the Castle comes from her. She has breathed upon it all, as the children blow upon the cold glass window-panes in winter; and as their warm breath crystallises into landscapes from fairyland, full of exquisite shapes and traceries upon the blank surface, so her spirit has transformed every grey stone of the old towers, every ancient tree and hedge in the gardens, every thought in my once melancholy self. All that was old is young, and all that was sad is glad, and I am the gladdest of all. Whatever heaven may be, there is no earthly paradise without woman, nor is there anywhere a place so desolate, so dreary, so unutterably miserable that a woman cannot make it seem heaven to the man she loves, and who loves her.

I hear certain cynics laugh, and cry that all that has been said before. Do not laugh, my good cynic. You are too small a man to laugh at such a great thing as love. Prayers have been said before now by many, and perhaps you say yours, too. I do not think they lose anything by being repeated, nor you by repeating them. You say that the world is bitter, and full of the Waters of Bitterness. Love, and so live that you may be loved—the world will turn sweet for you, and you shall rest like me by the Waters of Paradise.

THE DEAD SMILE

I

Sir Hugh Ockram smiled as he sat by the open window of his study, in the late August afternoon; and just then a curiously yellow cloud obscured the low sun, and the clear summer light turned lurid, as if it had been suddenly poisoned and polluted by the foul vapours of a plague. Sir Hugh's face seemed, at best, to be made of fine parchment drawn skin-tight over a wooden mask, in which two sunken eyes were sunk out of sight, and peered from far within through crevices under through crevices under the slanting, wrinkled lids, alive and watchful like two toads in their holes, side by side and exactly alike. But as the light changed, then a little yellow glare flashed in each. Nurse Macdonald said once that when Sir Hugh smiled he saw the faces of two women in hell—two dead women he had betrayed. Nurse Macdonald was a hundred years old. And the smile widened, stretching the pale lips across the discolored teeth in an expression of profound self-satisfaction, blended with the most unforgiving hatred and contempt for the human doll.

The hideous disease of which he was dying had touched his brain. His son stood beside him, tall, white and delicate as an angel in a primitive picture; and though there was deep distress in his violet eyes, as he looked at his father's face, he felt the shadow of that sickening smile stealing across his own lips and parting and drawing them against his will. It was like a bad dream, for he tried not to smile and smiled the more.

Beside him, strangely like him in her wan, angelic beauty, with
the same shadowy golden hair, the same sad violet eyes, the same
luminously pale face, Evelyn Warburton rested one hand upon his
arm. As she looked into her uncle's eyes, and could not turn her
own away, she knew that the deathly smile was hovering on her
own red lips, drawing them tightly across her little teeth, while
two bright tears ran down her cheeks to her mouth, and dropped
from the upper to the lower lip while she smiled—and the smile
was like the shadow of death and the seal of damnation upon her
pure young face.

"Of course," said Sir Hugh very slowly, still looking out at the
trees, "if you have made your mind up to be married, I cannot
hinder you, and I don't suppose you attach the smallest impor-
tance to my consent—"

"Father!" exclaimed Gabriel reproachfully.

"No. I do not deceive myself," continued the old man, smiling
terribly. "You will marry when I am dead, though there is a very
good reason why you had better not—why you had better not," he
repeated very emphatically, and he slowly turned his toad eyes
upon the lovers.

"What reason?" asked Evelyn in a frightened voice.

"Never mind the reason, my dear. You will marry just as if it
did not exist." There was a long pause.

"Two gone," he said, his voice lowering strangely, "and two
more will be four—all together—forever and ever, burning, burning, burning bright."

At the last words his head sank slowly back and the little glare
of his toad eyes disappeared under the swollen lids; and the lurid
cloud passed from the westering sun, so that the earth was green
again, and the light pure. Sir Hugh had fallen asleep, as he often
did in his illness, even while speaking.

Gabriel Ockram drew Evelyn away, and from the study they
went out into the dim hall, softly closing the door behind them,
and each audibly drew breath, as though some sudden danger had
been passed. As they laid their hands each in the other's, their
strangely-like eyes met in a long look, in which love and perfect

understanding were darkened by the secret terror of an unknown thing. Their pale faces reflected each other's fear.

"It is his secret," said Evelyn at last. "He will never tell us what it is."

"If he dies with it," answered Gabriel, "let it be on his own head!"

"On his head!" echoed the dim hall. It was a strange echo, and some were frightened by it, for they said that if it were a real echo it should repeat everything and not give back a phrase here and there, now speaking, now silent. But Nurse Macdonald said that the great hall would never echo a prayer when an Ockram was to die, though it would give back curses ten for one.

"On his head!" it repeated quite softly, and Evelyn started and looked round.

"It is only the echo," said Gabriel, leading her away.

They went out into the late afternoon light, and sat upon a stone seat behind the chapel, which had been built across the end of the east wing. It was very still, not a breath stirred, and there was no sound near them. Only far off in the park a songbird was whistling the high prelude to the evening chorus.

"It is very lonely here," said Evelyn, taking Gabriel's hand nervously and speaking as if she dreaded to disturb the silence. "If it were dark, I should be afraid."

"Of what? Of me?" Gabriel's sad eyes turned to her.

"Oh no! How could I be afraid of you! But of the old Ockrams—they say they are just under our feet here in the north vault outside the chapel, all in their shrouds with no coffins, as they used to bury them."

"As they always will—as they will bury my father, and me. They say an Ockram will not lie in a coffin."

"But it cannot be true—those are fairy tales—ghost stories!" Evelyn nestled nearer to her companion, grasping his hand more tightly, and the sun began to go down.

"Of course. But there is the story of old Sir Vernon, who was beheaded for treason under James the Second. The family brought his body back from the scaffold in an iron coffin with heavy locks, and they put it in the north vault. But ever afterwards, whenever the vault was opened to bury another of the family, they found the coffin wide open, and the body standing upright against the wall, and the head rolled away in a corner, smiling at it."

"As Uncle Hugh smiles?" Evelyn shivered.

"Yes, I suppose so," answered Gabriel, thoughtfully. "Of course I never saw it, and the vault has not been opened for thirty years—none of us have died since then."

"And if—if Uncle Hugh dies—shall you—" Evelyn stopped, and her beautiful thin face was quite white.

"Yes. I shall see him laid there too—with his secret, whatever it is." Gabriel sighed and pressed the girl's little hand.

"I do not like to think of it," she said unsteadily. "Oh, Gabriel, what can the secret be? He said we had better not marry—not that he forbade it—but he said it so strangely, and he smiled—ugh!" Her small white teeth chattered with fear, and she looked over her shoulder while drawing still closer to Gabriel. "And, somehow, I felt it in my own face—"

"So did I," answered Gabriel in a low, nervous voice. "Nurse Macdonald—" He stopped abruptly.

"What? What did she say?"

"Oh—nothing. She has told me things—they would frighten you, dear. Come, it is growing chilly." He rose, but Evelyn held his hand in both of hers, still sitting and looking up into his face.

"But we shall be married just the same—Gabriel! Say that we shall!"

"Of course, darling—of course. But while my father is so very ill, it is impossible—"

"Oh, Gabriel, Gabriel, dear! I wish we were married now!" cried Evelyn in sudden distress. "I know that something will prevent it and keep us apart."

"Nothing shall!"

"Nothing?"

"Nothing human," said Gabriel Ockram, as she drew him down to her.

And their faces, that were so strangely alike, met, and touched—and Gabriel knew that the kiss had a marvelous savor of evil, but on Evelyn's lips it was like the cool breath of a sweet and mortal fear. And neither of them understood, for they were innocent and young. Yet she drew him to her by her lightest touch, as a sensitive plant shivers and waves its thin leaves, and bends and closes softly upon what it wants; and he let himself be drawn to her willingly, as he would even if her touch had been deadly and poisonous; for she strangely loved that half voluptuous breath of fear, and he passionately desired the nameless evil something that lurked in her maiden lips.

"It is as if we loved in a strange dream," she said.

"I fear the waking," he murmured.

"We shall not wake, dear—when the dream is over it will have already turned into death, so softly that we shall not know it. But until then—"

She paused, and her eyes sought his, and their faces slowly came nearer. It was as if they had thoughts in their red lips that foresaw and foreknew the deep kiss of each other.

"Until then—" she said again, very low, and her mouth was nearer to his.

"Dream—till then," murmured his breath.

II

Nurse Macdonald was a hundred years old. She used to sleep sitting all bent together in a great old leathern arm-chair with wings, her feet in a bag foot-stool lined with sheepskin, and many warm blankets wrapped about her, even in summer. Beside her a little lamp always burned at night, by an old silver cup in which there was always something to drink.

Her face was very wrinkled, but the wrinkles were so small and fine and near together that they made shadows instead of lines. Two thin locks of hair, that was turning from white to a smoky yellow again, were drawn over her temples from under her starched white cap. Every now and then she woke and her eyelids were drawn up in tiny folds, like little pink silk curtains, and her queer blue eyes looked straight before her, through doors and walls and worlds to a far place beyond. Then she slept again, and her hands lay one upon the other on the edge of the blanket; the thumbs had grown longer than the fingers with age, and the joints shone in the low lamplight like polished crabapples.

It was nearly one o'clock in the night, and the summer breeze was blowing the ivy branch against the panes of the window with a hushing caress. In the small room beyond, with the door ajar, the young maid who took care of Nurse Macdonald was fast asleep. All was very quiet. The old woman breathed regularly, and her indrawn lips trembled each time as the breath went out, and her eyes were shut.

But outside the closed window there was a face, and violet eyes were looking steadily at the ancient sleeper, for it was like the face of Evelyn Warburton, though there were eighty feet from the sill of the window to the foot of the tower. Yet the cheeks were thinner than Evelyn's, and as white as a gleam, and the eyes stared, and the lips were not red with life; they were dead and painted with new blood.

Slowly Nurse Macdonald's wrinkled eyelids folded back, and she looked straight at the face at the window while one might count to ten.

"Is it time?" she asked, in her little old, far-away voice.

While she looked the face at the window changed; for the eyes opened wider and wider till the white glared all round the bright violet, and the bloody lips opened over gleaming teeth, and stretched and widened and stretched again, and the shadowy golden hair rose and streamed against the window in the night breeze. And in answer to Nurse Macdonald's question came the sound that freezes the living flesh.

That low-moaning voice that rises suddenly, like the scream of storm, from a moan to a wail, from a wail to a howl, from a howl to the fear-shriek of the tortured dead—he who has heard, knows, and can bear witness that the cry of the Banshee is an evil cry to hear alone in the deep night. When it was over and the face was gone, Nurse Macdonald shook a little in her great chair, and still she looked at the black square of the window, but there was nothing more there, nothing but the night, and the whispering ivy branch.

She turned her head to the door that was ajar, and there stood the girl, in her white gown, her teeth chattering with fright.

"It is time, child," said Nurse Macdonald. "I must go to him, for it is the end."

She rose slowly, leaning her withered hands upon the arms of the chair, and the girl brought her a woollen gown and a great mantle, and her crutch-stick, and made her ready. But very often the girl looked at the window and was unjointed with fear, and often Nurse Macdonald shook her head and said words which the maid could not understand.

"It was like the face of Miss Evelyn," said the girl at last, trembling.

But the ancient woman looked up sharply and angrily, and her queer blue eyes glared. She held herself up by the arm of the great chair with her left hand, and lifted up her crutch-stick to strike the maid with all her might. But she did not.

"You are a good girl," she said, "but you are a fool. Pray for wit, child, pray for wit—or else find service in another house than Ockram Hall. Bring the lamp and help me under my left arm."

The crutch-stick clacked on the wooden floor, and the low heels of the old woman's slippers clappered after, in slow triplets, as Nurse Macdonald got toward the door. And down the stairs each step she took was a labour in itself, and by the clacking noise the waking servants knew that she was coming very long before they saw her.

No one was sleeping now, and there were lights, and whisperings, and pale faces in the corridors near Sir Hugh's bedroom, and now someone went in, and now someone came out, but every one made way for Nurse Macdonald, who had nursed Sir Hugh's father more than eighty years ago.

The light was soft and clear in the room. There stood Gabriel Ockram by his father's bedside, and there knelt Evelyn Warburton, her hair lying like a golden shadow down her shoulders, and her hands clasped nervously together. And opposite Gabriel a nurse was trying to make Sir Hugh drink. But he would not, and though his lips were parted, his teeth were set. He was very, very thin and yellow now, and his eyes caught the light sideways and were as yellow coals.

"Do not torment him," said Nurse Macdonald to the woman who held the cup. "Let me speak to him, for his hour is come."

"Let her speak to him," said Gabriel, in a dull voice.

So the ancient woman leaned to the pillow and laid the feather-weight of her withered hand, that was like a brown moth, upon Sir Hugh's yellow fingers, and she spoke to him earnestly, while only Gabriel and Evelyn were left in the room to hear.

"Hugh Ockram," she said, "this is the end of your life, and as I saw you born, and saw your father born before you, I am come to see you die. Hugh Ockram, will you tell me the truth?"

The dying man recognized the little far-away voice he had known all his life, and he very slowly turned his yellow face to Nurse Macdonald; but he said nothing. Then she spoke again.

"Hugh Ockram, you will never see the daylight again. Will you tell the truth?"

His toad-like eyes were not yet dull. They fastened themselves on her face.

"What do you want of me?" he asked, and each word struck hollow upon the last. "I have no secrets. I have lived a good life."

Nurse Macdonald laughed—a tiny, cracked laugh, that made her old head bob and tremble a little, as if her neck were on a steel spring. But Sir Hugh's eyes grew red, and his pale lips began to twist.

"Let me die in peace," he said slowly.

But Nurse Macdonald shook her head, and her brown, moth-like hand left his and fluttered to his forehead.

"By the mother that bore you and died of grief for the sins you did, tell me the truth!"

Sir Hugh's lips tightened on his discolored teeth.

"Not on earth," he answered slowly.

"By the wife who bore your son and died heartbroken, tell me the truth!"

"Neither to you in life, nor to her in eternal death."

His lips writhed, as if the words were coals between them, and a great drop of sweat rolled across the parchment of his forehead. Gabriel Ockram bit his hand as he watched his father die. But Nurse Macdonald spoke a third time.

"By the woman whom you betrayed, and who waits for you this night, Hugh Ockram, tell me the truth!"

"It is too late. Let me die in peace."

His writhing lips began to smile across the set yellow teeth, and the toad eyes glowed like evil jewels in his head.

"There is time," said the ancient woman. "Tell me the name of Evelyn Warburton's father. Then I will let you die in peace."

Evelyn started back, kneeling as she was, and stared at Nurse Macdonald, and then at her uncle.

"The name of Evelyn's father?" he repeated slowly, while the awful smile spread upon his dying face.

The light was growing strangely dim in the great room. As Evelyn looked, Nurse Macdonald's crooked shadow on the wall grew gigantic. Sir Hugh's breath came thick, rattling in his throat, as death crept in like a snake and choked it back. Evelyn prayed aloud, high and clear.

Then something rapped at the window, and she felt her hair rise upon her head in a cool breeze, as she looked around, in spite of herself. And when she saw her own white face looking in at the window, and her own eyes staring at her through the glass, wide and fearful, and her own hair streaming against the pane, and her own lips dashed with blood, she rose slowly from the floor and stood rigid for one moment, till she screamed once and fell straight back into Gabriel's arms. But the shriek that answered hers was the fear-shriek of the tormented corpse, out of which the soul cannot pass for shame of deadly sins, though the devils fight in it with corruption, each for their due share.

Sir Hugh Ockram sat upright in his deathbed, and saw and cried aloud:

"Evelyn!" His harsh voice broke and rattled in his chest, as he sank down. But still Nurse Macdonald tortured him, for there was a little life left in him still.

"You have seen the mother, as she waits for you, Hugh Ockram. Who was this girl Evelyn's father? What was his name?"

For the last time the dreadful smile came upon the twisted lips, very slowly, very surely, now. The toad eyes glared red and the parchment face glowed a little in the flickering light. For the last time words came.

"They know it in hell."

Then the glowing eyes went out quickly, the yellow face turned waxen pale, and a great shiver ran through the thin body as Hugh Ockram died.

But in death he still smiled, for he knew his secret and kept it still, on the other side, and he would take it with him, to lie with him forever in the north vault of the chapel where the Ockrams lie uncoffined in their shrouds—all but one. Though he was dead, he smiled, for he had kept his treasure of evil truth to the end, and there was none left to tell the name he had spoken, but there was all the evil he had not undone left to bear fruit.

As they watched—Nurse Macdonald and Gabriel, who held Evelyn still unconscious in his arms while he looked at the father—they felt the dead smile crawling along their own lips—the ancient crone and the youth with the angel's face. Then they shivered a little, and both looked at Evelyn as she lay with her head on his shoulder, and though she was very beautiful, the same sickening smile was twisting her young mouth, too; and it was like the foreshadowing of a great evil which they could not understand.

But by and by they carried Evelyn out and she opened her eyes, and the smile was gone. From far away in the great house the sound of weeping and crooning came up the stairs and echoed along the dismal corridors, for the women had begun to mourn the dead master, after the Irish fashion, and the hall had echoes of its own all that night, like the far-off wail of the Banshee among forest trees.

When the time was come they took Sir Hugh in his winding-sheet on a trestle bier, and bore him to the chapel and through the iron door and down the long descent to the north vault, with tapers, to lay him by his father. And two men went in first to prepare the place, and came back staggering like drunken men, and white, leaving their lights behind them.

But Gabriel Ockram was not afraid, for he knew. When he went in alone and saw that the body of Sir Vernon Ockram was leaning upright against the stone wall, and that its head lay on the ground nearby with the face turned up, and the dried leathern lips smiled horribly at the dried-up corpse, while the iron coffin, lined with black velvet, stood open on the floor.

Then Gabriel took the thing in his hands, for it was very light, being quite dried by the air of the vault, and those who peeped in from the door saw him lay it in the coffin again, and it rustled a little, like a bundle of reeds, and sounded hollow as it touched the sides and the bottom. He also placed the head upon the shoulders, and shut down the lid, which fell to, with a rusty spring that snapped.

After that they laid Sir Hugh beside his father, with the trestle bier on which they had brought him; and they went back to the chapel.

But when they saw one another's faces, master and men, they were all smiling, with the dead smile of the corpse they had left in the vault, so that they could not bear to look at one another until it had faded away.

III

Gabriel Ockram became Sir Gabriel, inheriting the baronetcy with the half-ruined fortune left by his father, and still Evelyn Warburton lived at Ockram Hall, in the south room that had been hers ever since she could remember. She could not go away, for there were no relatives to whom she could have gone, and besides, there seemed to be no reason why she should not stay. The world would never trouble itself to care what the Ockrams did on their Irish estates, and it was long since the Ockrams had asked anything of the world.

So Sir Gabriel took his father's place at the dark old table in the dining-room, and Evelyn sat opposite to him, until such time as their mourning should be over, and they might be married at last. Meanwhile, their lives went on as before, since Sir Hugh had been a hopeless invalid during the last year of his life, and they had seen him but once a day for a little while, spending most of their time together in a strangely perfect companionship.

But though the late summer saddened into autumn, and autumn darkened into winter, and storm followed storm, and rain poured on rain through the short days and the long nights, yet Ockram Hall seemed less gloomy since Sir Hugh had been laid in the north vault beside his father. And at Christmastide Evelyn decked the great hall with holly and green boughs, and huge fires blazed on every hearth. Then the tenants were all bidden to come to a New Year's dinner, and they ate and drank well, while Sir Gabriel sat at the head of the table. Evelyn came in when the port wine was brought and the most respected of the tenants made a speech to propose her health.

It was long, he said, since there had been a Lady Ockram. Sir Gabriel shaded his eyes with his hand and looked down at the table, but a faint color came into Evelyn's transparent cheeks. But, said the gray-haired farmer, it was longer still since there had been a Lady Ockram so fair as the next was to be, and he gave the health of Evelyn Warburton.

Then the tenants all stood up and shouted for her, and Sir Gabriel stood up likewise, beside Evelyn. And when the men gave the last and loudest cheer of all there was a voice not theirs, above them all, higher, fiercer, louder—a scream not earthly, shrieking for the Bride of Ockram Hall. And the holly and the green boughs over the great chimney piece shook and slowly waved as if a cool breeze were blowing over them. But the men turned very pale, and many of them set down their glasses, but others let them fall upon the floor, for fear. And looking into one another's faces, they were all smiling strangely, a dead smile, like dead Sir Hugh's. One cried out words in Irish, and the fear of death was suddenly upon them all, so that they fled in panic, falling over one another like wild beasts in the burning forest, when the thick smoke runs along before the flame; and tables were overset, drinking glasses and bottles were broken in heaps, and the dark red wine crawled like blood upon the polished floor.

Sir Gabriel and Evelyn stood alone at the head of the table before the wreck of the feast, not daring to turn and see each other, for each knew that the other smiled. But his right arm held her and his left hand clasped her tight as they stared before them; and but for the shadows of her hair, one might not have told their two faces apart. They listened long, but the cry came not again, and the dead smile faded from their lips, while each remembered that Sir Hugh Ockram lay in the north vault, smiling in his winding-sheet, in the dark, because he had died with his secret.

So ended the tenants' New Year's dinner. But from that time on Sir Gabriel grew more and more silent, and his face grew even paler and thinner than before. Often, without warning and without words, he would rise from his seat, as if something moved him against his will, and he would go out into the rain or the sunshine to the north side of the chapel, and sit on the stone bench, staring at the ground as if he could see through it, and through the vault below, and through the white winding-sheet in the dark, to the dead smile that would not die.

Always when he went out in that way Evelyn came out presently and sat beside him. Once, too, as in the summer, their beautiful faces came suddenly near, and their lids drooped, and their red lips were almost joined together. But as their eyes met, they grew wide and wild, so that the white showed in a ring all round the deep violet, and their teeth chattered and their hands were like the hands of corpses, each in the other's, for the terror of what was under their feet, and of what they knew but could not see.

Once, also, Evelyn found Sir Gabriel in the chapel alone, standing before the iron door that led down to the place of death, and in his hand there was the key to the door; but he had not put it into the lock. Evelyn drew him away, shivering, for she had also been driven in waking dreams to see that terrible thing again, and to find out whether it had changed since it had lain there.

"I am going mad," said Sir Gabriel, covering his eyes with his hand as he went with her. "I see it in my sleep, I see it when I am awake—it draws me to it, day and night—and unless I see it I shall die!"

"I know," answered Evelyn, "I know. It is as if threads were spun from it like a spider's, drawing us down to it."

She was silent for a moment, and then she started violently and grasped his arm with a man's strength, and almost screamed the words she spoke.

"But we must not go there!" she cried. "We must not go!"

Sir Gabriel's eyes were half shut, and he was not moved by the agony of her face.

"I shall die, unless I see it again," he said, in a quiet voice not like his own. And all that day and that evening he scarcely spoke, thinking of it, always thinking, while Evelyn Warburton quivered from head to foot with a terror she had never known.

She went alone, on a grey winter's morning, to Nurse Macdonald's room in the tower, and sat down beside the great leathern easy chair, laying her thin white hand upon the withered fingers.

"Nurse," she said, "what was it that Uncle Hugh should have told you, that night before he died? It must have been an awful secret—and yet, though you asked him, I feel somehow that you know it, and that you know why he used to smile so dreadfully."

The old woman's head moved slowly from side to side.

"I only guess—I shall never know," she answered slowly in her cracked little voice.

"But what do you guess? Who am I? Why did you ask who my father was? You know I am Colonel Warburton's daughter, and my mother was Lady Ockram's sister, so that Gabriel and I are cousins. My father was killed in Afghanistan. What secret can there be?"

"I do not know. I can only guess."

"Guess what?" asked Evelyn imploringly, and pressing the soft withered hands, as she leaned forward. But Nurse Macdonald's wrinkled lids dropped suddenly over her queer blue eyes, and her lips shook a little with her breath, as if she were asleep.

Evelyn waited. By the fire the Irish maid was knitting fast, and the needles clicked like three or four clocks ticking against each other. And the real clock on the wall solemnly ticked alone, checking off the seconds of the woman who was a hundred years old, and had not many days left. Outside, the ivy branch beat the window in the wintry wind, as it had beaten against the glass a hundred years ago.

Then as Evelyn sat there she felt again the waking of a horrible desire—the sickening wish to go down, down to the thing in the north vault, and to open the winding-sheet, and see whether it had changed, and she held Nurse Macdonald's hands as if to keep herself in her place and fight against the appalling attraction of the evil dead.

But the old cat that kept Nurse Macdonald's feet warm, lying always on the bag footstool, got up and stretched itself, and looked up into Evelyn's eyes, while its back arched, and its tail thickened and bristled, and its ugly pink lips drew back in a devilish grin, showing its sharp teeth. Evelyn stared at it, half fascinated by its ugliness. Then the creature suddenly put out one paw with all its claws spread, and spat at the girl, and all at once the grinning cat was like the smiling corpse far down below, so that Evelyn shivered down to her small feet, and covered her face with her free hand, lest Nurse Macdonald should wake and see the dead smile there, for she could feel it.

The old woman had already opened her eyes again, and she touched her cat with the end of her crutch-stick, whereupon its back went down and its tail shrunk, and it sidled back to its place on the bag footstool. But its yellow eyes looked up sideways at Evelyn, between the slits of its lids.

"What is it that you guess, nurse?" asked the young girl again.

"A bad thing—a wicked thing. But I dare not tell you, lest it might not be true, and the very thought should blast your life. For if I guess right, he meant that you should not know, and that you two should marry, and pay for his old sin with your souls."

"He used to tell us that we ought not to marry—"

"Yes—he told you that, perhaps—but it was as if a man put poisoned meat before a starving beast, and said 'do not eat,' but never raised his hand to take the meat away. And if he told you that you should not marry, it was because he hoped you would; for of all men living or dead, Hugh Ockram was the falsest man that ever told a cowardly lie, and the cruelest that ever hurt a weak woman, and the worst that ever loved a sin."

"But Gabriel and I love each other," said Evelyn very sadly.

Nurse Macdonald's old eyes looked far away, at sights seen long ago, and that rose in the grey winter air amid the mists of an ancient youth.

"If you love, you can die together," she said, very slowly. "Why should you live, if it is true? I am a hundred years old. What has life given me? The beginning is fire; the end is a heap of ashes; and between the end and the beginning lies all the pain of the world. Let me sleep, since I cannot die."

Then the old woman's eyes closed again, and her head sank a little lower upon her breast.

So Evelyn went away and left her asleep, with the cat asleep on the bag footstool; and the young girl tried to forget Nurse Macdonald's words, but she could not, for she heard them over and over again in the wind, and behind her on the stairs. And as she grew sick with fear of the frightful unknown evil to which her soul was bound, she felt a bodily something pressing her, and pushing her, and forcing her on, and from the other side she felt the threads that drew her mysteriously; and when she shut her eyes, she saw in the chapel, behind the altar, the low iron door through which she must pass to go to the thing.

And as she lay awake at night, she drew the sheet over her face, lest she should see shadows on the wall beckoning to her; and the sound of her own warm breath made whisperings in her ears, while she held the mattress with her hands, to keep from getting up and going to the chapel. It would have been easier if there had not been a way thither through the library, by a door which was never locked. It would be fearfully easy to take her candle and go softly through the sleeping house. And the key of the vault lay under the altar behind a stone that turned. She knew the little secret. She could go alone and see.

But when she thought of it, she felt her hair rise on her head, and first she shivered so that the bed shook, and then the horror

went through her in a cold thrill that was agony again, like a myriad
of icy needles, boring into her nerves.

IV

The old clock in Nurse Macdonald's tower struck midnight.
From her room she could hear the creaking chains and weights in
their box in the corner of the staircase, and overhead the jarring
of the rusty lever that lifted the hammer. She had heard it all her
life. It struck eleven strokes clearly, and then came the twelfth,
with a dull half stroke, as though the hammer were too weary to go
on, and had fallen asleep against the bell.

The old cat got up from the bag footstool and stretched itself,
and Nurse Macdonald opened her ancient eyes and looked slowly
round the room by the dim light of the night lamp. She touched
the cat with her crutch-stick, and it lay down upon her feet. She
drank a few drops from her cup and went to sleep again.

But downstairs Sir Gabriel sat straight up as the clock struck,
for he had dreamed a fearful dream of horror, and his heart stood
still, till he awoke at its stopping, and it beat again furiously with
his breath, like a wild thing set free. No Ockram had ever known
fear waking, but sometimes it came to Sir Gabriel in his sleep.

He pressed his hands to his temples as he sat up in bed. His
hands were icy cold, but his head was hot. The dream faded far,
and in its place there came the master thought that racked his life;
with the thought also came the sick twisting of his lips in the dark
that would have been a smile. Far off, Evelyn Warburton dreamed
that the dead smile was on her mouth, and awoke, starting with a
little moan, her face in her hands, shivering.

But Sir Gabriel struck a light and got up, and began to walk up
and down his great room. It was midnight and he had barely slept
half an hour, and in the north of Ireland the winter nights are long.

"I shall go mad," he said to himself, holding his forehead. He
knew that it was true. For weeks and months the possession of the
thing had grown upon him like a disease, till he could think of nothing without thinking first of that. And now, all at once, it outgrew

his strength, and he knew that he must be its instrument or lose his mind—that he must do the deed he hated and feared, if he could fear anything, or that something would snap in his brain and divide him from life while he was yet alive. He took the candlestick in his hand, the old-fashioned heavy candlestick that had always been used by the head of the house. He did not think of dressing, but went as he was, in his silk night clothes and his slippers, and opened the door.

Everything was very still in the great old house. He shut the door behind him and walked noiselessly on the carpet through the long corridor. A cool breeze blew over his shoulder, and blew the flame of his candle straight out from him. Instinctively he stopped and looked round, but all was still, and the upright flame burned steadily. He walked on, and instantly a strong draught was behind him, almost extinguishing the light. It seemed to blow him on his way, ceasing whenever he turned, coming again when he went on— invisible, icy.

Down the great staircase to the echoing hall he went, seeing nothing but the flaring flame of the candle standing away from him over the guttering wax, while the cold wind blew over his shoulder and through his hair. On he passed through the open door into the library, dark with old books and carved bookcases; on through the door in the shelves, with painted shelves on it, and the imitated backs of books, so that one needed to know where to find it—and it shut itself after him with a soft click. He entered the low arched passage, and, though the door was shut behind him and fitted tightly in its frame, still the cold breeze blew the flame forward as he walked. And he was not afraid; but his face was very pale, and his eyes were wide and bright, looking before him, seeing already in the dark air the picture of the thing beyond. But in the chapel he stood still, his hand on the little turning stone tablet in the back of the stone altar. On the tablet were engraved the words: "*Clavis sepulchri Clarissimorum Dominorum De Ockram*"— "the key to the vault of the most illustrious Lords of Ockram." Sir Gabriel paused and listened. He fancied that he heard a sound far off in the great house where all had been so still, but it did not come

again. Yet he waited, at the last, and looked at the low iron door.
Beyond it, down the long descent, lay his father, uncoffined, six
months dead, corrupt, terrible in his clinging shroud. The strangely
preserving air of the vault could not yet have done its work completely. But on the thing's ghastly features, with their half-dried,
open eyes, there would still be the frightful smile with which the
man had died—the smile that haunted—

As the thought crossed Sir Gabriel's mind, he felt his lips writhing, and he struck his own mouth in wrath with the back of his
hand so fiercely that a drop of blood ran down to his chin, and
another, and more, falling black in the gloom upon the chapel pavement. But still his bruised lips twisted themselves. He turned the
tablet by the simple secret. It needed no safer fastening, for had
each Ockram been coffined in pure gold, and had the door been
open wide, there was not a man in Tyrone brave enough to go down
to that place, save Gabriel Ockram himself, with his angel's face,
his thin, white hands, and his sad unflinching eyes. He took the
great old key and set it into the lock of the iron door; and the heavy,
rattling noise echoed down the descent beyond like footsteps, as if
a watcher had stood behind the iron and were running away within,
with heavy dead feet. And though he was standing still, the cool
wind was from behind him, and blew the flame of the candle against
the iron panel. He turned the key.

Sir Gabriel saw that his candle was short. There were new ones
on the altar, with long candlesticks, and he lit one, and left his
own burning on the floor. As he set it down on the pavement his
lip began to bleed again, and another drop fell upon the stones.

He drew the iron door open and pushed it back against the
chapel wall, so that it should not shut of itself, while he was within;
and the horrible draught of the sepulchre came up out of the depths
in his face, foul and dark. He went in, but though the fetid air met
him, yet the flame of the tall candle was blown straight from him
against the wind while he walked down the easy incline with steady
steps, his loose slippers slapping the pavement as he trod.

He shaded the candle with his hand, and his fingers seemed to
be made of wax and blood as the light shone through them. And in

spite of him the unearthly draught forced the flame forward, till it was blue over the black wick, and it seemed as if it must go out. But he went straight on, with shining eyes.

The downward passage was wide, and he could not always see the walls by the struggling light, but he knew when he was in the place of death by the larger, drearier echo of his steps in the greater space, and by the sensation of a distant blank wall. He stood still, almost enclosing the flame of the candle in the hollow of his hand. He could see a little, for his eyes were growing used to the gloom. Shadowy forms were outlined in the dimness, where the biers of the Ockrams stood crowded together, side by side, each with its straight, shrouded corpse, strangely preserved by the dry air, like the empty shell that the locust sheds in summer. And a few steps before him he saw clearly the dark shape of headless Sir Vernon's iron coffin, and he knew that nearest to it lay the thing he sought.

He was as brave as any of those dead men had been, and they were his fathers, and he knew that sooner or later he should lie there himself, beside Sir Hugh, slowly drying to a parchment shell. But he was still alive, and he closed his eyes a moment as three great drops stood on his forehead.

Then he looked again, and by the whiteness of the winding-sheet he knew his father's corpse, for all the others were brown with age; and, moreover, the flame of the candle was blown toward it. He made four steps till he reached it, and suddenly the light burned straight and high, shedding a dazzling yellow glare upon the fine linen that was all white, save over the face, and where the joined hands were laid on the breast. And at those places ugly stains had spread, darkened with outlines of the features and of the tight-clasped fingers. There was a frightful stench of drying death.

As Sir Gabriel looked down, something stirred behind him, softly at first, then more noisily, and something fell to the stone floor with a dull thud and rolled up to his feet; he started back, and saw a withered head lying almost face upward on the pavement, grinning at him. He felt the cold sweat standing on his face, and his heart beat painfully.

For the first time in all his life that evil thing which men call
fear was getting hold of him, checking his heart-strings as a cruel
driver checks a quivering horse, clawing at his backbone with icy
hands, lifting his hair with freezing breath, climbing up and gathering in his midriff with leaden weight.

Yet presently he bit his lip and bent down, holding the candle
in one hand, to lift the shroud back from the head of the corpse
with the other. Slowly he lifted it. Then it clove to the half-dried
skin of the face, and his hand shook as if someone had struck him
on the elbow, but half in fear and half in anger at himself, he pulled
it, so that it came away with a little ripping sound. He caught his
breath as he held it, not yet throwing it back, and not yet looking.
The horror was working in him, and he felt that old Vernon Ockram
was standing up in his iron coffin, headless, yet watching him with
the stump of his severed neck.

While he held his breath he felt the dead smile twisting his lips.
In sudden wrath at his own misery, he tossed the death-stained
linen backward, and looked at last. He ground his teeth lest he
should shriek aloud.

There it was, the thing that haunted him, that haunted Evelyn
Warburton, that was like a blight on all that came near him.

The dead face was blotched with dark stains, and the thin, grey
hair was matted about the discoloured forehead. The sunken lids
were half open, and the candle light gleamed on something foul
where the toad eyes had lived.

But yet the dead thing smiled, as it had smiled in life; the
ghastly lips were parted and drawn wide and tight upon the wolf-
ish teeth, cursing still, and still defying hell to do its worst—defying, cursing, and always and forever smiling alone in the dark.

Sir Gabriel opened the winding-sheet where the hands were,
and the blackened, withered fingers were closed upon something
stained and mottled. Shivering from head to foot, but fighting like
a man in agony for his life, he tried to take the package from the
dead man's hold. But as he pulled at it the claw-like fingers seemed
to close more tightly, and when he pulled harder the shrunken

hands and arms rose from the corpse with a horrible look of life following his motion—then as he wrenched the sealed packet loose at last, the hands fell back into their place still folded.

He set down the candle on the edge of the bier to break the seals from the stout paper. And kneeling on one knee, to get a better light, he read what was within, written long ago in Sir Hugh's queer hand.

He was no longer afraid.

He read how Sir Hugh had written it all down that it might perchance be a witness of evil and of his hatred; how he had loved Evelyn Warburton, his wife's sister; and how his wife had died of a broken heart with his curse upon her, and how Warburton and he had fought side by side in Afghanistan, and Warburton had fallen; but Ockram had brought his comrade's wife back a full year later, and little Evelyn, her child, had been born in Ockram Hall. And next, how he had wearied of the mother and she had died like her sister with his curse on her. And then, how Evelyn had been brought up as his niece, and how he had trusted that his son Gabriel and his daughter, innocent and unknowing, might love and marry, that the souls of the women he had betrayed might suffer another anguish before eternity was out. And last of all, he hoped that some day, when nothing could be undone, the two might find his writing and live on, not daring to tell the truth for their children's sake and the world's word, man and wife.

This he read, kneeling beside the corpse in the north vault, by the light of the altar candle; and when he had read it all, he thanked God aloud that he had found the secret in time. But when he rose to his feet and looked down at the dead face it had changed, and the smile was gone from it forever, and the jaw had fallen a little, and the tired dead lips were relaxed. And then there was a breath behind him and close to him, not cold like that which had blown the flame of the candle as he came, but warm and human. He turned suddenly.

There she stood, all in white, with her shadowy golden hair—for she had risen from her bed and had followed him noiselessly, and had found him reading, and had herself read over his shoulder. He started violently when he saw her, for his nerves were un-strung—and then he cried out her name in that still place of death:

"Evelyn!"

"My brother!" she answered softly and tenderly, putting out both hands to meet his.

Man Overboard!

Yes—I have heard "Man overboard!" a good many times since I was a boy, and once or twice I have seen the man go. There are more men lost in that way than passengers on ocean steamers ever learn of. I have stood looking over the rail on a dark night, when there was a step beside me, and something flew past my head like a big black bat—and then there was a splash! Stokers often go like that. They go mad with the heat, and they slip up on deck and are gone before anybody can stop them, often without being seen or heard. Now and then a passenger will do it, but he generally has what he thinks a pretty good reason. I have seen a man empty his revolver into a crowd of emigrants forward, and then go over like a rocket. Of course, any officer who respects himself will do what he can to pick a man up, if the weather is not so heavy that he would have to risk his ship; but I don't think I remember seeing a man come back when he was once fairly gone more than two or three times in all my life, though we have often picked up the life-buoy, and sometimes the fellow's cap. Stokers and passengers jump over; I never knew a sailor to do that, drunk or sober. Yes, they say it has happened on hard ships, but I never knew a case myself. Once in a long time a man is fished out when it is just too late, and dies in the boat before you can get him aboard, and—well, I don't know that I ever told that story since it happened—I knew a fellow who went over, and came back dead. I didn't see him after he came back; only one of us did, but we all knew he was there.

No, I am not giving you "sharks." There isn't a shark in this story, and I don't know that I would tell it at all if we weren't alone, just you and I. But you and I have seen things in various parts, and maybe you will understand. Anyhow, you know that I am telling what I know about, and nothing else; and it has been on my mind to tell you ever since it happened, only there hasn't been a chance.

It's a long story, and it took some time to happen; and it began a good many years ago, in October, as well as I can remember. I was mate then; I passed the local Marine Board for master about three years later. She was the *Helen B. Jackson*, of New York, with lumber for the West Indies, four-masted schooner, Captain Hackstaff. She was an old-fashioned one, even then—no steam donkey, and all to do by hand. There were still sailors in the coasting trade in those days, you remember. She wasn't a hard ship, for the old man was better than most of them, though he kept to himself and had a face like a monkey-wrench. We were thirteen, all told, in the ship's company; and some of them afterwards thought that might have had something to do with it, but I had all that nonsense knocked out of me when I was a boy. I don't mean to say that I like to go to sea on a Friday, but I *have* gone to sea on a Friday, and nothing has happened; and twice before that we have been thirteen, because one of the hands didn't turn up at the last minute, and nothing ever happened either—nothing worse than the loss of a light spar or two, or a little canvas. Whenever I have been wrecked, we had sailed as cheerily as you please—no thirteens, no Fridays, no dead men in the hold. I believe it generally happens that way.

I dare say you remember those two Benton boys that were so much alike? It is no wonder, for they were twin brothers. They shipped with us as boys on the old *Boston Belle*, when you were mate and I was before the mast. I never was quite sure which was which of those two, even then; and when they both had beards it was harder than ever to tell them apart. One was Jim, and the other was Jack; James Benton and John Benton. The only difference I ever could see was, that one seemed to be rather more cheerful and inclined to talk than the other; but one couldn't even be sure of that. Perhaps they had moods. Anyhow, there was one of them that used to whistle when he was alone. He only knew one tune, and that was "Nancy Lee," and the other didn't know any tune at all; but I may be mistaken about that, too. Perhaps they both knew it.

Well, those two Benton boys turned up on board the *Helen B. Jackson*. They had been on half a dozen ships since the *Boston Belle*, and they had grown up and were good seamen. They had reddish beards and bright blue eyes and freckled faces; and they were quiet fellows, good workmen on rigging, pretty willing, and both good men at the wheel. They managed to be in the same watch—it was the port watch on the *Helen B.*, and that was mine, and I had great confidence in them both. If there was any job aloft that needed two hands, they were always the first to jump into the rigging; but that doesn't often happen on a fore-and-aft schooner. If it breezed up, and the jibtopsail was to be taken in, they never minded a wetting, and they would be out at the bowsprit end before there was a hand at the downhaul. The men liked them for that, and because they didn't blow about what they could do. I remember one day in a reefing job, the downhaul parted and came do on deck from the peak of the spanker. When the weather moderated, and we shook the reefs out, the downhaul was forgotten until we happened to think we might soon need it again. There was some sea on, and the boom was off and the gaff was slamming. One of those Benton boys was at the wheel, and before I knew what he was doing, the other was out on the gaff with the end of the new downhaul, trying to reeve it through its block. The one who was steering watched him, and got as white as cheese. The other one was swinging about on the gaff end, and every time she rolled to leeward he brought up with a jerk that would have sent anything but a monkey flying into space. But he didn't leave it until he had rove the new rope, and he got back all right. I think it was Jack at the wheel; the one that seemed more cheerful, the one that whistled "Nancy Lee." He had rather have been doing the job himself than watch his brother do it, and he had a scared look; but he kept her as steady as he could in the swell, and he drew a long breath when Jim had worked his way back to the peak-halliard block, and had something to hold on to. I think it was Jim.

They had good togs, too, and they were neat and clean men in the forecastle. I knew they had nobody belonging to them ashore,— no mother, no sisters, and no wives; but somehow they both looked as if a woman overhauled them now and then. I remember that they had one ditty bag between them, and they had a woman's thimble in it. One of the men said something about it to them, and they looked at each other; and one smiled, but the other didn't. Most of their clothes were alike, but they had one red guernsey between them. For some time I used to think it was always the same one that wore it, and I thought that might be a way to tell them apart. But then I heard one asking the other for it, and saying that the other had worn it last. So that was no sign either. The cook was a West Indiaman, called James Lawley; his father had been hanged for putting lights in cocoanut trees where they didn't belong. But he was a good cook, and knew his business; and it wasn't soup-and-bully and dog's-body every Sunday. That's what I meant to say. On Sunday the cook called both those boys Jim, and on week-days he called them Jack. He used to say he must be right sometimes if he did that, because even the hands on a painted clock point right twice a day.

What started me to trying for some way of telling the Bentons apart was this. I heard them talking about a girl. It was at night, in our watch, and the wind had headed us off a little rather suddenly, and when we had flattened in the jibs, we clewed down the topsails, while the two Benton boys got the spanker sheet aft. One of them was at the helm. I coiled down the mizzen-topsail downhaul myself, and was going aft to see how she headed up, when I stopped to look at a light, and leaned against the deck-house. While I was standing there I heard the two boys talking. It sounded as if they had talked of the same thing before, and as far as I could tell, the voice I heard first belonged to the one who wasn't quite so cheerful as the other—the one who was Jim when one knew which he was.

"Does Mamie know?" Jim asked.

"Not yet," Jack answered quietly. He was at the wheel. "I mean to tell her next time we get home."

"All right."

That was all I heard, because I didn't care to stand there listening while they were talking about their own affairs; so I went aft to look into the binnacle, and I told the one at the wheel to keep her so as long as she had way on her, for I thought the wind would back up again before long, and there was land to leeward. When he answered, his voice, somehow, didn't sound like the cheerful one. Perhaps his brother had relieved the wheel while they had been speaking, but what I had heard set me wondering which of them it was that had a girl at home. There's lots of time for wondering on a schooner in fair weather.

After that I thought I noticed that the two brothers were more silent when they were together. Perhaps they guessed that I had overheard something that night, and kept quiet when I was about. Some men would have amused themselves by trying to chaff them separately about the girl at home, and I suppose whichever one it was would have let the cat out of the bag if I had done that. But, somehow, I didn't like to. Yes, I was thinking of getting married myself at that time, so I had a sort of fellow-feeling for whichever one it was, that made me not want to chaff him.

They didn't talk much, it seemed to me; but in fair weather, when there was nothing to do at night, and one was steering, the other was everlastingly hanging round as if he were waiting to relieve the wheel, though he might have been enjoying a quiet nap for all I cared in such weather. Or else, when one was taking his turn at the lookout, the other would be sitting on an anchor beside him. One kept near the other, at night more than in the daytime. I noticed that. They were fond of sitting on that anchor, and they generally tucked away their pipes under it for the *Helen B.* was a dry boat in most weather, and like most fore-and-afters was better on a wind than going free. With a beam sea we sometimes shipped a little water aft. We were by the stern, anyhow, on that voyage, and that is one reason why we lost the man.

We fell in with a southerly gale, southeast at first; and then the barometer began to fall while you could watch it, and a long swell began to come up from the south'ard. A couple of months earlier we might have been in for a cyclone, but it's "October all over" in those waters, as you know better than I. It was just going to blow, and then it was going to rain, that was all; and we had plenty of time to make everything snug before it breezed up much. It blew harder after sunset, and by the time it was quite dark it was a full gale. We had shortened sail for it, but as we were by the stern we were carrying the spanker close reefed instead of the storm trysail. She steered better so, as long as we didn't have to heave to. I had the first watch with the Benton boys, and we had not been on deck an hour when a child might have seen that the weather meant business.

The old man came up on deck and looked round, and in less than a minute he told us to give her the trysail. That meant heaving to, and I was glad of it; for though the *Helen B.* was a good vessel enough, she wasn't a new ship by a long way, and it did her no good to drive her in that weather. I asked whether I should call all hands, but just then the cook came aft, and the old man said he thought we could manage the job without waking the sleepers, and the trysail was handy on deck already, for we hadn't been expecting anything better. We were all in oilskins, of course, and the night was as black as a coal mine, with only a ray of light from the slit in the binnacle shield, and you couldn't tell one man from another except by his voice. The old man took the wheel; we got the boom amidships, and he jammed her into the wind until she had hardly any way. It was blowing now, and it was all that I and two others could do to get in the slack of the downhaul, while the others lowered away at the peak and throat, and we had our hands full to get a couple of turns round the wet sail. It's all child's play on a fore-and-after compared with reefing topsails in anything like weather, but the gear of a schooner sometimes does unhandy things that you don't expect, and those everlasting long halliards get foul of everything if they get adrift. I remember thinking how unhandy that particular job was. Somebody unhooked the throat-halliard block, and thought he had hooked it into the head-cringle of the trysail, and sang out to hoist away, but he had missed it in the dark, and the heavy block went flying into the lee rigging, and nearly killed him when it swung back with the weather roll. Then the old man got her up in the wind until the jib was shaking like thunder; then he held her off, and she went off as soon as the head-sails filled, and he couldn't get her back again without the spanker. Then the *Helen B.* did her favourite trick, and before we had time to say much we had a sea over the quarter and were up to our waists, with the parrels of the trysail only half becketed round the mast, and the deck so full of gear that you couldn't put your foot on a plank, and the spanker beginning to get adrift again, being badly stopped, and the general confusion and hell's delight that you can only have on a fore-and-after when there's nothing really serious the matter. Of course, I don't mean to say that the old man couldn't have steered his trick as well as you or I or any other seaman; but I don't believe he had ever been on board the *Helen B.* before, or had his hand on her wheel till then; and he didn't know her ways. I don't mean to say that what happened was his fault. I don't know whose fault it was. Perhaps nobody was to blame. But I knew something happened somewhere on board when we shipped that sea, and you'll never get it out of my head. I hadn't any spare time myself, for I was becketing the rest of the trysail to the mast. We were on the starboard tack, and the throat-halliard came down to port as usual, and I suppose there were at least three men at it, hoisting away, while I was at the beckets.

Now I am going to tell you something. You have known me, man and boy, several voyages; and you are older than I am; and you have always been a good friend to me. Now, do you think I am the sort of man to think I hear things where there isn't anything to hear, or to think I see things when there is nothing to see? No, you don't. Thank you. Well now, I had passed the last becket, and I sang out to the men to sway away, and I was standing on the jaws of the spanker-gaff, with my left hand on the bolt-rope of the trysail, so that I could feel when it was board-taut, and I wasn't thinking of anything except being glad the job was over, and that we were going to heave her to. It was as black as a coal-pocket, except that you could see the streaks on the seas as they went by, and abaft the deck-house I could see the ray of light from the binnacle on the captain's yellow oilskin as he stood at the wheel—or rather I might have seen it if I had looked round at that minute. But I didn't look round. I heard a man whistling. It was "Nancy Lee," and I could have sworn that the man was right over my head in the crosstrees. Only somehow I knew very well that if anybody could have been up there, and could have whistled a tune, there were no living ears sharp enough to hear it on deck then. I heard it distinctly, and at the same time I heard the real whistling of the wind in the weather rigging, sharp and clear as the steam-whistle on a Dago's peanut-cart in New York. That was all right, that was as it should be; but the other wasn't right; and I felt queer and stiff, as if I couldn't move, and my hair was curling against the flannel lining of my sou'wester, and I thought somebody had dropped a lump of ice down my back.

I said that the noise of the wind in the rigging was real, as if the other wasn't, for I felt that it wasn't, though I heard it. But it was, all the same; for the captain heard it, too. When I came to relieve the wheel, while the men were clearing up decks, he was swearing. He was a quiet man, and I hadn't heard him swear before, and I don't think I did again, though several queer things happened after that. Perhaps he said all he had to say then; I don't see how he could have said anything more. I used to think nobody could swear like a Dane, except a Neapolitan or a South American; but when I had heard the old man I changed my mind. There's nothing afloat or ashore that can beat one of your quiet American skippers, if he gets off on that tack. I didn't need to ask him what was the matter, for I knew he had heard "Nancy Lee," as I had, only it affected us differently.

He did not give me the wheel, but told me to go forward and get the second bonnet off the staysail, so as to keep her up better. As we tailed on to the sheet when it was done, the man next me knocked his sou'wester off against my shoulder, and his face came so close to me that I could see it in the dark. It must have been very white for me to see it, but I only thought of that afterwards. I don't see how any light could have fallen upon it, but I knew it was one of the Benton boys. I don't know what made me speak to him. "Hullo, Jim! Is that you?" I asked. I don't know why I said Jim, rather than Jack.

"I am Jack," he answered.

We made all fast, and things were much quieter.

"The old man heard you whistling 'Nancy Lee,' just now," I said, "and he didn't like it."

It was as if there were a white light inside his face, and it was ghastly. I know his teeth chattered. But he didn't say anything, and the next minute he was somewhere in the dark trying to find his sou'wester at the foot of the mast.

When all was quiet, and she was hove to, coming to and falling off her four points as regularly as a pendulum, and the helm lashed a little to the lee, the old man turned in again, and I managed to light a pipe in the lee of the deckhouse, for there was nothing more to be done till the gale chose to moderate, and the ship was as easy as a baby in its cradle. Of course the cook had gone below, as he might have done an hour earlier; so there were supposed to be four of us in the watch. There was a man at the lookout, and there was a hand by the wheel, though there was no steering to be done, and I was having my pipe in the lee of the deck-house, and the fourth man was somewhere about decks, probably having a smoke too. I thought some skippers I had sailed with would have called the watch aft, and given them a drink after that job, but it wasn't cold, and I guessed that our old man wouldn't be particularly generous in that way. My hands and feet were red-hot, and it would be time enough to get into dry clothes when it was my watch below; so I stayed where I was, and smoked. But by and by, things being so quiet, I began to wonder why nobody moved on deck; just that sort of restless wanting to know where every man is that one some-times feels in a gale of wind on a dark night. So when I had fin-ished my pipe I began to move about. I went aft, and there was a man leaning over the wheel, with his legs apart and both hands hanging down in the light from the binnacle, and his sou'wester over his eyes. Then I went forward, and there was a man at the lookout, with his back against the foremast, getting what shelter he could from the staysail. I knew by his small height that he was not one of the Benton boys. Then I went round by the weather side, and poked about in the dark, for I began to wonder where the other man was. But I couldn't find him, though I searched the decks until I got right aft again. It was certainly one of the Benton boys that was missing, but it wasn't like either of them to go below to change his clothes in such warm weather. The man at the wheel was the other, of course. I spoke to him.

"Jim, what's become of your brother?"

"I am Jack, sir."

"Well, then, Jack, where's Jim? He's not on deck."

"I don't know, sir."

When I had come up to him he had stood up from force of instinct, and had laid his hands on the spokes as if he were steering, though the wheel was lashed; but he still bent his face down, and it was half hidden by the edge of his sou'wester, while he seemed to be staring at the compass. He spoke in a very low voice, but that was natural, for the captain had left his door open when he turned in, as it was a warm night in spite of the storm, and there was no fear of shipping any more water now.

"What put it into your head to whistle like that, Jack? You've been at sea long enough to know better."

He said something, but I couldn't hear the words; it sounded as if he were denying the charge.

"Somebody whistled," I said.

He didn't answer, and then, I don't know why, perhaps because the old man hadn't given us a drink, I cut half an inch off the plug of tobacco I had in my oilskin pocket, and gave it to him. He knew my tobacco was good, and he shoved it into his mouth with a word of thanks. I was on the weather side of the wheel.

"Go forward and see if you can find Jim," I said.

He started a little, and then stepped back and passed behind me, and was going along the weather side. Maybe his silence about the whistling had irritated me, and his taking it for granted that because we were hove to and it was a dark night, he might go forward any way he pleased. Anyhow, I stopped him, though I spoke good-naturedly enough.

"Pass to leeward, Jack," I said.

He didn't answer, but crossed the deck between the binnacle and the deckhouse to the lee side. She was only falling off and coming to, and riding the big seas as easily as possible, but the man was not steady on his feet and reeled against the corner of the deckhouse and then against the lee rail. I was quite sure he couldn't have had anything to drink, for neither of the brothers were the kind to hide rum from their shipmates, if they had any, and the only spirits that were aboard were locked up in the captain's cabin. I wondered whether he had been hit by the throat-halliard block and was hurt.

I left the wheel and went after him, but when I got to the corner of the deck-house I saw that he was on a full run forward, so I went back. I watched the compass for a while, to see how far she went off, and she must have come to again half a dozen times before I heard voices, more than three or four, forward; and then I heard the little West Indies cook's voice, high and shrill above the rest:— "Man overboard!"

There wasn't anything to be done, with the ship hove-to and the wheel lashed. If there was a man overboard, he must be in the water right alongside. I couldn't imagine how it could have happened, but I ran forward instinctively. I came upon the cook first, half-dressed in his shirt and trousers, just as he had tumbled out of his bunk. He was jumping into the main rigging, evidently hoping to see the man, as if any one could have seen anything on such a night, except the foam-streaks on the black water, and now and then the curl of a breaking sea as it went away to leeward. Several of the men were peering over the rail into the dark. I caught the cook by the foot, and asked who was gone.

"It's Jim Benton," he shouted down to me. "He's not aboard this ship!"

There was no doubt about that Jim Benton was gone; and I knew in a flash that he had been taken off by that sea when we were setting the storm trysail. It was nearly half an hour since then; she had run like wild for a few minutes until we got her hove-to, and no swimmer that ever swam could have lived as long as that in such a sea. The men knew it as well as I, but still they stared into the foam as if they had any chance of seeing the lost man. I let the cook get into the rigging and joined the men, and asked if they had made a thorough search on board, though I knew they had and that it could not take long, for he wasn't on deck, and there was only the forecastle below.

"That sea took him over, sir, as sure as you're born," said one of the men close beside me.

We had no boat that could have lived in that sea, of course, and we all knew it. I offered to put one over, and let her drift astern two or three cable's-lengths by a line, if the men thought they could haul me aboard again; but none of them would listen to that, and I should probably have been drowned if I had tried it, even with a life-belt; for it was a breaking sea. Besides, they all knew as well as I did that the man could not be right in our wake. I don't know why I spoke again.

"Jack Benton, are you there? Will you go if I will?"

"No, sir," answered a voice; and that was all.

By that time the old man was on deck, and I felt his hand on my shoulder rather roughly, as if he meant to shake me.

"I'd reckoned you had more sense, Mr. Torkeldsen," he said. "God knows I would risk my ship to look for him, if it were any use; but he must have gone half an hour ago."

He was a quiet man, and the men knew he was right, and that they had seen the last of Jim Benton when they were bending the trysail—if anybody had seen him then. The captain went below again, and for some time the men stood around Jack, quite near him, without saying anything, as sailors do when they are sorry for a man and can't help him; and then the watch below turned in again, and we were three on deck.

Nobody can understand that there can be much consolation in a funeral, unless he has felt that blank feeling there is when a man's gone overboard whom everybody likes. I suppose landsmen think it would be easier if they didn't have to bury their fathers and mothers and friends; but it wouldn't be. Somehow the funeral keeps up the idea of something beyond. You may believe in that something just the same; but a man who has gone in the dark, between two seas, without a cry, seems much more beyond reach than if he were still lying on his bed, and had only just stopped breathing. Perhaps Jim Benton knew that, and wanted to come back to us. I don't know, and I am only telling you what happened, and you may think what you like.

Jack stuck by the wheel that night until the watch was over. I don't know whether he slept afterwards, but when I came on deck four hours later, there he was again, in his oilskins, with his sou'wester over his eyes, staring into the binnacle. We saw that he would rather stand there, and we left him alone. Perhaps it was some consolation to him to get that ray of light when everything was so dark. It began to rain, too, as it can when a southerly gale is going to break up, and we got every bucket and tub on board, and set them under the booms to catch the fresh water for washing our clothes. The rain made it very thick, and I went and stood under the lee of the staysail, looking out. I could tell that day was breaking, because the foam was whiter in the dark where the seas crested, and little by little the black rain grew grey and steamy, and I couldn't see the red glare of the port light on the water when she went off and rolled to leeward. The gale had moderated considerably, and in another hour we should be under way again. I was still standing there when Jack Benton came forward. He stood still a few minutes near me. The rain came down in a solid sheet, and I could see his wet beard and a corner of his cheek, too, grey in the dawn. Then he stooped down and began feeling under the anchor for his pipe. We had hardly shipped any water forward, and I suppose he had some way of tucking the pipe in, so that the rain hadn't floated it off. Presently he got on his legs again, and I saw that he had two pipes in his hand. One of them had belonged to his brother, and after looking at them a moment I suppose he recognised his own, for he put it in his mouth, dripping with water. Then he looked at the other fully a minute without moving. When he had made up his mind, I suppose, he quietly chucked it over the lee rail, without even looking round to see whether I was watching him. I thought it was a pity, for it was a good wooden pipe, with a nickel ferrule, and somebody would have been glad to have it. But I didn't like to make any remark, for he had a right to do what he pleased with what had belonged to his dead brother. He blew the water out of his own pipe, and dried it against his jacket, putting his hand inside his oilskin; he filled it, standing under the lee of the foremast, got a light after wasting two or three matches, and turned the pipe upside down in his teeth, to keep the rain out of the bowl. I don't know why I noticed everything he did, and remember it now; but somehow I felt sorry for him, and I kept wondering whether there was anything I could say that would make him feel better. But I didn't think of anything, and as it was broad daylight I went aft again, for I guessed that the old man would turn out before long and order the spanker set and the helm up. But he didn't turn out before seven bells, just as the clouds broke and showed blue sky to leeward— "the Frenchman's barometer," you used to call it.

Some people don't seem to be so dead, when they are dead, as others are. Jim Benton was like that. He had been on my watch, and I couldn't get used to the idea that he wasn't about decks with me. I was always expecting to see him, and his brother was so exactly like him that I often felt as if I did see him and forgot he was dead, and made the mistake of calling Jack by his name; though I tried not to, because I knew it must hurt. If ever Jack had been the cheerful one of the two, as I had always supposed he had been, he had changed very much, for he grew to be more silent than Jim had ever been.

One fine afternoon I was sitting on the main-hatch, overhauling the clockwork of the taffrail-log, which hadn't been registering very well of late, and I had got the cook to bring me a coffee-cup to hold the small screws as I took them out, and a saucer for the sperm-oil I was going to use. I noticed that he didn't go away, but hung round without exactly watching what I was doing, as if he wanted to say something to me. I thought if it were worth much he would say it anyhow, so I didn't ask him questions; and sure enough he began of his own accord before long. There was nobody on deck but the man at the wheel, and the other man away forward.

"Mr. Torkeldsen," the cook began, and then stopped.

I supposed he was going to ask me to let the watch break out a barrel of flour, or some salt horse.

"Well, doctor?" I asked, as he didn't go on.

"Well, Mr. Torkeldsen," he answered, "I somehow want to ask you whether you think I am giving satisfaction on this ship, or not?"

"So far as I know, you are, doctor. I haven't heard any complaints from the forecastle, and the captain has said nothing, and I think you know your business, and the cabin-boy is bursting out of his clothes. That looks as if you are giving satisfaction. What makes you think you are not?"

I am not good at giving you that West Indies talk, and sha'n't try; but the doctor beat about the bush awhile, and then he told me he thought the men were beginning to play tricks on him, and he didn't like it, and thought he hadn't deserved it, and would like his discharge at our next port. I told him he was a d—d fool, of course, to begin with; and that men were more apt to try a joke with a chap they liked than with anybody they wanted to get rid of; unless it was a bad joke, like flooding his bunk, or filling his boots with tar. But it wasn't that kind of practical joke. The doctor said that the men were trying to frighten him, and he didn't like it, and that they put things in his way that frightened him. So I told him he was a d—d fool to be frightened, anyway, and I wanted to know what things they put in his way. He gave me a queer answer. He said they were spoons and forks, and odd plates, and a cup now and then, and such things.

I set down the taffrail-log on the bit of canvas I had put under it, and looked at the doctor. He was uneasy, and his eyes had a sort of hunted look, and his yellow face looked grey. He wasn't trying to make trouble. He was in trouble. So I asked him questions.

He said he could count as well as anybody, and do sums without using his fingers, but that when he couldn't count any other way he did use his fingers, and it always came out the same. He said that when he and the cabin-boy cleared up after the men's meals there were more things to wash than he had given out. There'd be a fork more, or there'd be a spoon more, and some-times there'd be a spoon and a fork, and there was always a plate more. It wasn't that he complained of that. Before poor Jim Benton was lost they had a man more to feed, and his gear to wash up after meals, and that was in the contract, the doctor said. It would have been if there were twenty in the ship's company; but he didn't think it was right for the men to play tricks like that. He kept his things in good order, and he counted them, and he was respon-sible for them, and it wasn't right that the men should take more things than they needed when his back was turned, and just soil them and mix them up with their own, so as to make him think—

He stopped there, and looked at me, and I looked at him. I didn't know what he thought, but I began to guess. I wasn't going to humour any such nonsense as that, so I told him to speak to the men himself, and not come bothering me about such things.

"Count the plates and forks and spoons before them when they sit down to table, and tell them that's all they'll get; and when they have finished, count the things again, and if the count isn't right, find out who did it. You know it must be one of them. You're not a green hand; you've been going to sea ten or eleven years, and don't want any lesson about how to behave if the boys play a trick on you."

"If I could catch him," said the cook, "I'd have a knife into him before he could say his prayers."

Those West India men are always talking about knives, espe-cially when they are badly frightened. I knew what he meant, and didn't ask him, but went on cleaning the brass cogwheels of the patent log and oiling the bearings with a feather. "Wouldn't it be better to wash it out with boiling water, sir?" asked the cook, in an insinuating tone. He knew that he had made a fool of himself, and was anxious to make it right again.

I heard no more about the odd platter and gear for two or three days, though I thought about his story a good deal. The doctor evi-dently believed that Jim Benton had come back, though he didn't quite like to say so. His story had sounded silly enough on a bright afternoon, in fair weather, when the sun was on the water, and every rag was drawing in the breeze, and the sea looked as pleasant and harmless as a cat that has just eaten a canary. But when it was toward the end of the first watch, and the waning moon had not risen yet, and the water was like still oil, and the jibs hung down flat and helpless like the wings of a dead bird—it wasn't the same then. More than once I have started then, and looked round when a fish jumped, expecting to see a face sticking up out of the water with its eyes shut. I think we all felt something like that at the time.

One afternoon we were putting a fresh service on the jib-sheet-pennant. It wasn't my watch, but I was standing by looking on. Just then Jack Benton came up from below, and went to look for his pipe under the anchor. His face was hard and drawn, and his eyes were cold like steel balls. He hardly ever spoke now, but he did his duty as usual and nobody had to complain of him, though we were all beginning to wonder how long his grief for his dead brother was going to last like that. I watched him as he crouched down, and ran his hand into the hiding-place for the pipe. When he stood up, he had two pipes in his hand.

Now, I remembered very well seeing him throw one of those pipes away, early in the morning after the gale; and it came to me now, and I didn't suppose he kept a stock of them under the anchor. I caught sight of his face, and it was greenish white, like the foam on shallow water, and he stood a long time looking at the two pipes. He wasn't looking to see which was his, for I wasn't five yards from him as he stood, and one of those pipes had been smoked that day, and was shiny where his hand had rubbed it, and the bone mouth-piece was chafed white where his teeth had bitten it. The other was water-logged. It was swelled and cracking with wet, and it looked to me as if there were a little green weed on it.

Jack Benton turned his head rather stealthily as I looked away, and then he hid the thing in his trousers pocket, and went aft on the lee side, out of sight. The men had got the sheet pennant on a stretch to serve it, but I ducked under it and stood where I could see what Jack did, just under the forestaysail. He couldn't see me, and he was looking about for something. His hand shook as he picked up a bit of half-bent iron rod, about a foot long, that had been used for turning an eyebolt, and had been left on the mainhatch. His hand shook as he got a piece of marline out of his pocket, and made the water-logged pipe fast to the iron. He didn't mean it to get adrift, either, for he took his turns carefully, and hove them taut and then rode them, so that they couldn't slip, and made the end fast with two half-hitches round the iron, and hitched it back on itself. Then he tried it with his hands, and looked up and down the deck furtively, and then quietly dropped the pipe and iron over the rail, so that I didn't even hear the splash. If anybody was playing tricks on board, they weren't meant for the cook.

I asked some questions about Jack Benton, and one of the men told me that he was off his feed, and hardly ate anything, and swallowed all the coffee he could lay his hands on, and had used up all his own tobacco and had begun on what his brother had left.

"The doctor says it ain't so, sir," said the man, looking at me shyly, as if he didn't expect to be believed; "the doctor says there's as much eaten from breakfast to breakfast as there was before Jim fell overboard, though there's a mouth less and another that eats nothing. I says it's the cabin-boy that gets it. He's bu'sting."

I told him that if the cabin-boy ate more than his share, he must work more than his share, so as to balance things. But the man laughed queerly, and looked at me again.

"I only said that, sir, just like that. We all know it ain't so."

"Well, how is it?"

"How is it?" asked the man, half-angry all at once. "I don't know how it is, but there's a hand on board that's getting his whack along with us as regular as the bells."

"Does he use tobacco?" I asked, meaning to laugh it out of him, but as I spoke I remembered the water-logged pipe.

"I guess he's using his own still," the man answered, in a queer, low voice. "Perhaps he'll take some one else's when his is all gone."

It was about nine o'clock in the morning, I remember, for just then the captain called to me to stand by the chronometer while he took his fore observation. Captain Hackstaff wasn't one of those old skippers who do everything themselves with a pocket watch, and keep the key of the chronometer in their waistcoat pocket, and won't tell the mate how far the dead reckoning is out. He was rather the other way, and I was glad of it, for he generally let me work the sights he took, and just ran his eye over my figures afterwards. I am bound to say his eye was pretty good, for he would pick out a mistake in a logarithm, or tell me that I had worked the "Equation of Time" with the wrong sign, before it seemed to me that he could have got as far as "half the sum, minus the altitude." He was always right, too, and besides he knew a lot about iron ships and local deviation, and adjusting the compass, and all that sort of thing. I don't know how he came to be in command of a fore-and-aft schooner. He never talked about himself, and maybe he had just been mate on one of those big steel square-riggers, and something had put him back. Perhaps he had been captain, and had got his ship aground, through no particular fault of his, and had to begin over again. Sometimes he talked just like you and me, and sometimes he would speak more like books do, or some of those Boston people I have heard. I don't know. We have all been shipmates now and then with men who have seen better days. Perhaps he had been in the Navy, but what makes me think he couldn't have been, was that he was a thorough good seaman, a regular old windjammer, and understood sail, which those Navy chaps rarely do. Why, you and I have sailed with men before the mast who had their master's certificates in their pockets,—English Board of Trade certificates, too,—who could work a double altitude if you would lend them a sextant and give them a look at the chronometer, as well as many a man who commands a big square-rigger. Navigation ain't everything, nor seamanship, either. You've got to have it in you, if you mean to get there.

I don't know how our captain heard that there was trouble forward. The cabin-boy may have told him, or the men may have talked outside his door when they relieved the wheel at night. Anyhow, he got wind of it, and when he had got his sight that morning he had all hands aft, and gave them a lecture. It was just the kind of talk you might have expected from him. He said he hadn't any complaint to make, and that so far as he knew everybody on board was doing his duty, and that he was given to understand that the men got their whack, and were satisfied. He said his ship was never a hard ship, and that he liked quiet, and that was the reason he didn't mean to have any nonsense, and the men might just as well understand that, too. We'd had a great misfortune, he said, and it was nobody's fault. We had lost a man we all liked and respected, and he felt that everybody in the ship ought to be sorry for the man's brother, who was left behind, and that it was rotten lubberly childishness, and unjust and unmanly and cowardly, to be playing schoolboy tricks with forks and spoons and pipes, and that sort of gear. He said it had got to stop right now, and that was all, and the men might go forward. And so they did.

It got worse after that, and the men watched the cook, and the cook watched the men, as if they were trying to catch each other; but I think everybody felt that there was something else. One evening, at supper-time, I was on deck, and Jack came aft to relieve the wheel while the man who was steering got his supper. He hadn't got past the main-hatch on the lee side, when I heard a man running in slippers that slapped on the deck, and there was a sort of a yell and I saw the coloured cook going for Jack, with a carving-knife in his hand. I jumped to get between them, and Jack turned round short, and put out his hand. I was too far to reach them, and the cook jabbed out with his knife. But the blade didn't get anywhere near Benton. The cook seemed to be jabbing it into the air again and again, at least four feet short of the mark. Then he dropped his right hand, and I saw the whites of his eyes in the dusk, and he reeled up against the pin-rail, and caught hold of a belaying-pin with his left. I had reached him by that time, and grabbed hold of his knife-hand and the other too, for I thought he was going to use the pin; but Jack Benton was standing staring stupidly at him, as if he didn't understand. But instead, the cook was holding on because he couldn't stand, and his teeth were chattering, and he let go of the knife, and the point stuck into the deck.

"He's crazy!" said Jack Benton, and that was all he said and he went aft.

When he was gone, the cook began to come to, and he spoke quite low, near my ear.

"There were two of them! So help me God, there were two of them!"

I don't know why I didn't take him by the collar, and give him a good shaking; but I didn't. I just picked up the knife and gave it to him, and told him to go back to his galley, and not to make a fool of himself. You see, he hadn't struck at Jack, but at something he thought he saw, and I knew what it was, and I felt that same thing, like a lump of ice sliding down my back, that I felt that night when we were bending the trysail.

When the men had seen him running aft, they jumped up after him, but they held off when they saw that I had caught him. By and by, the man who had spoken to me before told me what had happened. He was a stocky little chap, with a red head.

"Well," he said, "there isn't much to tell. Jack Benton had been eating his supper with the rest of us. He always sits at the after corner of the table, on the port side. His brother used to sit at the end, next him. The doctor gave him a thundering big piece of pie to finish up with, and when he had finished he didn't stop for a smoke, but went off quick to relieve the wheel. Just as he had gone, the doctor came in from the galley, and when he saw Jack's empty plate he stood stock still staring at it; and we all wondered what was the matter, till we looked at the plate. There were two forks in it, sir, lying side by side. Then the doctor grabbed his knife, and flew up through the hatch like a rocket. The other fork was there all right, Mr. Torkeldsen, for we all saw it and handled it; and we all had our own. That's all I know."

I didn't feel that I wanted to laugh when he told me that story; but I hoped the old man wouldn't hear it, for I knew he wouldn't believe it, and no captain that ever sailed likes to have stories like that going round about his ship. It gives her a bad name. But that was all anybody ever saw except the cook, and he isn't the first man who has thought he saw things without having any drink in him. I think, if the doctor had been weak in the head as he was afterwards, he might have done something foolish again, and there might have been serious trouble. But he didn't. Only, two or three times I saw him looking at Jack Benton in a queer, scared way, and once, I heard him talking to himself.

"There's two of them! So help me God, there's two of them!"

He didn't say anything more about asking for his discharge, but I knew well enough that if he got ashore at the next port we should never see him again, if he had to leave his kit behind him, and his money, too. He was scared all through, for good and all; and he wouldn't be right again till he got another ship. It's no use to talk to a man when he gets like that, any more than it is to send a boy to the main truck when he has lost his nerve.

Jack Benton never spoke of what happened that evening. I don't know whether he knew about the two forks, or not; or whether he understood what the trouble was. Whatever he knew from the other men, he was evidently living under a hard strain. He was quiet enough, and too quiet; but his face was set, and sometimes it twitched oddly when he was at the wheel, and he would turn his head round sharp to look behind him. A man doesn't do that naturally, unless there's a vessel that he thinks is creeping up on the quarter. When that happens, if the man at the wheel takes a pride in his ship, he will almost always keep glancing over his shoulder to see whether the other fellow is gaining. But Jack Benton used to look round when there was nothing there; and what is curious, the other men seemed to catch the trick when they were steering. One day the old man turned out just as the man at the wheel looked behind him.

"What are you looking at?" asked the captain.

"Nothing, sir," answered the man.

"Then keep your eye on the mizzenroyal," said the old man, as if he were forgetting that we weren't a square-rigger.

"Ay, ay, sir," said the man.

The captain told me to go below and work up the latitude from the dead-reckoning, and he went forward of the deckhouse and sat down to read, as he often did. When I came up, the man at the wheel was looking round again, and I stood beside him and just asked him quietly what everybody was looking at, for it was getting to be a general habit. He wouldn't say anything at first, but just answered that it was nothing. But when he saw that I didn't seem to care, and just stood there as if there were nothing more to be said, he naturally began to talk.

He said that it wasn't that he saw anything, because there wasn't anything to see except the spanker sheet just straining a little, and working in the sheaves of the blocks as the schooner rose to the short seas. There wasn't anything to be seen, but it seemed to him that the sheet made a queer noise in the blocks. It was a new manilla sheet; and in dry weather it did make a little noise, something between a creak and a wheeze. I looked at it and looked at the man, and said nothing; and presently he went on. He asked me if I didn't notice anything peculiar about the noise. I listened awhile, and said I didn't notice anything. Then he looked rather sheepish, but said he didn't think it could be his own ears, because every man who steered his trick heard the same thing now and then,—sometimes once in a day, sometimes once in a night, sometimes it would go on a whole hour.

"It sounds like sawing wood," I said, just like that.

"To us it sounds a good deal more like a man whistling 'Nancy Lee.'" He started nervously as he spoke the last words. "There, sir, don't you hear it?" he asked suddenly.

I heard nothing but the creaking of the manilla sheet. It was getting near noon, and fine, clear weather in southern waters,— just the sort of day and the time when you would least expect to feel creepy. But I remembered how I had heard that same tune overhead at night in a gale of wind a fortnight earlier, and I am not ashamed to say that the same sensation came over me now, and I wished myself well out of the *Helen B.*, and aboard of any old cargo-dragger, with a windmill on deck, and an eighty-nine-forty-eighter for captain, and a fresh leak whenever it breezed up.

Little by little during the next few days life on board that vessel came to be about as unbearable as you can imagine. It wasn't that there was much talk, for I think the men were shy even of speaking to each other freely about what they thought. The whole ship's company grew silent, until one hardly ever heard a voice, except giving an order and the answer. The men didn't sit over their meals when their watch was below, but either turned in at once or sat about on the forecastle smoking their pipes without saying a word. We were all thinking of the same thing. We all felt as if there were a hand on board, sometimes below, sometimes about decks, sometimes aloft, sometimes on the boom end; taking his full share of what the others got, but doing no work for it. We didn't only feel it, we knew it. He took up no room, he cast no shadow, and we never heard his footfall on deck; but he took his whack with the rest as regular as the bells, and he whistled "Nancy Lee." It was like the worst sort of dream you can imagine; and I dare say a good many of us tried to believe it was nothing else sometimes, when we stood looking over the weather rail in fine weather with the breeze in our faces; but if we happened to turn round and look into each other's eyes, we knew it was something worse than any dream could be; and we would turn away from each other with a queer, sick feeling, wishing that we could just for once see some-body who didn't know what we knew.

There's not much more to tell about the *Helen B. Jackson* so far as I am concerned. We were more like a shipload of lunatics than anything else when we ran in under Morro Castle, and anchored in Havana. The cook had brain fever and was raving mad in his delirium; and the rest of the men weren't far from the same state. The last three or four days had been awful, and we had been as near to having a mutiny on board as I ever want to be. The men didn't want to hurt anybody; but they wanted to get away out of that ship, if they had to swim for it; to get away from that whis-tling, from that dead shipmate who had come back, and who filled the ship with his unseen self. I know that if the old man and I hadn't kept a sharp lookout the men would have put a boat over quietly on one of those calm nights, and pulled away, leaving the captain and me and the mad cook to work the schooner into harbour. We should have done it somehow, of course, for we hadn't far to run if we could get a breeze; and once or twice I found myself wishing that the crew were really gone, for the awful state of fright in which they lived was beginning to work on me too. You see I partly believed and partly didn't; but anyhow I didn't mean to let the thing get the better of me, whatever it was. I turned crusty, too, and kept the men at work on all sorts of jobs, and drove them to it until they wished I was overboard, too. It wasn't that the old man and I were trying to drive them to desert without their pay, as I am sorry to say a good many skippers and mates do, even now. Captain Hackstaff was as straight as a string, and I didn't mean those poor fellows should be cheated out of a single cent; and I didn't blame them for wanting to leave the ship, but it seemed to me that the only chance to keep everybody sane through those last days was to work the men till they dropped. When they were dead tired they slept a little, and forgot the thing until they had to tumble up on deck and face it again. That was a good many years ago. Do you believe that I can't hear "Nancy Lee" now, without feeling cold down my back? For I heard it too, now and then, after the man had explained why he was always looking over his shoulder. Perhaps it was imagination. I don't know. When I look back it seems to me that I only remember a long fight against something I couldn't see, against an appalling presence, against something worse than cholera or Yellow Jack or the plague—and goodness knows the mildest of them is bad enough when it breaks out at sea. The men got as white as chalk, and wouldn't go about decks alone at night, no matter what I said to them. With the cook raving in his bunk the forecastle would have been a perfect hell, and there wasn't a spare cabin on board. There never is on a fore-and-after. So I put him into mine, and he was more quiet there, and at last fell into a sort of stupor as if he were going to die. I don't know what became of him, for we put him ashore alive and left him in the hospital.

The men came aft in a body, quiet enough, and asked the captain if he wouldn't pay them off, and let them go ashore. Some men wouldn't have done it, for they had shipped for the voyage, and had signed articles. But the captain knew that when sailors get an idea into their heads they're no better than children; and if he forced them to stay aboard he wouldn't get much work out of them, and couldn't rely on them in a difficulty. So he paid them off, and let them go. When they had gone forward to get their kits, he asked me whether I wanted to go too, and for a minute I had a sort of weak feeling that I might just as well. But I didn't, and he was a good friend to me afterwards. Perhaps he was grateful to me for sticking to him.

When the men went off he didn't come on deck; but it was my duty to stand by while they left the ship. They owed me a grudge for making them work during the last few days, and most of them dropped into the boat without so much as a word or a look, as sailors will. Jack Benton was the last to go over the side, and he stood still a minute and looked at me, and his white face twitched. I thought he wanted to say something.

"Take care of yourself, Jack," said I. "So long!"

It seemed as if he couldn't speak for two or three seconds; then his words came thick.

"It wasn't my fault, Mr. Torkeldsen. I swear it wasn't my fault!"

That was all; and he dropped over the side, leaving me to wonder what he meant.

The captain and I stayed on board, and the ship-chandler got a West India boy to cook for us.

That evening, before turning in, we were standing by the rail having a quiet smoke, watching the lights of the city, a quarter of a mile off, reflected in the still water. There was music of some sort ashore, in a sailors' dance-house, I dare say; and I had no doubt that most of the men who had left the ship were there, and already full of jiggy-jiggy. The music played a lot of sailors' tunes that ran into each other, and we could hear the men's voices in the chorus now and then. One followed another, and then it was "Nancy Lee," loud and clear, and the men singing "Yo-ho, heave-ho!"

"I have no ear for music," said Captain Hackstaff, "but it appears to me that's the tune that man was whistling the night we lost the man overboard. I don't know why it has stuck in my head, and of course it's all nonsense; but it seems to me that I have heard it all the rest of the trip."

I didn't say anything to that, but I wondered just how much the old man had understood. Then we turned in, and I slept ten hours without opening my eyes.

I stuck to the *Helen B. Jackson* after that as long as I could stand a fore-and-after; but that night when we lay in Havana was the last time I ever heard "Nancy Lee" on board of her. The spare hand had gone ashore with the rest, and he never came back, and he took his tune with him; but all those things are just as clear in my memory as if they had happened yesterday. After that I was in deep water for a year or more, and after I came home I got my certificate, and what with having friends and having saved a little money, and having had a small legacy from an uncle in Norway, I got the command of a coastwise vessel, with a small share in her. I was at home three weeks before going to sea, and Jack Benton saw my name in the local papers, and wrote to me.

He said that he had left the sea, and was trying farming, and he was going to be married, and he asked if I wouldn't come over for that, for it wasn't more than forty minutes by train; and he and Mamie would be proud to have me at the wedding. I remembered how I had heard one brother ask the other whether Mamie knew. That meant, whether she knew, he wanted to marry her, I suppose. She had taken her time about it, for it was pretty nearly three years then since we had lost Jim Benton overboard.

I had nothing particular to do while we were getting ready for sea; nothing to prevent me from going over for a day, I mean; and I thought I'd like to see Jack Benton, and have a look at the girl he was going to marry. I wondered whether he had grown cheerful again, and had got rid of that drawn look he had when he told me it wasn't his fault. How could it have been his fault, anyhow? So I wrote to Jack that I would come down and see him married; and when the day came I took the train, and got there about ten o'clock in the morning. I wish I hadn't. Jack met me at the station, and he told me that the wedding was to be late in the afternoon, and that they weren't going off on any silly wedding trip, he and Mamie, but were just going to walk home from her mother's house to his cottage. That was good enough for him, he said. I looked at him hard for a minute after we met. When we had parted I had a sort of idea that he might take to drink, but he hadn't. He looked very respectable and well-to-do in his black coat and high city collar; but he was thinner and bonier than when I had known him, and there were lines in his face, and I thought his eyes had a queer look in them, half shifty, half scared. He needn't have been afraid of me, for I didn't mean to talk to his bride about the *Helen B. Jackson.*

He took me to his cottage first, and I could see that he was proud of it. It wasn't above a cable's-length from highwater mark, but the tide was running out, and there was already a broad stretch of hard wet sand on the other side of the beach road. Jack's bit of land ran back behind the cottage about a quarter of a mile, and he said that some of the trees we saw were his. The fences were neat and well kept, and there was a fair-sized barn a little way from the cottage, and I saw some nice-looking cattle in the meadows; but it didn't look to me to be much of a farm, and I thought that before long Jack would have to leave his wife to take care of it, and go to sea again. But I said it was a nice farm, so as to seem pleasant, and as I don't know much about these things I dare say it was, all the same. I never saw it but that once. Jack told me that he and his brother had been born in the cottage, and that when their father and mother died they leased the land to Mamie's father, but had kept the cottage to live in when they came home from sea for a spell. It was as neat a little place as you would care to see: the floors as clean as the decks of a yacht, and the paint as fresh as a man-o'-war. Jack always was a good painter. There was a nice parlour on the ground floor, and Jack had papered it and had hung the walls with photographs of ships and foreign ports, and with things he had brought home from his voyages: a boomerang, a South Sea club, Japanese straw hats and a Gibraltar fan with a bull-fight on it, and all that sort of gear. It looked to me as if Miss Mamie had taken a hand in arranging it. There was a brand-new polished iron Franklin stove set into the old fireplace, and a red table-cloth from Alexandria, embroidered with those outlandish Egyptian letters. It was all as bright and homelike as possible, and he showed me everything, and was proud of everything, and I liked him the better for it. But I wished that his voice would sound more cheerful, as it did when we first sailed in the *Helen B.*, and that the drawn look would go out of his face for a minute. Jack showed me everything, and took me upstairs, and it was all the same: bright and fresh and ready for the bride. But on the upper landing there was a door that Jack didn't open. When we came out of the bedroom I noticed that it was ajar, and Jack shut it quickly and turned the key.

"That lock's no good," he said, half to himself. "The door is always open."

I didn't pay much attention to what he said, but as we went down the short stairs, freshly painted and varnished so that I was almost afraid to step on them, he spoke again.

"That was his room, sir. I have made a sort of store-room of it."

"You may be wanting it in a year or so," I said, wishing to be pleasant.

"I guess we won't use his room for that," Jack answered in a low voice.

Then he offered me a cigar from a fresh box in the parlour, and he took one, and we lit them, and went out; and as we opened the front door there was Mamie Brewster standing in the path as if she were waiting for us. She was a fine-looking girl, and I didn't wonder that Jack had been willing to wait three years for her. I could see that she hadn't been brought up on steam-heat and cold storage, but had grown into a woman by the sea-shore. She had brown eyes, and fine brown hair, and a good figure.

"This is Captain Torkeldsen," said Jack. "This is Miss Brewster, captain; and she is glad to see you."

"Well, I am," said Miss Mamie, "for Jack has often talked to us about you, captain."

She put out her hand, and took mine and shook it heartily, and I suppose I said something, but I know I didn't say much.

The front door of the cottage looked toward the sea, and there was a straight path leading to the gate on the beach road. There was another path from the steps of the cottage that turned to the right, broad enough for two people to walk easily, and it led straight across the fields through gates to a larger house about a quarter of a mile away. That was where Mamie's mother lived, and the wedding was to be there. Jack asked me whether I would like to look round the farm before dinner, but I told him I didn't know much about farms. Then he said he just wanted to look round himself a bit, as he mightn't have much more chance that day; and he smiled, and Mamie laughed.

"Show the captain the way to the house, Mamie," he said. "I'll be along in a minute."

So Mamie and I began to walk along the path, and Jack went up toward the barn.

"It was sweet of you to come, captain," Miss Mamie began, "for I have always wanted to see you."

"Yes," I said, expecting something more.

"You see, I always knew them both," she went on. "They used to take me out in a dory to catch codfish when I was a little girl, and I liked them both," she added thoughtfully. "Jack doesn't care to talk about his brother now. That's natural. But you won't mind telling me how it happened, will you? I should so much like to know."

Well, I told her about the voyage and what happened that night when we fell in with a gale of wind, and that it hadn't been anybody's fault, for I wasn't going to admit that it was my old captain's, if it was. But I didn't tell her anything about what happened afterwards. As she didn't speak, I just went on talking about the two brothers, and how like they had been, and how when poor Jim was drowned and Jack was left, I took Jack for him. I told her that none of us had ever been sure which was which.

"I wasn't always sure myself," she said, "unless they were together. Leastways, not for a day or two after they came home from sea. And now it seems to me that Jack is more like poor Jim, as I remember him, than he ever was, for Jim was always more quiet, as if he were thinking."

I told her I thought so, too. We passed the gate and went into the next field, walking side by side. Then she turned her head to look for Jack, but he wasn't in sight. I sha'n't forget what she said next.

"Are you sure now?" she asked.

I stood stock-still, and she went on a step, and then turned and looked at me. We must have looked at each other while you could count five or six.

"I know it's silly," she went on, "it's silly, and it's awful, too, and I have got no right to think it, but sometimes I can't help it. You see it was always Jack I meant to marry."

"Yes," I said stupidly, "I suppose so."

She waited a minute, and began walking on slowly before she went on again.

"I am talking to you as if you were an old friend, captain, and I have only known you five minutes. It was Jack I meant to marry, but now he is so like the other one."

When a woman gets a wrong idea into her head, there is only one way to make her tired of it, and that is to agree with her. That's what I did, and she went or, talking the same way for a little while, and I kept on agreeing and agreeing until she turned round on me.

"You know you don't believe what you say," she said, and laughed. "You know that Jack is Jack, right enough; and it's Jack I am going to marry."

Of course I said so, for I didn't care whether she thought me a weak creature or not. I wasn't going to say a word that could interfere with her happiness, and I didn't intend to go back on Jack Benton; but I remembered what he had said when he left the ship in Havana: that it wasn't his fault.

"All the same," Miss Mamie went on, as a woman will, without realising what she was saying, "all the same, I wish I had seen it happen. Then I should know."

Next minute she knew that she didn't mean that, and was afraid that I would think her heartless, and began to explain that she would really rather have died herself than have seen poor Jim go overboard. Women haven't got much sense, anyhow. All the same, I wondered how she could marry Jack if she had a doubt that he might be Jim after all. I suppose she had really got used to him

since he had given up the sea and had stayed ashore, and she cared
for him.

Before long we heard Jack coming up behind us, for we had
walked very slowly to wait for him.

"Promise not to tell anybody what I said, captain," said Mamie,
as girls do as soon as they have told their secrets.

Anyhow, I know I never did tell any one but you. This is the
first time I have talked of all that, the first time since I took the
train from that place. I am not going to tell you all about the day.
Miss Mamie introduced me to her mother, who was a quiet, hard-
faced old New England farmer's widow, and to her cousins and
relations; and there were plenty of them too at dinner, and there
was the parson besides. He was what they call a Hard-shell Bap-
tist in those parts, with a long, shaven upper lip and a whacking
appetite, and a sort of superior look, as if he didn't expect to see
many of us hereafter—the way a New York pilot looks round, and
orders things about when he boards an Italian cargo-dragger, as if
the ship weren't up to much anyway, though it was his business to
see that she didn't get aground. That's the way a good many par-
sons look, I think. He said grace as if he were ordering the men to
sheet home the topgallant-sail and get the helm up. After dinner
we went out on the piazza, for it was warm autumn weather; and
the young folks went off in pairs along the beach road, and the
tide had turned and was beginning to come in. The morning had
been clear and fine, but by four o'clock it began to look like a fog,
and the damp came up out of the sea and settled on everything.
Jack said he'd go down to his cottage and have a last look, for the
wedding was to be at five o'clock, or soon after, and he wanted to
light the lights, so as to have things look cheerful.

"I will just take a last look," he said again, as we reached the
house. We went in, and he offered me another cigar, and I lit it
and sat down in the parlour. I could hear him moving about, first
in the kitchen and then upstairs, and then I heard him in the
kitchen again; and then before I knew anything I heard somebody
moving upstairs again. I knew he couldn't have got up those stairs

as quick as that. He came into the parlour, and he took a cigar himself, and while he was lighting it I heard those steps again overhead. His hand shook, and he dropped the match.

"Have you got in somebody to help?" I asked.

"No," Jack answered sharply, and struck another match.

"There's somebody upstairs, Jack," I said. "Don't you hear footsteps?"

"It's the wind, captain," Jack answered; but I could see he was trembling.

"That isn't any wind, Jack," I said; "it's still and foggy. I'm sure there's somebody upstairs."

"If you are so sure of it, you'd better go and see for yourself, captain," Jack answered, almost angrily.

He was angry because he was frightened. I left him before the fireplace, and went upstairs. There was no power on earth that could make me believe I hadn't heard a man's footsteps overhead. I knew there was somebody there. But there wasn't. I went into the bedroom, and it was all quiet, and the evening light was streaming in, reddish through the foggy air; and I went out on the landing and looked in the little back room that was meant for a servant girl or a child. And as I came back again I saw that the door of the other room was wide open, though I knew Jack had locked it. He had said the lock was no good. I looked in. It was a room as big as the bedroom, but almost dark, for it had shutters, and they were closed. There was a musty smell, as of old gear, and I could make out that the floor was littered with sea chests, and that there were oilskins and such stuff piled on the bed. But I still believed that there was somebody upstairs, and I went in and struck a match and looked round. I could see the four walls and the shabby old paper, an iron bed and a cracked looking-glass, and the stuff on the floor. But there was nobody there. So I put out the match, and came out and shut the door and turned the key. Now, what I am telling you is the truth. When I had turned the key, I heard footsteps walking away from the door inside the room. Then I felt queer for a minute, and when I went downstairs I looked behind me, as the men at the wheel used to look behind them on board the *Helen B.*

Jack was already outside on the steps, smoking. I have an idea that he didn't like to stay inside alone.

"Well?" he asked, trying to seem careless.

"I didn't find anybody," I answered, "but I heard somebody moving about."

"I told you it was the wind," said Jack, contemptuously. "I ought to know, for I live here, and I hear it often."

There was nothing to be said to that, so we began to walk down toward the beach. Jack said there wasn't any hurry, as it would take Miss Mamie some time to dress for the wedding. So we strolled along, and the sun was setting through the fog, and the tide was coming in. I knew the moon was full, and that when she rose the fog would roll away from the land, as it does sometimes. I felt that Jack didn't like my having heard that noise, so I talked of other things, and asked him about his prospects, and before long we were chatting as pleasantly as possible. I haven't been at many weddings in my life, and I don't suppose you have, but that one seemed to me to be all right until it was pretty near over; and then, I don't know whether it was part of the ceremony or not, but Jack put out his hand and took Mamie's and held it a minute, and looked at her, while the parson was still speaking.

Mamie turned as white as a sheet and screamed. It wasn't a loud scream, but just a sort of stifled little shriek, as if she were half frightened to death; and the parson stopped, and asked her what was the matter, and the family gathered round.

"Your hand's like ice," said Mamie to Jack, "and it's all wet!"

She kept looking at it, as she got hold of herself again.

"It don't feel cold to me," said Jack, and he held the back of his hand against his cheek. "Try it again."

Mamie held out hers, and touched the back of his hand, timidly at first, and then took hold of it.

"Why, that's funny," she said.

"She's been as nervous as a witch all day," said Mrs. Brewster, severely.

"It is natural," said the parson, "that young Mrs. Benton should experience a little agitation at such a moment."

Most of the bride's relations lived at a distance, and were busy people, so it had been arranged that the dinner we'd had in the middle of the day was to take the place of a dinner afterwards, and that we should just have a bite after the wedding was over, and then that everybody should go home, and the young couple would walk down to the cottage by themselves. When I looked out I could see the light burning brightly in Jack's cottage, a quarter of a mile away. I said I didn't think I could get any train to take me back before half-past nine, but Mrs. Brewster begged me to stay until it was time, as she said her daughter would want to take off her wedding dress before she went home; for she had put on something white with a wreath, that was very pretty, and she couldn't walk home like that, could she?

So when we had all had a little supper the party began to break up, and when they were all gone Mrs. Brewster and Mamie went upstairs, and Jack and I went out on the piazza to have a smoke, as the old lady didn't like tobacco in the house.

The full moon had risen now, and it was behind me as I looked down toward Jack's cottage, so that everything was clear and white, and there was only the light burning in the window. The fog had rolled down to the water's edge, and a little beyond, for the tide was high, or nearly, and was lapping up over the last reach of sand, within fifty feet of the beach road.

Jack didn't say much as we sat smoking, but he thanked me for coming to his wedding, and I told him I hoped he would be happy; and so I did. I dare say both of us were thinking of those footsteps upstairs, just then, and that the house wouldn't seem so lonely with a woman in it. By and by we heard Mamie's voice talking to her mother on the stairs, and in a minute she was ready to go. She had put on again the dress she had worn in the morning, and it looked black at night, almost as black as Jack's coat.

Well, they were ready to go now. It was all very quiet after the day's excitement, and I knew they would like to walk down that path alone now that they were man and wife at last. I bade them good-night, although Jack made a show of pressing me to go with them by the path as far as the cottage, instead of going to the station by the beach road. It was all very quiet, and it seemed to me a sensible way of getting married; and when Mamie kissed her mother good-night I just looked the other way, and knocked my ashes over the rail of the piazza. So they started down the straight path to Jack's cottage, and I waited a minute with Mrs. Brewster, looking after them, before taking my hat to go. They walked side by side, a little shyly at first, and then I saw Jack put his arm round her waist. As I looked he was on her left, and I saw the outline of the two figures very distinctly against the moonlight on the path; and the shadow on Mamie's right was broad and black as ink, and it moved along, lengthening and shortening with the unevenness of the ground beside the path.

I thanked Mrs. Brewster, and bade her good-night; and though she was a hard New England woman her voice trembled a little as she answered, but being a sensible person she went in and shut the door behind her as I stepped out on the path. I looked after the couple in the distance a last time, meaning to go down to the road, so as not to overtake them; but when I had made a few steps I stopped and looked again, for I knew I had seen something queer, though I had only realised it afterwards. I looked again, and it was plain enough now; and I stood stock-still, staring at what I saw. Mamie was walking between two men. The second man was just the same height as Jack, both being about a half ahead taller than she; Jack on her left in his black tail-coat and round hat, and the other man on her right—well, he was a sailor-man in wet oilskins. I could see the moonlight shining on the water that ran down him, and on the little puddle that had settled where the flap of his sou'wester was turned up behind: and one of his wet, shiny arms was round Mamie's waist, just above Jack's. I was fast to the spot where I stood, and for a minute I thought I was crazy. We'd had nothing but some cider for dinner, and tea in the evening, otherwise I'd have thought something had got into my head, though I was never drunk in my life. It was more like a bad dream after that.

I was glad Mrs. Brewster had gone in. As for me, I couldn't help following the three, in a sort of wonder to see what would happen, to see whether the sailorman in his wet togs would just melt away into the moonshine. But he didn't.

I moved slowly, and I remembered afterwards that I walked on the grass, instead of on the path, as if I were afraid they might hear me coming. I suppose it all happened in less than five minutes after that, but it seemed as if it must have taken an hour. Neither Jack nor Mamie seemed to notice the sailor. She didn't seem to know that his wet arm was round her, and little by little they got near the cottage, and I wasn't a hundred yards from them when they reached the door. Something made me stand still then. Perhaps it was fright, for I saw everything that happened just as I see you now.

Mamie set her foot on the step to go up, and as she went forward I saw the sailor slowly lock his arm in Jack's, and Jack didn't move to go up. Then Mamie turned round on the step, and they all three stood that way for a second or two. She cried out then,—I heard a man cry like that once, when his arm was taken off by a steam-crane,—and she fell back in a heap on the little piazza.

I tried to jump forward, but I couldn't move, and I felt my hair rising under my hat. The sailor turned slowly where he stood, and swung Jack round by the arm steadily and easily, and began to walk him down the pathway from the house. He walked him straight down that path, as steadily as Fate; and all the time I saw the moonlight shining on his wet oilskins. He walked him through the gate, and across the beach road, and out upon the wet sand, where the tide was high. Then I got my breath with a gulp, and ran for them across the grass, and vaulted over the fence, and stumbled across the road. But when I felt the sand under my feet, the two were at the water's edge; and when I reached the water they were far out, and up to their waists; and I saw that Jack Benton's head had fallen forward on his breast, and his free arm hung limp beside him, while his dead brother steadily marched him to his death. The moonlight was on the dark water, but the fog-bank was white beyond, and I saw them against it; and they went slowly and steadily down. The water was up to their armpits, and then up to their shoulders, and then I saw it rise up to the black rim of Jack's hat. But they never wavered; and the two heads went straight on, straight on, till they were under, and there was just a ripple in the moonlight where Jack had been.

It has been on my mind to tell you that story, whenever I got a chance. You have known me, man and boy, a good many years; and I thought I would like to hear your opinion. Yes, that's what I always thought. It wasn't Jim that went overboard; it was Jack, and Jim just let him go when he might have saved him; and then Jim passed himself off for Jack with us, and with the girl. If that's what happened, he got what he deserved. People said the next day that Mamie found it out as they reached the house, and that her husband just walked out into the sea, and drowned himself; and they would have blamed me for not stopping him if they'd known that I was there. But I never told what I had seen, for they wouldn't have believed me. I just let them think I had come too late.

When I reached the cottage and lifted Mamie up, she was raving mad. She got better afterwards, but she was never right in her head again.

Oh, you want to know if they found Jack's body? I don't know whether it was his, but I read in a paper at a Southern port where I was with my new ship that two dead bodies had come ashore in a gale down East, in pretty bad shape. They were locked together, and one was a skeleton in oilskins.

For the Blood is the Life

We had dined at sunset on the broad roof of the old tower, because it was cooler there during the great heat of summer. Besides, the little kitchen was built at one corner of the great square platform, which made it more convenient than if the dishes had to be carried down the steep stone steps broken in places and everywhere worn with age. The tower was one of those built all down the west coast of Calabria by the Emperor Charles V. early in the sixteenth century, to keep off the Barbary pirates, when the unbelievers were allied with Francis I. against the Emperor and the Church. They have gone to ruin, a few still stand intact, and mine is one of the largest. How it came into my possession ten years ago, and why I spend a part of each year in it, are matters which do not concern this tale. The tower stands in one of the loneliest spots in Southern Italy, at the extremity of a curving, rocky promontory, which forms a small but safe natural harbour at the southern extremity of the Gulf of Policastro, and just north of Cape Scalea, the birthplace of Judas Iscariot, according to the old local legend. The tower stands alone on this hooked spur of the rock, and there is not a house to be seen within three miles of it. When I go there I take a couple of sailors, one of whom is a fair cook, and when I am away it is in charge of a gnome-like little being who was once a miner and who attached himself to me long ago.

My friend, who sometimes visits me in my summer solitude, is an artist by profession, a Scandinavian by birth, and a cosmopolitan by force of circumstances. We had dined at sunset; the sunset glow had reddened and faded again, and the evening purple steeped the vast chain of the mountains that embrace the deep gulf to eastward and rear themselves higher and higher towards the south. It was hot, and we sat at the landward corner of the platform, waiting for the night breeze to come down from the lower hills. The colour sank out of the air, there was a little interval of deep-grey twilight, and a lamp sent a yellow streak from the open door of the kitchen, where the men were getting their supper.

Then the moon rose suddenly above the crest of the promontory, flooding the platform and lighting up every little spur of rock and knoll of grass below us, down to the edge of the motionless water. My friend lighted his pipe and sat looking at a spot on the hillside. I knew that he was looking at it, and for a long time past I had wondered whether he would ever see anything there that would fix his attention. I knew that spot well. It was clear that he was interested at last, though it was a long time before he spoke. Like most painters, he trusts to his own eyesight, as a lion trusts his strength and a stag his speed, and he is always disturbed when he cannot reconcile what he sees with what he believes that he ought to see.

"It's strange," he said. "Do you see that little mound just on this side of the boulder?"

"Yes," I said, and I guessed what was coming.

"It looks like a grave," observed Holger.

"Very true. It does look like a grave."

"Yes," continued my friend, his eyes still fixed on the spot. "But the strange thing is that I see the body lying on the top of it. Of course," continued Holger, turning his head on one side as artists do, "it must be an effect of light. In the first place, it is not a grave at all. Secondly, if it were, the body would be inside and not outside. Therefore, it's an effect of the moonlight. Don't you see it?"

"Perfectly; I always see it on moonlight nights."

"It doesn't seem it interest you much," said Holger.

"On the contrary, it does interest me, though I am used to it. You're not so far wrong, either. The mound is really a grave."

"Nonsense!" cried Holger incredulously. "I suppose you'll tell me that what I see lying on it is really a corpse!"

"No," I answered, "it's not. I know, because I have taken the trouble to go down and see."

"Then what is it?" asked Holger.

"It's nothing."

"You mean that it's an effect of light, I suppose?"

"Perhaps it is. But the inexplicable part of the matter is that it makes no difference whether the moon is rising or setting, or waxing or waning. If there's any moonlight at all, from east or west or overhead, so long as it shines on the grave you can see the outline of the body on top."

Holger stirred up his pipe with the point of his knife, and then used his finger for a stopper. When the tobacco burned well, he rose from his chair.

"If you don't mind," he said, "I'll go down and take a look at it."

He left me, crossed the roof, and disappeared down the dark steps. I did not move, but sat looking down until he came out of the tower below. I heard him humming an old Danish song as he crossed the open space in the bright moonlight, going straight to the mysterious mound. When he was ten paces from it, Holger stopped short, made two steps forward, and then three or four backward, and then stopped again. I know what that meant. He had reached the spot where the Thing ceased to be visible—where, as he would have said, the effect of light changed.

Then he went on till he reached the mound and stood upon it. I could see the Thing still, but it was no longer lying down; it was on its knees now, winding its white arms round Holger's body and looking up into his face. A cool breeze stirred my hair at that moment, as the night wind began to come down from the hills, but it felt like a breath from another world.

The Thing seemed to be trying to climb to its feet helping itself up by Holger's body while he stood upright, quite unconscious of it and apparently looking toward the tower, which is very picturesque when the moonlight falls upon it on that side.

"Come along!" I shouted. "Don't stay there all night!"

It seemed to me that he moved reluctantly as he stepped from the mound, or else with difficulty. That was it. The Thing's arms were still round his waist, but its feet could not leave the grave. As he came slowly forward it was drawn and lengthened like a wreath of mist, thin and white, till I saw distinctly that Holger shook himself, as a man does who feels a chill. At the same instant a little wail of pain came to me on the breeze—it might have been the cry of the small owl that lives amongst the rocks—and the misty presence floated swiftly back from Holger's advancing figure and lay once more at its length upon the mound.

Again I felt the cool breeze in my hair, and this time an icy thrill of dread ran down my spine. I remembered very well that I had once gone down there alone in the moonlight; that presently, being near, I had seen nothing; that, like Holger, I had gone and had stood upon the mound; and I remembered how when I came back, sure that there was nothing there, I had felt the sudden conviction that there was something after all if I would only look back, a temptation I had resisted as unworthy of a man of sense, until, to get rid of it, I had shaken myself just as Holger did.

And now I knew that those white, misty arms had been round me, too; I knew it in a flash, and I shuddered as I remembered that I had heard the night owl then, too. But it had not been the night owl. It was the cry of the Thing.

I refilled my pipe and poured out a cup of strong southern wine; in less than a minute Holger was seated beside me again.

"Of course there's nothing there," he said, "but it's creepy, all the same. Do you know, when I was coming back I was so sure that there was something behind me that I wanted to turn around and look? It was an effort not to."

He laughed a little, knocked the ashes out of his pipe, and poured himself out some wine. For a while neither of us spoke, and the moon rose higher and we both looked at the Thing that lay on the mound.

"You might make a story about that," said Holger after a long time.

"There is one," I answered. "If you're not sleepy, I'll tell it to you."

"Go ahead," said Holger, who likes stories.

Old Alario was dying up there in the village beyond the hill. You remember him, I have no doubt. They say that he made his money by selling sham jewelry in South America, and escaped with his gains when he was found out. Like all those fellows, if they bring anything back with them, he at once set to work to enlarge his house, and as there are no masons here, he sent all the way to Paola for two workmen. They were a rough-looking pair of scoundrels—a Neapolitan who had lost one eye and a Sicilian with an old scar half an inch deep across his left cheek. I often saw them, for on Sundays they used to come down here and fish off the rocks. When Alario caught the fever that killed him the masons were still at work. As he had agreed that part of their pay should be their board and lodging, he made them sleep in the house. His wife was dead, and he had an only son called Angelo, who was a much better sort than himself. Angelo was to marry the daughter of the richest man in the village, and, strange to say, though the marriage was arranged by their parents, the young people were said to be in love with each other.

For that matter, the whole village was in love with Angelo, and among the rest a wild, good-looking creature called Cristina, who was more like a gipsy than any girl I ever saw about here. She had very red lips and very black eyes, she was built like a greyhound, and had the tongue of the devil. But Angelo did not care a straw for her. He was rather a simple-minded fellow, quite different from his old scoundrel of a father, and under what I should call normal circumstances I really believe that he would never have looked at any girl except the nice plump little creature, with a fat dowry, whom his father meant him to marry. But things turned up which were neither normal nor natural.

On the other hand, a very handsome young shepherd from the hills above Maratea was in love with Cristina, who seems to have been quite indifferent to him. Cristina had no regular means of subsistence, but she was a good girl and willing to do any work or go on errands to any distance for the sake of a loaf of bread or a mess of beans, and permission to sleep under cover. She was especially glad when she could get something to do about the house of Angelo's father. There is no doctor in the village, and when the neighbours saw that old Alario was dying they sent Cristina to Scalea to fetch one. That was late in the afternoon, and if they had waited so long it was because the dying miser refused to allow any such extravagance while he was able to speak. But while Cristina was gone matters grew rapidly worse, the priest was brought to the bedside, and when he had done what he could he gave it as his opinion to the bystanders that the old man was dead, and left the house.

You know these people. They have a physical horror of death. Until the priest spoke, the room had been full of people. The words were hardly out of his mouth before it was empty. It was night now. They hurried down the dark steps and out into the street.

Angelo, as I have said, was away, Cristina had not come back—the simple woman-servant who had nursed the sick man fled with the rest, and the body was left alone in the flickering light of the earthen oil lamp.

Five minutes later two men looked in cautiously and crept forward toward the bed. They were the one-eyed Neapolitan mason and his Sicilian companion. They knew what they wanted. In a moment they had dragged from under the bed a small but heavy iron-bound box, and long before anyone thought of coming back to the dead man they had left the house and the village under cover of darkness. It was easy enough, for Alario's house is the last toward the gorge which leads down here, and the thieves merely went out by the back door, got over the stone wall, and had nothing to risk after that except that possibility of meeting some belated countryman, which was very small indeed, since few of the people use that path. They had a mattock and shovel, and they made their way without accident.

I am telling you this story as it must have happened, for, of course, there were no witnesses to this part of it. The men brought the box down by the gorge, intending to bury it on the beach in the wet sand, where it would have been much safer. But the paper would have rotted if they had been obliged to leave it there long, so they dug their hole down there, close to that boulder. Yes, just where the mound is now.

Cristina did not find the doctor in Scalea, for he had been sent for from a place up the valley, half-way to San Domenico. If she had found him we would have come on his mule by the upper road, which is smoother but much longer. But Cristina took the short cut by the rocks, which passes about fifty feet above the mound, and goes round that corner. The men were digging when she passed, and she heard them at work. It would not have been like her to go by without finding out what the noise was, for she was never afraid of anything in her life, and, besides, the fishermen sometimes come ashore here at night to get a stone for an anchor or to gather sticks to make a little fire. The night was dark and Cristina probably came close to the two men before she could see what they were doing. She knew them, of course, and they knew her, and understood instantly that they were in her power. There was only one thing to be done for their safety, and they did it. They knocked her on the head, they dug the hole deep, and they buried her quickly with the iron-bound chest. They must have understood that their only chance of escaping suspicion lay in getting back to the village before their absence was noticed, for they returned immediately, and were found half and hour later gossiping quietly with the man who was making Alario's coffin. He was a crony of theirs, and had been working at the repairs in the old man's house. So far as I have been able to make out, the only persons who were supposed to know where Alario kept his treasure were Angelo and the one woman-servant I have mentioned. Angelo was away; it was the woman who discovered the theft.

It was easy enough to understand why no one else knew where the money was. The old man kept his door locked and the key in his pocket when he was out, and did not let the woman enter to clean the place unless he was there himself. The whole village knew that he had money somewhere, however, and the masons had

probably discovered the whereabouts of the chest by climbing in
at the window in his absence. If the old man had not been delirious until he lost consciousness he would have been in frightful
agony of mind for his riches. The faithful woman-servant forgot
their existence only for a few moments when she fled with the rest,
overcome by the horror of death. Twenty minutes had not passed
before she returned with the two hideous old hags who are always
called in to prepare the dead for burial. Even then she had not at
first the courage to go near the bed with them, but she made a pretence of dropping something, went down on her knees as if to find
it, and looked under the bedstead. The walls of the room were newly
whitewashed down to the floor and she saw at a glance that the
chest was gone. It had been there in the afternoon, it had therefore been stolen in the short interval since she had left the room.

There are no carabineers stationed in the village; there is not
so much as a municipal watchman, for there is no municipality.
There never was such a place, I believe. Scalea is supposed to look
after it in some mysterious way, and it takes a couple of hours to
get anybody from there. As the old woman had lived in the village
all her life, it did not even occur to her to apply to any civil authority for help. She simply set up a howl and ran through the village
in the dark, screaming out that her dead master's house had been
robbed. Many of the people looked out, but at first no one seemed
inclined to help her. Most of them, judging her by themselves,
whispered to each other that she had probably stolen the money
herself. The first man to move was the father of the girl whom
Angelo was to marry; having collected his household, all of whom
felt a personal interest in the wealth which was to have come into
the family, he declared it to be his opinion that the chest had been
stolen by the two journeymen masons who lodged in the house.
He headed a search for them, which naturally began in Alario's
house and ended in the carpenter's workshop, where the thieves
were found discussing a measure of wine with the carpenter over
the half-finished coffin, by the light of one earthen lamp filled with
oil and tallow. The search-party at once accused the delinquents
of the crime, and threatened to lock them up in the cellar till the

carabineers could be fetched from Scalea. The two men looked at each other for one moment, and then without the slightest hesitation they put out the single light, seized the unfinished coffin between them, and using it as a sort of battering ram, dashed upon their assailants in the dark. In a few moments they were beyond pursuit.

That is the end of the first part of the story. The treasure had disappeared, and as no trace of it could be found the people supposed that the thieves had succeeded in carrying it off. The old man was buried, and when Angelo came back at last he had to borrow money to pay for the miserable funeral, and had some difficulty in doing so. He hardly needed to be told that in losing his inheritance he had lost his bride. In this part of the world marriages are made on strictly business principles, and if the promised cash is not forthcoming on the appointed day, the bride or the bridegroom whose parents have failed to produce it may as well take themselves off, for there will be no wedding. Poor Angelo knew that well enough. His father had been possessed of hardly any land, and now that the hard cash which he had brought from South America was gone, there was nothing left but debts for the building materials that were to have been used for enlarging and improving the old house. Angelo was beggared, and the nice plump little creature who was to have been his, turned up her nose at him in the most approved fashion. As for Cristina, it was several days before she was missed, for no one remembered that she had been sent to Scalea for the doctor, who had never come. She often disappeared in the same way for days together, when she could find a little work here and there at the distant farms among the hills. But when she did not come back at all, people began to wonder, and at last made up their minds that she had connived with the masons and had escaped with them.

I paused and emptied my glass.

"That sort of thing could not happen anywhere else," observed Holger, filling his everlasting pipe again. "It is wonderful what a natural charm there is about murder and sudden death in a romantic country like this. Deeds that would be simply brutal and disgusting anywhere else become dramatic and mysterious because this is Italy, and we are living in a genuine tower of Charles V. built against Barbary pirates."

"There's something in that," I admitted. Holger is the most romantic man in the world inside of himself, but he always thinks it necessary to explain why he feels anything.

"I suppose the found the poor girl's body with the box," he said presently.

"As it seems to interest you," I answered, "I'll tell you the rest of the story."

The moon had risen by this time; the outline of the Thing on the mound was clearer to our eyes than before.

The village very soon settled down to its small dull life. No one missed old Alario, who had been away so much on his voyages to South America that he had never been a familiar figure in his native place. Angelo lived in the half-finished house, and because he had no money to pay the old woman-servant, she would not stay with him, but once in a long time she would come and wash a shirt for him for old acquaintance' sake. Besides the house, he had inherited a small patch of ground at some distance from the village; he tried to cultivate it, but he had no heart in the work, for he knew he could never pay the taxes on it and on the house, which would certainly be confiscated by the Government, or seized for the debt of the building material, which the man who had supplied it refused to take back.

Angelo was very unhappy. So long as his father had been alive and rich, every girl in the village had been in love with him; but that was all changed now. It had been pleasant to be admired and courted, and invited to drink wine by fathers who had girls to marry. It was hard to be stared at coldly, and sometimes laughed at because he had been robbed of his inheritance. He cooked his miserable meals for himself, and from being sad became melancholy and morose.

At twilight, when the day's work was done, instead of hanging about in the open space before the church with young fellows of his own age, he took to wandering in lonely places on the outskirts of the village till it was quite dark. Then he slunk home and went to bed to save the expense of a light. But in those lonely twilight hours he began to have strange waking dreams. He was not always alone, for often when he sat on the stump of a tree, where the narrow path turns down the gorge, he was sure that a woman came up noiselessly over the rough stones, as if her feet were bare; and she stood under a clump of chestnut trees only half a dozen yards down the path, and beckoned to him without speaking. Though she was in the shadow he knew that her lips were red, and that when they parted a little and smiled at him she showed two small sharp teeth. He knew this at first rather than saw it, and he knew that it was Cristina, and that she was dead. Yet he was not afraid; he only wondered whether it was a dream, for he thought that if he had been awake he should have been frightened.

Besides, the dead woman had red lips, and that could only happen in a dream. Whenever he went near the gorge after sunset she was already there waiting for him, or else she very soon appeared, and he began to be sure of her blood-red mouth, but now each feature grew distinct, and the pale face looked at him with deep and hungry eyes.

It was the eyes that grew dim. Little by little he came to know that someday the dream would not end when he turned away to go home, but would lead him down the gorge out of which the vision rose. She was nearer now when she beckoned to him. Her cheeks were not livid like those of the dead, but pale with starvation, with the furious and unappeased physical hunger of her eyes that devoured him. They feasted on his soul and cast a spell over him, and at last they were close to his own and held him. He could not tell whether her breath was as hot as fire, or as cold as ice; he could not tell whether her red lips burned his or froze them, or whether her five fingers on his wrists seared scorching scars or bit his flesh like frost; he could not tell whether he was awake or asleep, whether she was alive or dead, but he knew that she loved him, she alone of all creatures, earthly or unearthly, and her spell had power over him.

When the moon rose high that night the shadow of that Thing was not alone down there upon the mound.

Angelo awoke in the cool dawn, drenched with dew and chilled through flesh, and blood, and bone. He opened his eyes to the faint grey light, and saw the stars were still shining overhead. He was very weak, and his heart was beating so slowly that he was almost like a man fainting. Slowly he turned his head on the mound, as on a pillow, but the other face was not there. Fear seized him suddenly, a fear unspeakable and unknown; he sprang to his feet and fled up the gorge, and he never looked behind him until he reached the door of the house on the outskirts of the village. Drearily he went to his work that day, and wearily the hours dragged themselves after the sun, till at last it touched the sea and sank, and the great sharp hills above Maratea turned purple against the dove-coloured eastern sky.

Angelo shouldered his heavy hoe and left the field. He felt less tired now than in the morning when he had begun to work, but he promised himself that he would go home without lingering by the gorge, and eat the best supper he could get himself, and sleep all night in his bed like a Christian man. Not again would he be tempted down the narrow way by a shadow with red lips and icy breath; not again would he dream that dream of terror and delight. He was near the village now; it was half an hour since the sun had set, and the cracked church bell sent little discordant echoes across the rocks and ravines to tell all good people that the day was done. Angelo stood still a moment where the path forked, where it led toward the village on the left, and down to the gorge on the right, where a clump of chestnut trees overhung the narrow way. He stood still a minute, lifting his battered hat from his head and gazing at the fast-fading sea westward, and his lips moved as he silently repeated the familiar evening prayer. His lips moved, but the words that followed them in his brain lost their meaning and turned into others, and ended in a name that he spoke aloud—

Cristina! With the name, the tension of his will relaxed suddenly, reality went out and the dream took him again, and bore him on swiftly and surely like a man walking in his sleep, down, down, by the steep path in the gathering darkness. And as she glided beside him, Cristina whispered strange, sweet things in his ear, which somehow, if he had been awake, he knew that he could not quite have understood; but now they were the most wonderful words he had ever heard in his life. And she kissed him also, but not upon his mouth. He felt her sharp kisses upon his white throat, and he knew that her lips were red. So the wild dream sped on through twilight and darkness and moonrise, and all the glory of the summer's night. But in the chilly dawn he lay as one half dead upon the mound down there, recalling and not recalling, drained of his blood, yet strangely longing to give those red lips more. Then came the fear, the awful nameless panic, the mortal horror that guards the confines of the world we see not, neither know of as we know of other things, but which we feel when its icy chill freezes our bones and stirs our hair with the touch of a ghostly hand. Once more Angelo sprang from the mound and fled up the gorge in the breaking day, but his step was less sure this time, and he panted for breath as he ran; and when he came to the bright spring of water that rises half way up the hillside, he dropped upon his knees and hands and plunged his whole face in and drank as he had never drunk before—for it was the thirst of the wounded man who has lain bleeding all night upon the battle-field.

She had him fast now, and he could not escape her, but would come to her every evening at dusk until she had drained him of his last drop of blood. It was in vain that when the day was done he tried to take another turning and to go home by a path that did not lead near the gorge. It was in vain that he made promises to himself each morning at dawn when he climbed the lonely way up from the shore to the village. It was all in vain, for when the sun sank burning into the sea, and the coolness of the evening stole out as from a hiding-place to delight the weary world, his feet turned toward the old way, and she was waiting for him in the shadow under the chestnut trees; and then all happened as before, and she fell to kissing his white throat even as she flitted lightly down the way, winding one arm about him. And as his blood failed, she grew more hungry and more thirsty every day, and every day when he awoke in the early dawn it was harder to rouse himself to the effort of climbing the steep path to the village; and when he went to his work his feet dragged painfully, and there was hardly strength in his arms to wield the heavy hoe. He scarcely spoke to anyone now, but the people said he was "consuming himself" for love of the girl he was to have married when he lost his inheritance; and they laughed heartily at the thought, for this is not a very romantic country. At this time Antonio, the man who stays here to look after the tower, returned from a visit to his people, who live near Salerno. He had been away all the time since before Alario's death and knew nothing of what had happened. He has told me that he came back late in the afternoon and shut himself up in the tower to eat and sleep, for he was very tired. It was past midnight when he awoke, and when he looked out toward the mound, and he saw something, and he did not sleep again that night. When he went out again in the morning it was broad daylight, and there was nothing to be seen on the mound but loose stones and driven sand. Yet he did not go very near it; he went straight up the path to the village and directly to the house of the old priest.

"I have seen an evil thing this night," he said; "I have seen how the dead drink the blood of the living. And the blood is the life."

"Tell me what you have seen," said the priest in reply.

Antonio told him everything he had seen.

"You must bring your book and your holy water to-night," he added. "I will be here before sunset to go down with you, and if it pleases your reverence to sup with me while we wait, I will make ready."

"I will come," the priest answered, "for I have read in old books of these strange beings which are neither quick nor dead, and which lie ever fresh in their graves, stealing out in the dusk to taste life and blood."

Antonio cannot read, but he was glad to see that the priest understood the business; for, of course, the books must have instructed him as to the best means of quieting the half-living Thing for ever.

So Antonio went away to his work, which consists largely in sitting on the shady side of the tower, when he is not perched upon a rock with a fishing-line catching nothing. But on that day he went twice to look at the mound in the bright sunlight, and he searched round and round it for some hole through which the being might get in and out; but he found none. When the sun began to sink and the air was cooler in the shadows, he went up to fetch the old priest, carrying a little wicker basket with him; and in this they placed a bottle of holy water, and the basin, and sprinkler, and the stole which the priest would need; and they came down and waited in the door of the tower till it should be dark. But while the light still lingered very grey and faint, they saw something moving, just there, two figures, a man's that walked, and a woman's that flitted beside him, and while her head lay on his shoulder she kissed his throat. The priest has told me that, too, and that his teeth chattered and he grasped Antonio's arm. The vision passed and disappeared into the shadow. Then Antonio got the leathern flask of strong liquor, which he kept for great occasions, and poured such a draught as made the old man feel almost young again; and gave the priest his stole to put on and the holy water to carry, and they went out together toward the spot where the work was to be done. Antonio says that in spite of the rum his own knees shook together, and the priest stumbled over his Latin. For when they were yet a few yards from the mound the flickering light of the lantern fell upon Angelo's white face, unconscious as if in sleep, and on his upturned throat, over which a very thin red line of blood trickled down into his collar; and the flickering light of the lantern played upon another face that looked up from the feast, upon two deep, dead eyes that saw in spite of death—upon parted lips, redder than life itself—upon two gleaming teeth on which glistened a rosy drop. Then the priest, good old man, shut his eyes tight and showered holy water before him, and his cracked voice rose almost to a scream; and then Antonio, who is no coward after all, raised his pick in one hand and the lantern in the other, as he sprang forward, not knowing what the end should be; and then he swears that he heard a woman's cry, and the Thing was gone, and Angelo lay alone on the mound unconscious, with the red line on his throat and the beads of deathly sweat on his cold forehead. They lifted him, half-dead as he was, and laid him on the ground close by; then Antonio went to work, and the priest helped him, thought he was old and could not do much; and they dug deep, and at last Antonio, stand-ing in the grave, stooped down with his lantern to see what he might see.

His hair used to be dark brown, with grizzled streaks about the temples; in less than a month from that day he was as grey as a badger. He was a miner when he was young, and most of these fellows have seen ugly sights now and then, when accidents have happened, but he had never seen what he saw that night—that Thing which is neither alive nor dead, that Thing that will abide neither above ground nor in the grave. Antonio had brought some-thing with him which the priest had not noticed—a sharp stake shaped from a piece of tough old driftwood. He had it with him now, and he had his heavy pick, and he had taken the lantern down into the grave. I don't think any power on earth could make him speak of what happened then, and the old priest was too fright-ened to look in. He says he heard Antonio breathing like a wild beast, and moving as if he were fighting with something almost as strong as himself; and he heard an evil sound also, with blows, as of something violently driven through flesh and bone; and then, the most awful sound of all—a woman's shriek, the unearthly scream of a woman neither dead nor alive, but buried deep for many days. And he, the poor old priest, could only rock himself as he knelt there in the sand, crying aloud his prayers and exorcisms to drown these dreadful sounds. Then suddenly a small iron-bound chest was thrown up and rolled over against the old man's knee, and in a moment more Antonio was beside him, his face as white as tallow in the flickering light of the lantern, shoveling the sand and pebbles into the grave with furious haste, and looking over the edge till the pit was half full; and the priest said that there was much fresh blood on Antonio's hands and on his clothes.

I had come to the end of my story. Holger finished his wine and leaned back in his chair.

"So Angelo got his own again," he said. "Did he marry the prim and plump young person to whom he had been betrothed?"

"No; he had been badly frightened. He went to South America, and has not been heard of since."

"And that poor thing's body is there still, I suppose," said Holger. "Is it quite dead yet, I wonder?"

I wonder, too. But whether it be dead or alive, I should hardly care to see it, even in broad daylight. Antonio is as grey as a badger, and he has never been quite the same man since that night.

THE KING'S MESSENGER

It was rather a dim daylight dinner. I remember that quite distinctly, for I could see the glow of the sunset over the trees in the park through the high window at the west end of the dining-room. I had expected to find a larger party, I believe, for I recollect being a little surprised at seeing only a dozen people assembled at table. It seemed to me that in old times, ever so long ago, when I had last stayed in that house, there had been as many as thirty or forty guests. I recognised some of them among a number of beautiful portraits that hung on the walls. There was room for a great many, because there was only one huge window at one end, and the large door at the other. I was very much surprised, too, to see a portrait of myself, evidently painted about twenty years ago, by Lenbach. It seemed very strange that I should have so completely forgotten the picture, and that I should not be able to remember having sat for it. We were good friends, it is true, and he might have painted it from memory without my knowledge, but it was certainly strange that he should never have told me about it. The portraits that hung in the dining-room were all very good indeed, and all, I should say, by the best painters of that time.

My left-hand neighbour was a lovely girl, whose name I had forgotten, though I had known her long, and I fancied that she looked a little disappointed when she saw that I was beside her. On my right there was a vacant seat, and beyond it sat an elderly woman with features as hard as the overwhelmingly splendid diamonds she wore. Her eyes made me think of grey glass marbles cemented into a stone mask. It was odd that her name should have escaped me, too, for I had often met her.

The table looked irregular, and I counted the guests mechanically while I ate my soup. We were only twelve, but the empty chair beside me was the thirteenth place.

I suppose it was not very tactful of me to mention this, but I wanted to say something to the beautiful girl on my left, and no other subject for a general remark suggested itself. Just as I was going to speak, I remembered who she was.

"Miss Lorna," I said, to attract her attention, for she was looking away from me towards the door, though she turned when I spoke— "I hope you are not superstitious about being thirteen at table, are you?"

"We are only twelve," she said, in the sweetest voice in the world.

"Yes; but someone else is coming. There's an empty chair here beside me."

"Oh, he doesn't count," said Miss Lorna quietly. "At least, not for everybody. When did you get here? Just in time for dinner, I suppose."

"Yes," I answered, "I'm in luck to be beside you. It seems an age since we were last here together."

"It does indeed!" Miss Lorna sighed and looked at the pictures on the opposite wall. "I've lived a lifetime since I saw you last."

I smiled at the exaggeration. "When you are thirty, you won't talk of having your life behind you," I said.

"I shall never be thirty," Miss Lorna answered, with such an odd little air of conviction that I did not think of anything to say. "Besides, life isn't made up of years or months or hours, or of anything that has to do with time." she continued. "You ought to know that. Our bodies are something better than mere clocks, wound up to show just how old we are at every moment, by our hair turning grey and our teeth falling out and our faces getting wrinkled and yellow, or puffy and red! Look at your own portrait over there. I don't mind saying that you must have been twenty years younger when that was painted, but I'm sure you are just the same man to-day—improved by age, perhaps!"

I heard a sweet little echoing laugh that seemed very far away; and indeed I could not have sworn that it rippled from Miss Lorna's beautiful lips, for though they were parted and smiling, my impression is that they did not move, even as most women's lips are moved by laughter.

"Thank you for thinking me improved," I said. "I find you a little changed, too. I was just going to say that you seem sadder, but you laughed just then."

"Did I? I suppose that's the right thing to do when the play is over, isn't it?"

"If it has been an amusing play," I answered, humoring her.

The wonderful violet eyes turned to me, full of light. "It's not been a bad play. I don't complain."

"Why do you speak of it as over?"

"I'll tell you, because I'm sure you will keep my secret. You will, won't you? We were always such good friends, you and I, even two years ago when I was young and silly! Will you promise not to tell anyone till I'm gone?"

"Gone?"

"Yes. Will you promise?"

"Of course I will. But—" I did not finish the sentence, because Miss Lorna bent nearer to me, so as to speak in a much lower tone. While I listened, I felt her sweet young breath on my cheek.

"I'm going away to-night with the man who is to sit on your other side," she said. "He's a little late—he often is, for he is tremendously busy; but he'll come presently, and after dinner we shall just stroll out into the garden and never come back. That's my secret. You won't betray me, will you?"

Again, as she looked at me, I heard that far-off silver laugh, sweet and low. I was almost too much surprised by what she had told me to notice how still her parted lips were, but that comes back to me now, with my other details.

"My dear Miss Lorna," I said, "do you think of your parents before taking such a step?"

"I have thought of them," she answered. "Of course, they would never consent, and I am very sorry to leave them, but it can't be helped."

At this moment, as often happens when two people are talking in low tones at a large dinner table, there was a momentary lull in the general conversation, and I was spared the trouble of making any further answer to what Miss Lorna had told me so unexpectedly, and with such profound confidence in my discretion.

To tell the truth, she would very probably not have listened, whether my words expressed sympathy or protest, for she had turned suddenly pale, and her eyes were wide and dark. The drop in the talk at table was due to the appearance of the man who was to occupy the vacant place beside me.

He had entered the room very quietly, and he made no elaborate apology for being late, as he sat down, bending his head courteously to our hostess and her husband, and smiling in a gentle sort of way as he nodded to the others.

"Please forgive me," he said quietly. "I was detained by a funeral and missed the train."

It was not until he had taken his place that he looked across me at Miss Lorna and exchanged a glance of recognition with her. I noticed that the lady with the hard face and the splendid diamonds, who was on his other side, drew away from him a little, as if not wishing even to let his sleeve brush against her bare arm. It occurred to me at the same time that Miss Lorna must be wishing me anywhere else except between the man with whom she was just going to run away, and I wished, for their sake and mine, that I could change places with him.

He was certainly not like other men, though few people would have called him handsome. There was something about him that instantly fixed the attention; rarely beautiful as Miss Lorna was, almost everyone would have noticed him first on entering the room, and most persons, I think, would have been more interested by his face than by hers. I could well imagine that some women might love him, even to distraction, though it was just as easy to understand that others might be strongly repelled by him, and might even fear him.

For my part, I shall not try to describe him as one describes an ordinary man, with a dozen or so adjectives that leave nothing to the imagination but yet offer it no picture which it can grasp. My instinct was to fear him rather than think of him as a possible friend, but I could not help feeling instant admiration for him, as one does at first sight for anything which is very complete, harmonious, and strong. He was dark, and pale, with a shadowy pallor I never saw in any other face; the features of thrice-great Hermes were not modelled in more perfect symmetry; his luminous eyes were not unkind, but there was something fateful in them, and they were set very deep under the grand white brow. His age I could not guess, but I should have called him young; standing, I had seen that he was tall and sinewy, and now that he was seated, he had the unmistakable look of a man accustomed to be in authority, to be heard and to be obeyed. His hands were white, his fingers straight, lean, and very strong.

Everyone at the table seemed to know him, but, as often happens among civilised people, no one called him by name in speaking to him.

"We were beginning to be afraid that you might not get here," said our host.

"Really?" The Thirteenth Guest smiled quietly, but shook his head. "Did you ever know me to break an engagement, under any circumstances?"

The master of the house laughed, though not very cordially, I thought.

"No," he answered. "Your reputation for keeping your appointments is proverbial. Even your enemies must admit that!"

The Guest nodded, and smiled again. Miss Lorna bent towards me.

"What do you think of him?" she asked, almost in a whisper.

"Very striking sort of man," I answered in a low tone. "But I'm inclined to be a little afraid of him."

"So was I, at first," she said, and I heard the silver laugh again. "But that soon wears off," she went on. "You'll know him better some day!"

"Shall I?"

"Yes. I'm quite sure you will. Oh, I don't pretend that I fell in love with him at first sight! I went through a phase of feeling afraid of him, as almost everyone does. You see, when people first meet him, they cannot possibly know how kind and gentle he can be, though he is so tremendously strong. I've heard him called cruel, and ruthless, and cold—but it's not true! Indeed, it's not! He can be as gentle as a woman, and he's the truest friend in all the world."

I was going to ask her to tell me his name, but just then I saw that she was looking at him, across me, and I sat as far back in my chair as I could, so that they might speak to each other if they wished to. Their eyes met, and there was a longing light in both— I could not help glancing from one to the other—and Miss Lorna's sweet lips moved almost imperceptibly, though no sound came from them. I have seen young lovers make that small sign to one another even across a room, the signal of a kiss given and returned in the heart's thoughts.

If she had been less beautiful and young, if the man she loved had not been so magnificently manly, it would have irritated me; but it seemed natural that they should love and not be ashamed of it, and I only hoped that no one else at the table had noticed the tenderly quivering little contraction of the young girl's exquisite mouth.

"You remembered," said the man, quietly. "I got your message this morning. Thank you."

"I hope it's not going to be very hard," murmured Miss Lorna, smiling. "Not that it would make any great difference if it were," she added, more thoughtfully.

"It's the easiest thing in life," he said, "and I promise that you shall never regret it."

"I trust you," the young girl answered, simply.

Then she turned away, for she, no doubt felt the awkwardness of talking to him across me of a secret which she had confided to me without letting him know that she had done so. Instinctively I turned to him, feeling that the moment had come for breaking the ice and making acquaintance, since we were neighbours at table in a friend's house, and I had known Miss Lorna so long. Besides, it is always interesting to talk with a man who is just going to do something very dangerous or dramatic, and who does not guess that you know what he is about.

"I suppose you motored here from town, as you said you missed the train," I said. "It's a good road, isn't it?"

"Yes, I literally flew," replied the dark man, with his gentle smile. "I hope you're not superstitious about thirteen at table?"

"Not in the least," I answered. "In the first place, I'm a fatalist about everything that doesn't depend on my own free will. As I have not the slightest intention of doing anything to shorten my life, it will certainly not come to an abrupt end by any auto-suggestion arising from a silly superstition like that about thirteen!"

"Autosuggestion? That's rather a new light on the old belief."

"And secondly," I continued, "I don't believe in death. There is no such thing."

"Really?" My neighbour seemed greatly surprised "How do you mean?" he asked. "I don't think I understand you."

"I'm sure *I* don't," put in Miss Lorna, and the silvery laugh followed. She had overheard the conversation, and some of the others were listening, too.

"You don't kill a book by translating it," I said, rather glad to expound my views. "Death is only a translation of life into another language. That's what I mean."

"That's a most interesting point of view," observed the Thirteenth Guest thoughtfully. "I never thought of the matter in that way before, though I've often seen the expression 'translated' in epitaphs. Are you sure that you are not indulging in a little paranomasia?"

"What's that?" inquired the hard-faced lady, with all the contempt which a scholarly word deserves in polite society.

"It means punning," I answered. "No. I am not making a pun. Grave subjects do not lend themselves to low forms of humour. I assure you, I am quite in earnest. Death, in the ordinary sense, is not a real phenomenon at all, so long as there is any life in the universe. It's a name we apply to a change we only partly understand."

"Learned discussions are an awful bore," said the hard-faced lady, very audibly.

"I don't advise you to argue the question too sharply with your neighbour there," laughed the master of house, leaning forward and speaking to me. "He'll get the better of you! He's an expert at what you call 'translating people into another language.'"

If the man beside me was a famous surgeon, as our host, perhaps, meant, it seemed to me that the remark was not in very good taste. He looked more like a soldier.

"Does our friend mean that you are in the army, and that you are a dangerous person?" I asked of him.

"No," he answered, quietly. "I'm only a King's Messenger, and in my own opinion, I'm not at all dangerous."

"It must be rather an active life," I said, in order to say something— "constantly coming and going, I suppose?"

"Yes, constantly."

I felt that Miss Lorna was watching and listening, and I turned to her, only to find that she was again looking beyond me, at my neighbour, though he did not see her. I remember her face very distinctly as it was just then; the recollection is, in fact, the last impression I retained of her matchless beauty, for I never saw her after that evening.

It is something to have seen one of the most beautiful women in the world gazing at the man who was more to her than life and all it held; it is something I cannot forget. But he did not return her look just then, for he had joined in the general conversation, and very soon afterwards he practically absorbed it.

He talked well; more than well, marvellously; but before long, even the lady with the hard face was listening, spellbound with the rest of us, to his stories of nations, and tales of men, brilliant descriptions, anecdotes of heroism and tenderness that were each a perfect coin from the mint of humanity, and dashes of daring wit, and glimpses of a profound insight into the great mystery of the beyond, and now and then a manly comment on life, that came straight from the heart: never, in all my long experience, did I hear poet, or scholar, or soldier, or ruler of men talk as he did that evening. And as I listened, I was more and more amazed that such a man should be but a simple King's Messenger, as he said he was, earning a poor gentleman's living by carrying his majesty's despatches from London to the ends of the earth, and I made some sad and sober inward reflections on the vast difference between the gift of talking supremely well and the genius a man must have to accomplish even one little thing in history, in literature, or in art.

"Do you wonder that I love him?" whispered Miss Lorna.

Even in the whisper I heard the glorious pride of the woman who loves altogether, and wholly believes that there is no one like her chosen man.

"No," I answered, "for it is no wonder! I only hope—" I stopped, feeling that it would be foolish and unkind to express the doubt I felt.

"You hope that I may not be disappointed," said Miss Lorna, still almost in a whisper. "That was what you were going to say, I'm sure."

I nodded in spite of myself, and met her eyes; they were full of a wonderful light.

"No one was ever disappointed in him," she murmured— "no living being, neither man, nor woman, nor child. With him I shall have peace and love without end."

"Without end?"

"Yes. Forever and ever!"

After dinner we scattered through the great rooms in the soft evening light of mid June, and by and by I was standing in an open window with the mistress of the house, looking across the garden.

In the distance, Lorna was walking slowly away down the broad avenue with a tall man; and while they were still in sight, though far away, I am sure that I saw his arm steal around her, as if he were drawing her on, and her head bent lovingly to his shoulder; and so they glided away into the twilight and disappeared.

Then at last I turned to my hostess. "Do you mind telling me the name of that man who came in late and talked so well?" I asked. "You all seemed to know him like an old friend."

She looked at me in profound surprise. "Do you mean to say that you do not know who he is?" she asked.

"No. I never met him before. He is a most extraordinary man to be only a King's Messenger."

"He is, indeed, a King's Messenger, my dear friend. His name is Death."

I dreamed this dream one afternoon last summer, dozing in my chair on deck, under the double awning, when the *Alda* was anchored off Goletta, in sight of Carthage, and the cool north breeze was blowing down the deep gulf of Tunis. I must have been awakened by some slight sound from a boat alongside, for when I opened my eyes my man was standing a little way off, evidently waiting till I should finish my nap. He brought me a telegram which had just come on board, and I opened it rather drowsily, not expecting any particular news.

It was from England, from a very dear friend.

LORNA DIED SUDDENLY LAST NIGHT AT CHURCH HADLEY.

That was all; the dream had been a message.

"With him I shall have peace and love without end."

Thank God, I hear those words in her own voice, whenever I think of her.

The Screaming Skull

I have often heard it scream. No, I am not nervous, I am not imaginative, and I never believed in ghosts, unless that thing is one. Whatever it is, it hates me almost as much as it hated Luke Pratt, and it screams at me.

If I were you, I would never tell ugly stories about ingenious ways of killing people, for you never can tell but that some one at the table may be tired of his or her nearest and dearest. I have always blamed myself for Mrs. Pratt's death, and I suppose I was responsible for it in a way, though heaven knows I never wished her anything but long life and happiness. If I had not told that story she might be alive yet. That is why the thing screams at me, I fancy.

She was a good little woman, with a sweet temper, all things considered, and a nice gentle voice; but I remember hearing her shriek once when she thought her little boy was killed by a pistol that went off though everyone was sure that it was not loaded. It was the same scream; exactly the same, with a sort of rising quaver at the end; do you know what I mean? Unmistakable.

The truth is, I had not realized that the doctor and his wife were not on good terms. They used to bicker a bit now and then when I was here, and I often noticed that little Mrs. Pratt got very red and bit her lip hard to keep her temper, while Luke grew pale and said the most offensive things. He was that sort when he was in the nursery, I remember, and afterwards at school. He was my cousin, you know; that is how I came by this house; after he died, and his boy Charley was killed in South Africa, there were no relations left.

Yes, it's a pretty little property, just the sort of thing for an old sailor like me who has taken to gardening.

One always remembers one's mistakes much more vividly than one's cleverest things, doesn't one? I've often noticed it. I was dining with the Pratts one night, when I told them the story that afterwards made so much difference. It was a wet night in November, and the sea was moaning. Hush!—if you don't speak you will hear it now. . . .

Do you hear the tide? Gloomy sound, isn't it? Sometimes, about this time of year—hallo!—there it is! Don't be frightened, man—it won't eat you—it's only a noise, after all! But I'm glad you've heard it, because there are always people who think it's the wind, or my imagination, or something. You won't hear it again tonight, I fancy, for it doesn't often come more than once. Yes—that's right. Put another stick on the fire, and a little more stuff into that weak mixture you're so fond of. Do you remember old Blauklot the carpenter, on that German ship that picked us up when the *Clontarf* went to the bottom? We were hove to in a howling gale one night, as snug as you please, with no land within five hundred miles, and the ship coming up and falling off as regularly as clockwork— "Biddy te boor beebles ashore tis night, poys!" old Blauklot sang out, as he went off to his quarters with the sail-maker. I often think of that, now that I'm ashore for good and all.

Yes, it was on a night like this, when I was at home for a spell, waiting to take the *Olympia* out on her first trip—it was on the next voyage that she broke the record, you remember—but that dates it. Ninety-two was the year, early in November.

The weather was dirty, Pratt was out of temper, and the dinner was bad, very bad indeed, which didn't improve matters, and cold, which made it worse. The poor little lady was very unhappy about it, and insisted on making a Welsh rarebit on the table to counteract the raw turnips and the half-boiled mutton. Pratt must have had a hard day. Perhaps he had lost a patient. At all events, he was in a nasty temper.

"My wife is trying to poison me, you see!" he said. "She'll succeed some day." I saw that she was hurt, and I made believe to laugh, and said that Mrs. Pratt was much too clever to get rid of her husband in such a simple way; and then I began to tell them about Japanese tricks with spun glass and chopped horsehair and the like.

Pratt was a doctor, and knew a lot more than I did about such things, but that only put me on my mettle, and I told a story about a woman in Ireland who did for three husbands before anyone suspected foul play.

Did you never hear that tale? The fourth husband managed to keep awake and caught her, and she was hanged. How did she do it? She drugged them, and poured melted lead into their ears through a little horn funnel when they were asleep. . . . No—that's the wind whistling. It's backing up to the southward again. I can tell by the sound. Besides, the other thing doesn't often come more than once in an evening even at this time of year—when it happened. Yes, it was in November. Poor Mrs. Pratt died suddenly in her bed not long after I dined here. I can fix the date, because I got the news in New York by the steamer that followed the *Olympia* when I took her out on her first trip. You had the *Leofric* the same year? Yes, I remember. What a pair of old buffers we are coming to be, you and I. Nearly fifty years since we were apprentices together on the *Clontarf*. Shall you ever forget old Blauklot? "Biddy te boor beebles ashore, poys!" Ha, ha! Take a little more, with all that water. It's the old Hulstkamp I found in the cellar when this house came to me, the same I brought Luke from Amsterdam five-and-twenty years ago. He had never touched a drop of it. Perhaps he's sorry now, poor fellow.

Where did I leave off? I told you that Mrs. Pratt died suddenly—yes. Luke must have been lonely here after she was dead, I should think; I came to see him now and then, and he looked worn and nervous, and told me that his practice was growing too heavy for him, though he wouldn't take an assistant on any account. Years went on, and his son was killed in South Africa, and after that he began to be queer. There was something about him not like other people. I believe he kept his senses in his profession to the end;

there was no complaint of his having made bad mistakes in cases, or anything of that sort, but he had a look about him—

Luke was a red-headed man with a pale face when he was young, and he was never stout; in middle age he turned a sandy grey, and after his son died he grew thinner and thinner, till his head looked like a skull with parchment stretched over it very tight, and his eyes had a sort of glare in them that was very disagreeable to look at.

He had an old dog that poor Mrs. Pratt had been fond of, and that used to follow her everywhere. He was a bulldog, and the sweetest tempered beast you ever saw, though he had a way of hitching his upper lip behind one of his fangs that frightened strangers a good deal. Sometimes, of an evening, Pratt and Bumble—that was the dog's name—used to sit and look at each other a long time, thinking about old times, I suppose, when Luke's wife used to sit in that chair you've got. That was always her place, and this was the doctor's, where I'm sitting. Bumble used to climb up by the footstool—he was old and fat by that time, and could not jump much, and his teeth were getting shaky. He would look steadily at Luke, and Luke looked steadily at the dog, his face growing more and more like a skull with two little coals for eyes; and after about five minutes or so, though it may have been less, old Bumble would suddenly begin to shake all over, and all on a sudden he would set up an awful howl, as if he had been shot, and tumble out of the easy-chair and trot away, and hide himself under the sideboard, and lie there making odd noises.

Considering Pratt's looks in those last months, the thing is not surprising, you know. I'm not nervous or imaginative, but I can quite believe he might have sent a sensitive woman into hysterics—his head looked so much like a skull in parchment.

At last I came down one day before Christmas, when my ship was in dock and I had three weeks off. Bumble was not about, and I said casually that I supposed the old dog was dead.

"Yes," Pratt answered, and I thought there was something odd in his tone even before he went on after a little pause. "I killed him," he said presently. "I could stand it no longer."

I asked what it was that Luke could not stand, though I guessed well enough.

"He had a way of sitting in her chair and glaring at me, and then howling," Luke shivered a little. "He didn't suffer at all, poor old Bumble," he went on in a hurry, as if he thought I might imagine he had been cruel. "I put dionine into his drink to make him sleep soundly, and then I chloroformed him gradually, so that he could not have felt suffocated even if he was dreaming. It's been quieter since then."

I wondered what he meant, for the words slipped out as if he could not help saying them. I've understood since. He meant that he did not hear that noise so often after the dog was out of the way. Perhaps he thought at first that it was old Bumble in the yard howling at the moon, though it's not that kind of noise, is it? Besides, I know what it is, if Luke didn't. It's only a noise after all, and a noise never hurt anybody yet. But he was much more imaginative than I am. No doubt there really is something about this place that I don't understand; but when I don't understand a thing, I call it a phenomenon, and I don't take it for granted that it's going to kill me, as he did. I don't understand everything, by long odds, nor do you, nor does any man who has been to sea. We used to talk of tidal waves, for instance, and we could not account for them; now we account for them by calling them submarine earthquakes, and we branch off into fifty theories, any one of which might make earthquakes quite comprehensible if we only knew what they were. I fell in with one of them once, and the inkstand flew straight up from the table against the ceiling of my cabin. The same thing happened to Captain Lecky—I dare say you've read about it in his "Wrinkles." Very good. If that sort of thing took place ashore, in this room for instance, a nervous person would talk about spirits and levitation and fifty things that mean nothing, instead of just quietly setting it down as a "phenomenon" that has not been explained yet. My view of that voice, you see.

Besides, what is there to prove that Luke killed his wife? I would not even suggest such a thing to anyone but you. After all, there was nothing but the coincidence that poor little Mrs. Pratt died suddenly in her bed a few days after I told that story at dinner. She was not the only woman who ever died like that. Luke got the doctor over from the next parish, and they agreed that she had died of something the matter with her heart. Why not? It's common enough.

Of course, there was the ladle. I never told anybody about that, and, it made me start when I found it in the cupboard in the bedroom. It was new, too—a little tinned iron ladle that had not been in the fire more than once or twice, and there was some lead in it that had been melted, and stuck to the bottom of the bowl, all grey, with hardened dross on it. But that proves nothing. A country doctor is generally a handy man, who does everything for himself, and Luke may have had a dozen reasons for melting a little lead in a ladle. He was fond of sea-fishing, for instance, and he may have cast a sinker for a night-line; perhaps it was a weight for the hall clock, or something like that. All the same, when I found it I had a rather queer sensation, because it looked so much like the thing I had described when I told them the story. Do you understand? It affected me unpleasantly, and I threw it away; it's at the bottom of the sea a mile from the Spit, and it will be jolly well rusted beyond recognizing if it's ever washed up by the tide.

You see, Luke must have bought it in the village, years ago, for the man sells just such ladles still. I suppose they are used in cooking. In any case, there was no reason why an inquisitive housemaid should find such a thing lying about, with lead in it, and wonder what it was, and perhaps talk to the maid who heard me tell the story at dinner—for that girl married the plumber's son in the village, and may remember the whole thing.

You understand me, don't you? Now that Luke Pratt is dead and gone, and lies buried beside his wife, with an honest man's tombstone at his head, I should not care to stir up anything that could hurt his memory. They are both dead, and their son, too. There was trouble enough about Luke's death, as it was.

How? He was found dead on the beach one morning, and there was a coroner's inquest. There were marks on his throat, but he had not been robbed. The verdict was that he had come to his end "by the hands or teeth of some person or animal unknown," for half the jury thought it might have been a big dog that had thrown him down and gripped his windpipe, though the skin of his throat was not broken. No one knew at what time he had gone out, nor where he had been. He was found lying on his back above high-water mark, and an old cardboard bandbox that had belonged to his wife lay under his hand, open. The lid had fallen off. He seemed to have been carrying home a skull in the box—doctors are fond of collecting such things. It had rolled out and lay near his head, and it was a remarkably fine skull, rather small, beautifully shaped and very white, with perfect teeth. That is to say, the upper jaw was perfect, but there was no lower one at all, when I first saw it.

Yes, I found it here when I came. You see, it was very white and polished, like a thing meant to be kept under a glass case, and the people did not know where it came from, nor what to do with it; so they put it back into the bandbox and set it on the shelf of the cupboard in the best bedroom, and of course they showed it to me when I took possession. I was taken down to the beach, too, to be shown the place where Luke was found, and the old fisherman explained just how he was lying, and the skull beside him. The only point he could not explain was why the skull had rolled up the sloping sand towards Luke's head instead of rolling downhill to his feet. It did not seem odd to me at the time, but I have often thought of it since, for the place is rather steep. I'll take you there tomorrow if you like—I made a sort of cairn of stones there afterwards.

When he fell down, or was thrown down—whichever happened—the bandbox struck the sand, and the lid came off, and the thing came out and ought to have rolled down. But it didn't. It was close to his head almost touching it, and turned with the face towards it. I say it didn't strike me as odd when the man told me; but I could not help thinking about it afterwards, again and again, till I saw a picture of it all when I closed my eyes; and then I began to ask myself why the plaguey thing had rolled up instead of down, and why it had stopped near Luke's head instead of anywhere else, a yard away, for instance.

You naturally want to know what conclusion I reached, don't you? None that at all explained the rolling, at all events. But I got something else into my head, after a time, that made me feel downright uncomfortable.

Oh, I don't mean as to anything supernatural! There may be ghosts, or there may not be. If there are, I'm not inclined to believe that they can hurt living people except by frightening them, and, for my part, I would rather face any shape of ghost than a fog in the Channel when it's crowded. No. What bothered me was just a foolish idea, that's all, and I cannot tell how it began, nor what made it grow till it turned into a certainty.

I was thinking about Luke and his poor wife one evening over my pipe and a dull book, when it occurred to me that the skull might possibly be hers, and I have never got rid of the thought since. You'll tell me there's no sense in it, no doubt, that Mrs. Pratt was buried like a Christian and is lying in the churchyard where they put her, and that it's perfectly monstrous to suppose her husband kept her skull in her old bandbox in his bedroom. All the same, in the face of reason, and common sense, and probability, I'm convinced that he did. Doctors do all sorts of queer things that would make men like you and me feel creepy, and those are just the things that don't seem probable, nor logical, nor sensible to us.

Then, don't you see?—if it really was her skull, poor woman, the only way of accounting for his having it is that he really killed her, and did it in that way, as the woman killed her husbands in the story, and that he was afraid there might be an examination some day which would betray him. You see, I told that too, and I believe it had really happened some fifty or sixty years ago. They dug up the three skulls, you know, and there was a small lump of lead rattling about in each one. That was what hanged the woman. Luke remembered that, I'm sure. I don't want to know what he did when he thought of it; my taste never ran in the direction of horrors, and I don't fancy you care for them either, do you? No. If you did, you might supply what is wanting to the story.

It must have been rather grim, eh? I wish I did not see the whole thing so distinctly, just as everything must have happened. He took it the night before she was buried, I'm sure, after the coffin had been shut, and when the servant girl was asleep. I would bet anything, that when he'd got it, he put something under the sheet in its place, to fill up and look like it. What do you suppose he put there, under the sheet?

I don't wonder you take me up on what I'm saying! First I tell you that I don't want to know what happened, and that I hate to think about horrors, and then I describe the whole thing to you as if I had seen it. I'm quite sure that it was her work-bag that he put there. I remember the bag very well, for she always used it of an evening; it was made of brown plush, and when it was stuffed full it was about the size of—you understand. Yes, there I am, at it again! You may laugh at me, but you don't live here alone, where it was done, and you didn't tell Luke the story about the melted lead. I'm not nervous, I tell you, but sometimes I begin to feel that I understand why some people are. I dwell on all this when I'm alone, and I dream of it, and when that thing screams—well, frankly, I don't like the noise any more than you do, though I should be used to it by this time.

I ought not to be nervous. I've sailed in a haunted ship. There was a Man in the Top, and two-thirds of the crew died of the West Coast fever inside of ten days after we anchored; but I was all right, then and afterwards. I have seen some ugly sights, too, just as you have, and all the rest of us. But nothing ever stuck in my head in the way this does.

You see, I've tried to get rid of the thing, but it doesn't like that. It wants to be there in its place, in Mrs. Pratt's bandbox in the cupboard in the best bedroom. It's not happy anywhere else. How do I know that? Because I've tried it. You don't suppose that I've not tried, do you? As long as it's there it only screams now and then, generally at this time of year, but if I put it out of the house it goes on all night, and no servant will stay here twenty-four hours. As it is, I've often been left alone and have been obliged to shift for myself for a fortnight at a time. No one from the village would ever pass a night under the roof now, and as for selling the place, or even letting it, that's out of the question. The old women say that if I stay here I shall come to a bad end myself before long.

I'm not afraid of that. You smile at the mere idea that anyone could take such nonsense seriously. Quite right. It's utterly blatant nonsense, I agree with you. Didn't I tell you that it's only a noise after all when you started and looked round as if you expected to see a ghost standing behind your chair?

I may be all wrong about the skull, and I like to think that I am when I can. It may be just a fine specimen which Luke got somewhere long ago, and what rattles about inside when you shake it may be nothing but a pebble, or a bit of hard clay, or anything. Skulls that have lain long in the ground generally have something inside them that rattles don't they? No, I've never tried to get it out, whatever it is; I'm afraid it might be lead, don't you see? And if it is, I don't want to know the fact, for I'd much rather not be sure. If it really is lead, I killed her quite as much as if I had done the deed myself. Anybody must see that, I should think. As long as I don't know for certain, I have the consolation of saying that it's all utterly ridiculous nonsense, that Mrs. Pratt died a natural death and that the beautiful skull belonged to Luke when he was a student in London. But if I were quite sure, I believe I should have to leave the house; indeed I do, most certainly. As it is, I had to give up trying to sleep in the best bedroom where the cupboard is.

You ask me why I don't throw it into the pond—yes, but please don't call it a "confounded bugbear"—it doesn't like being called names.

There! Lord, what a shriek! I told you so! You're quite pale, man. Fill up your pipe and draw your chair nearer to the fire, and take some more drink. Old Hollands never hurt anybody yet. I've seen a Dutchman in Java drink half a jug of Hulstkamp in a morning without turning a hair. I don't take much rum myself, because it doesn't agree with my rheumatism, but you are not rheumatic and it won't damage you. Besides, it's a very damp night outside. The wind is howling again, and it will soon be in the south-west; do you hear how the windows rattle? The tide must have turned too, by the moaning.

We should not have heard the thing again if you had not said that. I'm pretty sure we should not. Oh yes, if you choose to describe it as a coincidence, you are quite welcome, but I would rather that you should not call the thing names again, if you don't mind. It may be that the poor little woman hears, and perhaps it hurts her, don't you know? Ghosts? No! You don't call anything a ghost that you can take in your hands and look at in broad daylight, and that rattles when you shake it. Do you, now? But it's something that hears and understands; there's no doubt about that.

I tried sleeping in the best bedroom when I first came to the house just because it was the best and most comfortable, but I had to give it up It was their room, and there's the big bed she died in, and the cupboard is in the thickness of the wall, near the head, on the left. That's where it likes to be kept, in its bandbox. I only used the room for a fortnight after I came, and then I turned out and took the little room downstairs, next to the surgery, where Luke used to sleep when he expected to be called to a patient during the night.

I was always a good sleeper ashore; eight hours is my dose, eleven to seven when I'm alone, twelve to eight when I have a friend with me. But I could not sleep after three o'clock in the morning in that room—a quarter past, to be accurate—as a matter of fact, I timed it with my old pocket chronometer, which still keeps good time, and it was always at exactly seventeen minutes past three. I wonder whether that was the hour when she died?

It was not what you have heard. If it had been that, I could not have stood it two nights. It was just a start and a moan and hard breathing for a few seconds in the cupboard, and it could never have waked me under ordinary circumstances, I'm sure. I suppose you are like me in that, and we are just like other people who have been to sea. No natural sounds disturb us at all, not all the racket of a square-rigger hove to in a heavy gale, or rolling on her beam ends before the wind. But if a lead pencil gets adrift and rattles in the drawer of your cabin table you are awake in a moment. Just so—you always understand. Very well, the noise in the cupboard was no louder than that, but it waked me instantly.

I said it was like a "start." I know what I mean, but it's hard to explain without seeming to talk nonsense. Of course you cannot exactly "hear" a person "start"; at the most, you might hear the quick drawing of the breath between the parted lips and closed teeth, and the almost imperceptible sound of clothing that moved suddenly though very slightly. It was like that.

You know how one feels what a sailing vessel is going to do, two or three seconds before she does it, when one has the wheel. Riders say the same of a horse, but that's less strange, because the horse is a live animal with feelings of its own, and only poets and landsmen talk about a ship being alive, and all that. But I have always felt somehow that besides being a steaming machine or a sailing machine for carrying weights, a vessel at sea is a sensitive instrument, and a means of communication between nature and man, and most particularly the man at the wheel, if she is steered by hand. She takes her impressions directly from wind and sea, tide and stream, and transmits them to the man's hand, just as the wireless telegraphy picks up the interrupted currents aloft and turns them out below in the form of a message.

You see what I am driving at; I felt that something started in the cupboard, and I felt it so vividly that I heard it, though there may have' been nothing to hear, and the sound inside my head waked me suddenly. But I really heard the other noise. It was as if it were muffled inside a box, as far away as if it came through a long-distance telephone; and yet I knew that it was inside the cupboard near the head of my bed. My hair did not bristle and my blood did not run cold that time. I simply resented being waked up by something that had no business to make a noise, any more than a pencil should rattle in the drawer of my cabin table on board ship. For I did not understand; I just supposed that the cupboard had some communication with the outside air, and that the wind had got in and was moaning through it with a sort of very faint screech. I struck a light and looked at my watch, and it was seventeen minutes past three. Then I turned over and went to sleep on my right ear. That's my good one; I'm pretty deaf with the other, for I struck the water with it when I was a lad in diving from the fore-topsail yard. Silly thing to do, it was, but the result is very convenient when I want to go to sleep when there's a noise.

That was the first night, and the same thing happened again and several times afterwards, but not regularly, though it was always at the same time, to a second; perhaps I was sometimes sleeping on my good ear, and sometimes not. I overhauled the cupboard and there was no way by which the wind could get in, or anything else, for the door makes a good fit, having been meant to keep out moths, I suppose; Mrs. Pratt must have kept her winter things in it, for it still smells of camphor and turpentine.

After about a fortnight I had had enough of the noises. So far I had said to myself that it would be silly to yield to it and take the skull out of the room. Things always look differently by daylight, don't they? But the voice grew louder—I suppose one may call it a voice—and it got inside my deaf ear, too, one night. I realized that when I was wide awake, for my good ear was jammed down on the pillow, and I ought not to have heard a foghorn in that position. But I heard that, and it made me lose my temper, unless it scared me, for sometimes the two are not far apart. I struck a light and got up, and I opened the cupboard, grabbed the bandbox and threw it out of the window, as far as I could.

Then my hair stood on end. The thing screamed in the air, like a shell from a twelve-inch gun. It fell on the other side of the road. The night was very dark, and I could not see it fall, but I know it fell beyond the road. The window is just over the front door, it's fifteen yards to the fence, more or less, and the road is ten yards wide. There's a thick-set hedge beyond, along the glebe that belongs to the vicarage.

I did not sleep much more than night. It was not more than half an hour after I had thrown the bandbox out when I heard a shriek outside—like what we've had tonight, but worse, more despairing, I should call it; and it may have been my imagination, but I could have sworn that the screams came nearer and nearer each time. I lit a pipe, and walked up and down for a bit, and then took a book and sat up reading, but I'll be hanged if I can remember what I read nor even what the book was, for every now and then a shriek came up that would have made a dead man turn in his coffin.

A little before dawn someone knocked at the front door. There was no mistaking that for anything else, and I opened my window and looked down, for I guessed that someone wanted the doctor, supposing that the new man had taken Luke's house. It was rather a relief to hear a human knock after that awful noise.

You cannot see the door from above, owing to the little porch. The knocking came again, and I called out, asking who was there, but nobody answered, though the knock was repeated. I sang out again, and said that the doctor did not live here any longer. There was no answer, but it occurred to me that it might be some old countryman who was stone deaf. So I took my candle and went down to open the door. Upon my word, I was not thinking of the thing yet, and I had almost forgotten the other noises. I went down convinced that I should find somebody outside, on the doorstep, with a message. I set the candle on the hall table, so that the wind should not blow it out when I opened. While I was drawing the old-fashioned bolt I heard the knocking again. It was not loud, and it had a queer, hollow sound, now that I was close to it, I remember, but I certainly thought it was made by some person who wanted to get in.

It wasn't. There was nobody there, but as I opened the door inward, standing a little on one side, so as to see out at once, something rolled across the threshold and stopped against my foot.

I drew back as I felt it, for I knew what it was before I looked down. I cannot tell you how I knew, and it seemed unreasonable, for I am still quite sure that I had thrown it across the road. It's a French window, that opens wide, and I got a good swing when I flung it out. Besides, when I went out early in the morning, I found the bandbox beyond the thick hedge.

You may think it opened when I threw it, and that the skull dropped out; but that's impossible, for nobody could throw an empty cardboard box so far. It's out of the question; you might as well try to fling a ball of paper twenty-five yards, or a blown bird's egg.

To go back, I shut and bolted the hall door, picked the thing up carefully, and put it on the table beside the candle. I did that mechanically, as one instinctively does the right thing in danger without thinking at all—unless one does the opposite. It may seem odd, but I believe my first thought had been that somebody might come and find me there on the threshold while it was resting against my foot, lying a little on its side, and turning one hollow eye up at my face, as if it meant to accuse me. And the light and shadow from the candle played in the hollows of the eyes as it stood on the table, so that they seemed to open and shut at me. Then the candle went out quite unexpectedly, though the door was fastened and there was not the least draught; and I used up at least half a dozen matches before it would burn again.

I sat down rather suddenly, without quite knowing why. Probably I had been badly frightened, and perhaps you will admit there was no great shame in being scared. The thing had come home, and it wanted to go upstairs, back to its cupboard. I sat still and stared at it for a bit till I began to feel very cold; then I took it and carried it up and set it in its place, and I remember that I spoke to it, and promised that it should have its bandbox again in the morning.

You want to know whether I stayed in the room till daybreak? Yes, but I kept a light burning, and sat up smoking and reading, most likely out of fright; plain, undeniable fear, and you need not call it cowardice either, for that's not the same thing. I could not have stayed alone with that thing in the cupboard; I should have been scared to death, though I'm not more timid than other people. Confound it all, man, it had crossed the road alone, and had got up the doorstep and had knocked to be let in.

When the dawn came, I put on my boots and went out to find the bandbox. I had to go a good way round, by the gate near the high road, and I found the box open and hanging on the other side of the hedge. It had caught on the twigs by the string, and the lid had fallen off and was lying on the ground below it. That shows that it did not open till it was well over; and if it had not opened as soon as it left my hand, what was inside it must have gone beyond the road too.

That's all. I took the box upstairs to the cupboard, and put the skull back and locked it up. When the girl brought me my breakfast she said she was sorry, but that she must go, and she did not care if she lost her month's wages. I looked at her, and her face was a sort of greenish yellowish white. I pretended to be surprised, and asked what was the matter; but that was of no use, for she just turned on me and wanted to know whether I meant to stay in a haunted house, and how long I expected to live if I did, for though she noticed I was sometimes a little hard of hearing, she did not believe that even I could sleep through those screams again—and if I could, why had I been moving about the house and opening and shutting the front door, between three and four in the morning? There was no answering that, since she had heard me, so off she went, and I was left to myself. I went down to the village during the morning and found a woman who was willing to come and do the little work there is and cook my dinner, on condition that she might go home every night. As for me, I moved downstairs that day, and I have never tried to sleep in the best bedroom since. After a little while I got a brace of middle-aged Scotch servants from London, and things were quiet enough for a long time. I began by telling them that the house was in a very exposed position, and that the wind whistled round it a good deal in the autumn and winter, which had given it a bad name in the village, the Cornish people being inclined to superstition and telling ghost stories. The two hard-faced, sandy-haired sisters almost smiled, and they answered with great contempt that they had no great opinion of any Southern bogey whatever, having been in service in two English haunted houses, where they had never seen so much as the Boy in Grey, whom they reckoned no very particular rarity in Forfarshire.

They stayed with me several months, and while they were in the house we had peace and quiet. One of them is here again now, but she went away with her sister within the year. This one—she was the cook—married the sexton, who works in my garden. That's the way of it. It's a small village and he has not much to do, and he knows enough about flowers to help me nicely, besides doing most of the hard work; for though I'm fond of exercise, I'm getting a little stiff in the hinges. He's a sober, silent sort of fellow, who minds his own business, and he was a widower when I came here—Trehearn is his name, James Trehearn. The Scottish sisters would not admit that there was anything wrong about the house, but when November came they gave me warning that they were going, on the ground that the chapel was such a long walk from here, being in the next parish, and that they could not possibly go to our church. But the younger one came back in the spring, and as soon as the banns could be published she was married to James Trehearn by the vicar, and she seems to have had no scruples about hearing him preach since then. I'm quite satisfied, if she is! The couple live in a small cottage that looks over the churchyard.

I suppose you are wondering what all this has to do with what I was talking about. I'm alone so much that when an old friend comes to see me, I sometimes go on talking just for the sake of hearing my own voice. But in this case there is really a connection of ideas. It was James Trehearn who buried poor Mrs. Pratt, and her husband after her in the same grave, and it's not far from the back of his cottage. That's the connection in my mind, you see. It's plain enough. He knows something; I'm quite sure that he does, though he's such a reticent beggar.

Yes, I'm alone in the house at night now, for Mrs. Trehearn does everything herself, and when I have a friend the sexton's niece comes in to wait on the table. He takes his wife home every evening in winter, but in summer, when there's light, she goes by herself. She's not a nervous woman, but she's less sure than she used to be that there are no bogies in England worth a Scotch-woman's notice. Isn't it amusing, the idea that Scotland has a monopoly of the supernatural? Odd sort of national pride, I call that, don't you?

That's a good fire, isn't it? When driftwood gets started at last there's nothing like it, I think. Yes, we get lots of it, for I'm sorry to say there are still a great many wrecks about here. It's a lonely coast, and you may have all the wood you want for the trouble of bringing it in. Trehearn and I borrow a cart now and then, and load it between here and the Spit. I hate a coal fire when I can get wood of any sort. A log is company, even if it's only a piece of a deck beam or timber sawn off, and the salt in it makes pretty sparks. See how they fly, like Japanese hand-fireworks! Upon my word, with an old friend and a good fire and a pipe, one forgets all about that thing upstairs, especially now that the wind has moderated. It's only a lull, though, and it will blow a gale before morning.

You think you would like to see the skull? I've no objection. There's no reason why you shouldn't have a look at it, and you never saw a more perfect one in your life, except that there are two front teeth missing in the lower jaw.

Oh yes—I had not told you about the jaw yet. Trehearn found it in the garden last spring when he was digging a pit for a new asparagus bed. You know we make asparagus beds six or eight feet deep here. Yes, yes—I had forgotten to tell you that. He was digging straight down, just as he digs a grave; if you want a good asparagus bed made, I advise you to get a sexton to make it for you. Those fellows have a wonderful knack at that sort of digging.

Trehearn had got down about three feet when he cut into a mass of white lime in the side of the trench. He had noticed that the earth was a little looser there, though he says it had not been disturbed for a number of years. I suppose he thought that even old lime might not be good for asparagus, so he broke it out and threw it up. It was pretty hard, he says, in biggish lumps, and out of sheer force of habit he cracked the lumps with his spade as they lay outside the pit beside him; the jaw bone of the skull dropped out of one of the pieces. He thinks he must have knocked out the two front teeth in breaking up the lime, but he did not see them anywhere. He's a very experienced man in such things, as you may imagine, and he said at once that the jaw had probably belonged to a young woman, and that the teeth had been complete when she died. He brought it to me, and asked me if I wanted to keep it; if I did not, he said he would drop it into the next grave he made in the churchyard, as he supposed it was a Christian jaw, and ought to have decent burial, wherever the rest of the body might be. I told him that doctors often put bones into quicklime to whiten them nicely, and that I supposed Dr Pratt had once had a little lime pit in the garden for that purpose, and had forgotten the jaw. Trehearn looked at me quietly.

"Maybe it fitted that skull that used to be in the cupboard upstairs, sir," he said. "Maybe Dr Pratt had put the skull into the lime to clean it, or something, and when he took it out he left the lower jaw behind. There's some human hair sticking in the lime, sir."

I saw there was, and that was what Trehearn said. If he did not suspect something, why in the world should he have suggested that the jaw might fit the skull? Besides, it did. That's proof that he knows more than he cares to tell. Do you suppose he looked before she was buried? Or perhaps—when he buried Luke in the same grave—

Well, well, it's of no use to go over that, is it? I said I would keep the jaw with the skull, and I took it upstairs and fitted it into its place. There's not the slightest doubt about the two belonging together, and together they are.

Trehearn knows several things. We were talking about plastering the kitchen a while ago, and he happened to remember that it had not been done since the very week when Mrs. Pratt died. He did not say that the mason must have left some lime on the place, but he thought it, and that it was the very same lime he had found in the asparagus pit. He knows a lot. Trehearn is one of your silent beggars who can put two and two together. That grave is very near the back of his cottage, too, and he's one of the quickest men with a spade I ever saw. If he wanted to know the truth, he could, and no one else would ever be the wiser unless he chose to tell. In a quiet village like ours, people don't go and spend the night in the churchyard to see whether the sexton potters about by himself between ten o'clock and daylight.

What is awful to think of, is Luke's deliberation, if he did it; his cool certainty that no one would find him out; above all, his nerve, for that must have been extraordinary. I sometimes think it's bad enough to live in the place where it was done, if it really was done. I always put in the condition, you see, for the sake of his memory, and a little bit for my own sake, too.

I'll go upstairs and fetch the box in a minute. Let me light my pipe; there's no hurry! We had supper early, and it's only half-past nine o'clock. I never let a friend go to bed before twelve, or with less than three glasses—you may have as many more as you like, but you shan't have less, for the sake of old times.

It's breezing up again, do you hear? That was only a lull just now, and we are going to have a bad night.

A thing happened that made me start a little when I found that the jaw fitted exactly. I'm not very easily startled in that way myself, but I have seen people make a quick movement, drawing their breath sharply, when they had thought they were alone and suddenly turned and saw someone very near them. Nobody can call that fear. You wouldn't, would you? No. Well, just when I had set the jaw in its place under the skull, the teeth closed sharply on my finger. It felt exactly as if it were biting me hard, and I confess that I jumped before I realized that I had been pressing the jaw and the skull together with my other hand. I assure you I was not at all nervous. It was broad daylight, too, and a fine day, and the sun was streaming into the best bedroom. It would have been absurd to be nervous, and it was only a quick mistaken impression, but it really made me feel queer. Somehow it made me think of the funny verdict of the coroner's jury on Luke's death, "by the hand or teeth of some person or animal unknown". Ever since that I've wished I had seen those marks on his throat, though the lower jaw was missing then.

I have often seen a man do insane things with his hands that he does not realize at all. I once saw a man hanging on by an old awning stop with one hand, leaning backward, outboard, with all his weight on it, and he was just cutting the stop with the knife in his other hand when I got my arms round him. We were in midocean, going twenty knots. He had not the smallest idea what he was doing; neither had I when I managed to pinch my finger between the teeth of that thing. I can feel it now. It was exactly as if it were alive and were trying to bite me. It would if it could, for I know it hates me, poor thing! Do you suppose that what rattles about inside is really a bit of lead? Well, I'll get the box down presently, and if whatever it is happens to drop out into your hands, that's your affair. If it's only a clod of earth or a pebble, the whole matter would be off my mind, and I don't believe I should ever think of the skull again; but somehow I cannot bring myself to shake out the bit of hard stuff myself. The mere idea that it may be lead makes me confoundedly uncomfortable, yet I've got the conviction that I shall know before long. I shall certainly know. I'm sure Trehearn knows, but he's such a silent beggar.

I'll go upstairs now and get it. What? You had better go with me? Ha, ha! do you think I'm afraid of a bandbox and a noise? Nonsense!

Bother the candle, it won't light! As if the ridiculous thing understood what it's wanted for! Look at that—the third match. They light fast enough for my pipe. There, do you see? It's a fresh box, just out of the tin safe where I keep the supply on account of the dampness. Oh, you think the wick of the candle may be damp, do you? All right, I'll light the beastly thing in the fire. That won't go out, at all events. Yes, it sputters a bit, but it will keep lighted now. It burns just like any other candle, doesn't it? The fact is, candles are not very good about here. I don't know where they come from, but they have a way of burning low occasionally, with a greenish flame that spits tiny sparks, and I'm often annoyed by their going out of themselves. It cannot be helped, for it will be long before we have electricity in our village. It really is rather a poor light, isn't it?

You think I had better leave you the candle and take the lamp, do you? I don't like to carry lamps about, that's the truth. I never dropped one in my life, but I have always thought I might, and it's so confoundedly dangerous if you do. Besides, I am pretty well used to these rotten candles by this time.

You may as well finish that glass while I'm getting it, for I don't mean to let you off with less than three before you go to bed. You won't have to go upstairs, either, for I've put you in the old study next to the surgery—that's where I live myself. The fact is, I never ask a friend to sleep upstairs now. The last man who did was

Crackenthorpe, and he said he was kept awake all night. You re-member old Crack, don't you? He stuck to the Service, and they've just made him an admiral. Yes, I'm off now—unless the candle goes out. I couldn't help asking if you remembered Crackenthorpe. If anyone had told us that the skinny little idiot he used to be was to turn out the most successful of the lot of us, we should have laughed at the idea, shouldn't we? You and I did not do badly, it's true—but I'm really going now. I don't mean to let you think that I've been putting it off by talking! As if there were anything to be afraid of! If I were scared, I should tell you so quite frankly, and get you to go upstairs with me.

Here's the box. I brought it down very carefully, so as not to disturb it, poor thing. You see, if it were shaken, the jaw might get separated from it again, and I'm sure it wouldn't like that. Yes, the candle went out as I was coming downstairs, but that was the draught from the leaky window on the landing. Did you hear any-thing? Yes, there was another scream. Am I pale, do you say? That's nothing. My heart is a little queer sometimes, and I went upstairs too fast. In fact, that's one reason why I really prefer to live alto-gether on the ground floor.

Wherever the shriek came from, it was not from the skull, for I had the box in my hand when I heard the noise, and here it is now; so we have proved definitely that the screams are produced by something else. I've no doubt I shall find out some day what makes them. Some crevice in the wall, of course, or a crack in a chimney, or a chink in the frame of a window. That's the way all ghost sto-ries end in real life. Do you know, I'm jolly glad I thought of going up and bringing it down for you to see, for that last shriek settles the question. To think that I should have been so weak as to fancy that the poor skull could really cry out like a living thing!

Now I'll open the box, and we'll take it out and look at it under the bright light. It's rather awful to think that the poor lady used to sit there, in your chair, evening after evening, in just the same light, isn't it? But then—I've made up my mind that it's all rubbish from beginning to end, and that it's just an old skull that Luke had when he was a student and perhaps he put it into the lime merely to whiten it, and could not find the jaw.

I made a seal on the string, you see, after I had put the jaw in its place, and I wrote on the cover. There's the old white label on it still, from the milliner's, addressed to Mrs. Pratt when the hat was sent to her, and as there was room I wrote on the edge: "A skull, once the property of the late Luke Pratt, MD." I don't quite know why I wrote that, unless it was with the idea of explaining how the thing happened to be in my possession. I cannot help wondering sometimes what sort of hat it was that came in the bandbox. What colour was it, do you think? Was it a gay spring hat with a bobbing feather and pretty ribands? Strange that the very same box should hold the head that wore the finery—perhaps. No—we made up our minds that it just came from the hospital in London where Luke did his time. It's far better to look at it in that light, isn't it? There's no more connection between that skull and poor Mrs. Pratt than there was between my story about the lead and—

Good Lord! Take the lamp—don't let it go out, if you can help it— I'll have the window fastened again in a second—I say, what a gale! There, it's out! I told you so! Never mind, there's the fire-light— I've got the window shut—the bolt was only half down. Was the box blown off the table? Where the deuce is it? There! That won't open again, for I've put up the bar. Good dodge, an old-fashioned bar—there's nothing like it. Now, you find the bandbox while I light the lamp. Confound those wretched matches! Yes, a pipe spill is better—it must light in the fire—hadn't thought of it—thank you—there we are again. Now, where's the box? Yes, put it back on the table, and we'll open it.

That's the first time I have ever known the wind to burst that window open; but it was partly carelessness on my part when I last shut it. Yes, of course I heard the scream. It seemed to go all round the house before it broke in at the window. That proves that it's always been the wind and nothing else, doesn't it? When it was not the wind, it was my imagination I've always been a very imaginative man: I must have been, though I did not know it. As we grow older we understand ourselves better, don't you know?

I'll have a drop of the Hulstkamp neat, by way of an exception, since you are filling up your glass. That damp gust chilled me, and with my rheumatic tendency I'm very much afraid of a chill, for the cold sometimes seems to stick in my joints all winter when it once gets in.

By George, that's good stuff! I'll just light a fresh pipe, now that everything is snug again, and then we'll open the box. I'm so glad we heard that last scream together, with the skull here on the table between us, for a thing cannot possibly be in two places at the same time, and the noise most certainly came from outside, as any noise the wind makes must. You thought you heard it scream through the room after the window was burst open? Oh yes, so did I, but that was natural enough when everything was open. Of course we heard the wind. What could one expect?

Look here, please. I want you to see that the seal is intact before we open the box together. Will you take my glasses? No, you have your own. All right. The seal is sound, you see, and you can read the words of the motto easily. "Sweet and low"—that's it—because the poem goes on "Wind of the Western Sea", and says, "blow him again to me", and all that. Here is the seal on my watch chain, where it's hung for more than forty years. My poor little wife gave it to me when I was courting, and I never had any other. It was just like her to think of those words—she was always fond of Tennyson.

It's no use to cut the string, for it's fastened to the box, so I'll just break the wax and untie the knot, and afterwards we'll seal it up again. You see, I like to feel that the thing is safe in its place, and that nobody can take it out. Not that I should suspect Trehearn of meddling with it, but I always feel that he knows a lot more than he tells.

You see, I've managed it without breaking the string, though when I fastened it I never expected to open the bandbox again. The lid comes off easily enough. There! Now look!

What! Nothing in it! Empty! It's gone, man, the skull is gone!

No, there's nothing the matter with me. I'm only trying to collect my thoughts. It's so strange. I'm positively certain that it was inside when I put on the seal last spring. I can't have imagined that: it's utterly impossible. If I ever took a stiff glass with a friend now and then, I would admit that I might have made some idiotic mistake when I had taken too much. But I don't, and I never did. A pint of ale at supper and half a go of rum at bedtime was the most I ever took in my good days. I believe it's always we sober fellows who get rheumatism and gout! Yet there was my seal, and there is the empty bandbox. That's plain enough.

I say, I don't half like this. It's not right. There's something wrong about it, in my opinion. You needn't talk to me about super-natural manifestations, for I don't believe in them, not a little bit! Somebody must have tampered with the seal and stolen the skull. Sometimes, when I go out to work in the garden in summer, I leave my watch and chain on the table. Trehearn must have taken the seal then, and used it, for he would be quite sure that I should not come in for at least an hour.

If it was not Trehearn—oh, don't talk to me about the possibil-ity that the thing has got out by itself! If it has, it must be some-where about the house, in some out-of-the-way corner, waiting. We may come upon it anywhere, waiting for us, don't you know?—just waiting in the dark. Then it will scream at me; it will shriek at me in the dark, for it hates me, I tell you!

The bandbox is quite empty. We are not dreaming, either of us. There, I turn it upside down.

What's that? Something fell out as I turned it over. It's on the floor, it's near your feet. I know it is, and we must find it. Help me to find it, man. Have you got it? For God's sake, give it to me, quickly!

Lead! I knew it when I heard it fall. I knew it couldn't be any-thing else by the little thud it made on the hearthrug. So it was lead after all and Luke did it.

I feel a little bit shaken up—not exactly nervous, you know, but badly shaken up, that's the fact. Anybody would, I should think. After all, you cannot say that it's fear of the thing, for I went up and brought it down—at least, I believed I was bringing it down, and that's the same thing, and by George, rather than give in to such silly nonsense, I'll take the box upstairs again and put it back in its place. It's not that. It's the certainty that the poor little woman came to her end in that way, by my fault, because I told the story. That's what is so dreadful. Somehow, I had always hoped that I should never be quite sure of it, but there is no doubting it now. Look at that!

Look at it! That little lump of lead with no particular shape. Think of what it did, man! Doesn't it make you shiver? He gave her something to make her sleep, of course, but there must have been one moment of awful agony. Think of having boiling lead poured into your brain. Think of it. She was dead before she could scream, but only think of—oh! there it is again—it's just outside—I know it's just outside—I can't keep it out of my head!—oh!—oh!

You thought I had fainted? No, I wish I had, for it would have stopped sooner. It's all very well to say that it's only a noise, and that a noise never hurt anybody—you're as white as a shroud yourself. There's only one thing to be done, if we hope to close an eye tonight. We must find it and put it back into its bandbox and shut it up in the cupboard, where it likes to be I don't know how it got out, but it wants to get in again. That's why it screams so awfully tonight—it was never so bad as this—never since I first—

Bury it? Yes, if we can find it, we'll bury it, if it takes us all night. We'll bury it six feet deep and ram down the earth over it, so that it shall never get out again, and if it screams, we shall hardly hear it so deep down. Quick, we'll get the lantern and look for it. It cannot be far away; I'm sure it's just outside—it was coming in when I shut the window, I know it.

Yes, you're quite right. I'm losing my senses, and I must get hold of myself. Don't speak to me for a minute or two; I'll sit quite still and keep my eyes shut and repeat something I know. That's the best way.

"Add together the altitude, the latitude, and the polar distance, divide by two and subtract the altitude from the half-sum; then add the logarithm of the secant of the latitude, the cosecant of the polar distance, the cosine of the half-sum and the sine of the half-sum minus the altitude"—there! Don't say that I'm out of my senses, for my memory is all right, isn't it?

Of course, you may say that it's mechanical, and that we never forget the things we learned when we were boys and have used almost every day for a lifetime. But that's the very point. When a man is going crazy, it's the mechanical part of his mind that gets out of order and won't work right; he remembers things that never happened, or he sees things that aren't real, or he hears noises when there is perfect silence. That's not what is the matter with either of us, is it?

Come, we'll get the lantern and go round the house. It's not raining—only blowing like old boots, as we used to say. The lantern is in the cupboard under the stairs in the hall, and I always keep it trimmed in case of a wreck.

No use to look for the thing? I don't see how you can say that. It was nonsense to talk of burying it, of course, for it doesn't want to be buried; it wants to go back into its bandbox and be taken upstairs, poor thing! Trehearn took it out, I know, and made the seal over again. Perhaps he took it to the churchyard, and he may have meant well. I dare say he thought that it would not scream any more if it were quietly laid in consecrated ground, near where it belongs. But it has come home. Yes, that's it. He's not half a bad fellow, Trehearn, and rather religiously inclined, I think. Does not that sound natural, and reasonable, and well meant? He supposed it screamed because it was not decently buried—with the rest. But he was wrong. How should he know that it screams at me because it hates me, and because it's my fault that there was that little lump of lead in it?

No use to look for it, anyhow? Nonsense! I tell you it wants to be found—Hark! what's that knocking? Do you hear it? Knock—knock—knock—three times, then a pause, and then again. It has a hollow sound, hasn't it?

It has come home. I've heard that knock before. It wants to come in and be taken upstairs in its box. It's at the front door.

Will you come with me? We'll take it in. Yes, I own that I don't like to go alone and open the door. The thing will roll in and stop against my foot, just as it did before, and the light will go out. I'm a good deal shaken by finding that bit of lead, and, besides, my heart isn't quite right—too much strong tobacco, perhaps. Besides, I'm quite willing to own that I'm a bit nervous tonight, if I never was before in my life.

That's right, come along! I'll take the box with me, so as not to come back. Do you hear the knocking? It's not like any other knocking I ever heard. If you will hold this door open, I can find the lantern under the stairs by the light from this room without bringing the lamp into the hall—it would only go out.

The thing knows we are coming—hark! It's impatient to get in. Don't shut the door till the lantern is ready, whatever you do. There will be the usual trouble with the matches, I suppose—no, the first one, by Jove! I tell you it wants to get in, so there's no trouble. All right with that door now; shut it, please. Now come and hold the lantern, for it's blowing so hard outside that I shall have to use both hands. That's it, hold the light low. Do you hear the knocking still? Here goes—I'll open just enough with my foot against the bottom of the door—now!

Catch it! it's only the wind that blows it across the floor, that's all—there's half a hurricane outside, I tell you! Have you got it? The bandbox is on the table. One minute, and I'll have the bar up. There!

Why did you throw it into the box so roughly? It doesn't like that, you know.

What do you say? Bitten your hand? Nonsense, man! You did just what I did. You pressed the jaws together with your other hand and pinched yourself. Let me see. You don't mean to say you have drawn blood? You must have squeezed hard by Jove, for the skin is certainly torn. I'll give you some carbolic solution for it before we go to bed, for they say a scratch from a skull's tooth may go bad and give trouble.

Come inside again and let me see it by the lamp. I'll bring the bandbox—never mind the lantern, it may just as well burn in the hall for I shall need it presently when I go up the stairs. Yes, shut the door if you will; it makes it more cheerful and bright. Is your finger still bleeding? I'll get you the carbolic in an instant; just let me see the thing.

Ugh! There's a drop of blood on the upper jaw. It's on the eye-tooth. Ghastly, isn't it? When I saw it running along the floor of the hall, the strength almost went out of my hands, and I felt my knees bending, then I understood that it was the gale, driving it over the smooth boards. You don't blame me? No, I should think not! We were boys together, and we've seen a thing or two, and we may just as well own to each other that we were both in a beastly funk when it slid across the floor at you. No wonder you pinched your finger picking it up, after that, if I did the same thing out of sheer nervousness, in broad daylight, with the sun streaming in on me.

Strange that the jaw should stick to it so closely, isn't it? I sup-pose it's the dampness, for it shuts like a vice—I have wiped off the drop of blood, for it was not nice to look at. I'm not going to try to open the jaws, don't be afraid! I shall not play any tricks with the poor thing, but I'll just seal the box again, and we'll take it upstairs and put it away where it wants to be. The wax is on the writing-table by the window. Thank you. It will be long before I leave my seal lying about again, for Trehearn to use, I can tell you. Explain? I don't explain natural phenomena, but if you choose to think that Trehearn had hidden it somewhere in the bushes, and that the gale blew it to the house against the door, and made it knock, as if it wanted to be let in, you're not thinking the impos-sible, and I'm quite ready to agree with you.

Do you see that? You can swear that you've actually seen me seal it this time, in case anything of the kind should occur again. The wax fastens the strings to the lid, which cannot possibly be lifted, even enough to get in one finger. You're quite satisfied, aren't you? Yes. Besides, I shall lock the cupboard and keep the key in my pocket hereafter.

Now we can take the lantern and go upstairs. Do you know? I'm very much inclined to agree with your theory that the wind blew it against the house. I'll go ahead, for I know the stairs; just hold the lantern near my feet as we go up. How the wind howls and whistles! Did you feel the sand on the floor under your shoes as we crossed the hall?

Yes—this is the door of the best bedroom. Hold up the lantern, please. This side, by the head of the bed. I left the cupboard open when I got the box. Isn't it queer how the faint odour of women's dresses will hang about an old closet for years? This is the shelf. You've seen me set the box there, and now you see me turn the key and put it into my pocket. So that's done!

Goodnight. Are you sure you're quite comfortable? It's not much of a room, but I dare say you would as soon sleep here as upstairs tonight. If you want anything, sing out; there's only a lath and plaster partition between us. There's not so much wind on this side by half. There's the Hollands on the table, if you'll have one more nightcap. No? Well, do as you please. Goodnight again, and don't dream about that thing, if you can.

The following paragraph appeared in the *Penraddon News*, 23rd November 1906:

MYSTERIOUS DEATH OF A RETIRED SEA CAPTAIN

The village of Tredcombe is much disturbed by the strange death of Captain Charles Braddock, and all sorts of impossible stories are circulating with regard to the circumstances, which certainly seem difficult of explanation. The retired captain, who had successfully commanded in his time the largest and fastest liners belonging to one of the principal transatlantic steamship companies, was found dead in his bed on Tuesday morning in his own cottage, a quarter of a mile from the village. An examination was made at once by the local practitioner, which revealed the horrible fact that the deceased had been bitten in the throat by a human assailant, with such amazing force as to crush the windpipe and cause death. The marks of the teeth of both jaws were so plainly visible on the skin that they could be counted, but the perpetrator of the deed had evidently lost the two lower middle incisors. It is hoped that this peculiarity may help to identify the murderer, who can only be a dangerous escaped maniac. The deceased, though over sixty-five years of age, is said to have been a hale man of considerable physical strength, and it is remarkable that no signs of any struggle were visible in the room, nor could it be ascertained how the murderer had entered the house. Warning has been sent to all the insane asylums in the United Kingdom, but as yet no information has been received regarding the escape of any dangerous patient.

The coroner's Jury returned the somewhat singular verdict that Captain Braddock came to his death "by the hands or teeth of some person unknown." The local surgeon is said to have expressed privately the opinion that the maniac is a woman, a view he deduces from the small size of the jaws, as shown by the marks of the teeth. The whole affair is shrouded in mystery. Captain Braddock was a widower, and lived alone. He leaves no children.

(*Note.*—Students of ghost lore and haunted houses will find the foundation of the foregoing story in the legends about a skull which is still preserved in the farmhouse called Bettiscombe Manor, situated, I believe, on the Dorsetshire coast.)

THE DOLL'S GHOST

It was a terrible accident, and for one moment the splendid machinery of Cranston House got out of gear and stood still. The butler emerged from the retirement in which he spent his elegant leisure. Two grooms of the chambers appeared simultaneously from opposite directions. There were actually housemaids on the grand staircase, and those who remember the facts most exactly assert that Mrs. Pringle herself positively stood upon the landing. Mrs. Pringle was the housekeeper. As for the head nurse, the under nurse, and the nursery-maid, their feelings cannot be described. The head nurse laid one hand upon the polished marble balustrade and stared stupidly before her. The under nurse stood rigid and pale, leaning against the polished marble wall, and the nursery-maid collapsed and sat down upon the polished marble step, just beyond the limits of the velvet carpet, and burst into tears.

The Lady Gwendolen Lancaster-Douglas-Scroop, youngest daughter of the ninth Duke of Cranston, and aged six years and three months, picked herself up quite alone, and sat down on the third step from the foot of the grand staircase in Cranston House.

"Oh!" exclaimed the butler, and he disappeared again.

"Ah!" responded the grooms of the chambers, as they also went away.

"It's only that doll," Mrs. Pringle was distinctly heard to say, in a tone of contempt.

The under nurse heard her say it. Then the three nurses gathered round Lady Gwendolen and patted her, and gave her unhealthy things out of their pockets, and hurried her out of Cranston House as fast as they could, lest it should be found out upstairs that they had allowed the Lady Gwendolen Lancaster-Douglas-Scroop to tumble down the grand staircase with her doll in her arms. And as the doll was badly broken, the nursery-maid carried it, with the pieces, wrapped up in Lady Gwendolen's little cloak. It was not far to Hyde Park, and when they had reached a quiet place they took means to find out that Lady Gwendolen had no bruises. For the carpet was very thick and soft, and there was thick stuff under it to make it softer.

Lady Gwendolen Douglas-Scroop sometimes yelled, but she never cried. It was because she had yelled that the nurse had allowed her to go downstairs alone with Nina, the doll, under one arm, while she steadied herself with her other hand on the balustrade, and trod upon the polished marble steps beyond the edge of the carpet. So she had fallen, and Nina had come to grief.

When the nurses were quite sure that she was not hurt, they unwrapped the doll and looked at her in her turn. She had been a very beautiful doll, very large, and fair, and healthy, with real yellow hair, and eyelids that would open and shut over very grown-up dark eyes. Moreover, when you moved her right arm up and down she said "Pa-pa," and when you moved the left she said "Mama," very distinctly.

"I heard her say 'Pa' when she fell," said the under nurse, who heard everything. "But she ought to have said 'Pa-pa.'"

"That's because her arm went up when she hit the step," said the head nurse. "She'll say the other 'Pa' when I put it down again."

"Pa," said Nina, as her right arm was pushed down, and speaking through her broken face. It was cracked right across, from the upper corner of the forehead, with a hideous gash, through the nose and down to the little frilled collar of the pale green silk Mother Hubbard frock, and two little three-cornered pieces of porcelain had fallen out.

"I'm sure it's a wonder she can speak at all, being all smashed," said the under nurse.

"You'll have to take her to Mr. Puckler," said her superior. "It's not far, and you'd better go at once."

Lady Gwendolen was occupied with digging a hole in the ground with a little spade, and paid no attention to the nurses.

"What are you doing?" inquired the nursery-maid, looking on.

"Nina's dead, and I'm diggin' her a grave," replied her ladyship thoughtfully.

"Oh, she'll come to life again all right," said the nursery-maid.

The under nurse wrapped Nina up again and departed. Fortunately a kind soldier, with very long legs and a very small cap, happened to be there; and as he had nothing to do, he offered to see the under nurse safely to Mr. Puckler's and back.

Mr. Bernard Puckler and his little daughter lived in a little house in a little alley, which led out off a quiet little street not very far from Belgrave Square. He was the great doll doctor whose extensive practice lay in the most aristocratic quarter. He mended dolls of all sizes and ages, boy dolls and girl dolls, baby dolls in long clothes, and grown-up dolls in fashionable gowns, talking dolls and dumb dolls, those that shut their eyes when they lay down, and those whose eyes had to be shut for them by means of a mysterious wire. His daughter Else was only twelve years old, but she was already very clever at mending dolls' clothes and at doing their hair, which is harder than you might think, though the dolls sit quite still while it is being done.

Mr. Puckler had originally been a German, but he had dissolved his nationality in the ocean of London many years ago, like a great many foreigners. He still had one or two German friends, however, who came on Saturday evenings, and smoked with him and played picquet or "skat" with him for farthing points, and called him "Herr Doctor," which seemed to please Mr. Puckler very much.

He looked older than he was, for his beard was rather long and ragged, his hair was grizzled and thin, and he wore horn-rimmed spectacles. As for Else, she was a thin, pale child, very quiet and neat, with dark eyes and brown hair that was plaited down her back and tied with a bit of black ribbon. She mended the dolls' clothes and took the dolls back to their homes when they were quite strong again.

The house was a little one, but too big for the two people who lived in it. There was a small sitting-room facing the street, and the workshop was at the back, and there were three rooms upstairs. But the father and daughter lived most of their time in the workshop, because they were generally at work, even in the evenings.

Mr. Puckler laid Nina on the table and looked at her a long time, till the tears began to fill his eyes behind the horn-rimmed spectacles. He was a very susceptible man, and he often fell in love with the dolls he mended, and found it hard to part with them when they had smiled at him for a few days. They were real little people to him, with characters and thoughts and feelings of their own, and he was very tender with them all. But some attracted him especially from the first, and when they were brought to him maimed and injured, their state seemed so pitiful to him that the tears came easily. You must remember that he had lived among dolls during a great part of his life, and understood them.

"How do you know that they feel nothing?" he went on to say to Else. "You must be gentle with them. It costs nothing to be kind to the little beings, and perhaps it makes a difference to them."

And Else understood him, because she was a child, and she knew that she was more to him than all the dolls.

He fell in love with Nina at first sight, perhaps because her beautiful brown glass eyes were something like Else's, and he loved Else first and best, with all his heart. And, besides, it was a very sorrowful case. Nina had evidently not been long in the world, for her complexion was perfect, her hair was smooth where it should be smooth, and curly where it should be curly, and her silk clothes were perfectly new. But across her face was that frightful gash, like a sabre-cut, deep and shadowy within, but clean and sharp at the edges. When he tenderly pressed her head to close the gaping wound, the edges made a fine grating sound that was painful to hear, and the lids of the dark eyes quivered and trembled as though Nina were suffering dreadfully.

"Poor Nina!" he exclaimed sorrowfully. "But I shall not hurt you much, though you will take a long time to get strong."

He always asked the names of the broken dolls when they were brought to him, and sometimes the people knew what the children called them, and told him. He liked "Nina" for a name. Altogether and in every way she pleased him more than any doll he had seen for many years, and he felt drawn to her, and made up his mind to make her perfectly strong and sound, no matter how much labor it might cost him.

Mr. Puckler worked patiently a little at a time, and Else watched him. She could do nothing for poor Nina, whose clothes needed no mending. The longer the doll doctor worked, the more fond he became of the yellow hair and the beautiful brown glass eyes. He sometimes forgot all the other dolls that were waiting to be mended, lying side by side on a shelf, and sat for an hour gazing at Nina's face while he racked his ingenuity for some new invention by which to hide even the smallest trace of the terrible accident.

She was wonderfully mended. Even he was obliged to admit that; but the scar was still visible to his keen eyes, a very fine line right across the face, downwards from right to left. Yet all the conditions had been most favorable for a cure, since the cement had set quite hard at the first attempt and the weather had been fine and dry, which makes a great difference in a dolls' hospital.

At last he knew that he could do no more, and the under nurse had already come twice to see whether the job was finished, as she coarsely expressed it.

"Nina is not quite strong yet," Mr. Puckler had answered each time, for he could not make up his mind to face the parting.

And now he sat before the square table at which he worked, and Nina lay before him for the last time with a big brown paper box beside her. It stood there like her coffin, waiting for her, he thought. He must put her into it, and lay tissue paper over her dear face, and then put on the lid, and at the though of tying the string his sight was dim with tears again. He was never to look into the glassy depths of the beautiful brown eyes any more, nor to hear the little wooden voice say "Pa-pa" and "Ma-ma." It was a very painful moment.

In the vain hope of gaining time before the separation, he took up the little sticky bottles of cement and glue and gum and colour, looking at each one in turn, and then at Nina's face. And all his small tools lay there, neatly arranged in a row, but he knew that he could not use them again for Nina. She was quite strong at last, and in a country where there should be no cruel children to hurt her she might live a hundred years, with only that almost imperceptible line across her face to tell of the fearful thing that had befallen her on the marble steps of Cranston House.

Suddenly Mr. Puckler's heart was quite full, and he rose abruptly from his seat and turned away.

"Else," he said unsteadily, "you must do it for me. I cannot bear to see her go into the box."

So he went and stood at the window with his back turned, while Else did what he had not the heart to do.

"Is it done?" he asked, not turning round. "Then take her away, my dear. Put on your hat, and take her to Cranston House quickly. When you are gone I will turn round."

Else was used to her father's queer ways with the dolls, and though she had never seen him so much moved by a parting, she was not much surprised.

"Come back quickly," he said, when he heard her hand on the latch. "It is growing late. I should not send you at this hour. But I cannot bear to look forward to it any more."

When Else was gone, he left the window and sat down in his place before the table again, to wait for the child to come back. He touched the place where Nina had lain, very gently, and he recalled the softly tinted pink face, the glass eyes, and the ringlets of yellow hair, till he could almost see them.

The evenings were long, for it was late in the spring, but it began to grow dark soon and Else had not come back. She had been gone an hour and a half, and that was much longer than he had expected, for it was barely half a mile from Belgrave Square to

Cranston House. He reflected that the child might have been kept waiting, but as the twilight deepened he grew anxious and walked up and down in the dim workshop, no longer thinking of Nina, but of Else, his own living child, whom he loved.

An undefinable, disquieting sensation came upon him by fine degrees, a chilliness and a faint stirring of his thin hair, joined with a wish to be in any company rather than to be alone much longer. It was the beginning of fear.

He told himself in strong German-English that he was a foolish old man, and he began to feel about for the matches in the dusk. He knew just where they should be, for he always kept them in the same place, close to the little tin box that held bits of sealing-wax of various colours for some kinds of mending. But somehow he could not find the matches in the gloom.

Something had happened to Else, he was sure, and as his fear increased, he felt as though it might be allayed if he could get a light and see what time it was. Then he called himself a foolish old man again, and the sound of his own voice startled him in the dark. He could not find the matches.

The window was grey still; he might see what time it was if he went close to it, and he could go and get matches out of the cupboard afterwards. He stood back from the table, to get out of the way of the chair, and began to cross the board floor.

He stopped. Something was following him in the dark. There was a small pattering, as of tiny feet, upon the boards. He stopped and listened, and the roots of his hair tingled. It was nothing, and he was a foolish old man. He made two steps more, and he was sure that he heard the little pattering again. He turned his back to the window, leaning against the sash so that the panes began to crack, and he faced the dark. Everything was quite still, and it smelt of paste and cement and wood-filings as usual.

"Is that you, Else?" he asked, and he was surprised by the fear in his voice.

There was no answer in the room, and he held up his watch and tried to make out what time it was by the grey dusk that was just not quite darkness. So far as he could see, it was within two or three minutes of ten o'clock. He had been a long time alone. He was shocked, and frightened for Else, out in London, so late, and he almost ran across the room to the door. As he fumbled for the latch, he distinctly heard the running of the little feet after him.

"Mice!" he exclaimed feebly, just as he got the door open.

He shut it quickly behind him, and felt as though some cold thing had settled on his back and was writhing upon him. The passage was quite dark, but he found his hat and was out in the alley in a moment, breathing more freely, and surprised to find how much light there still was in the open air. He could see the pavement clearly under his feet, and far off in the street to which the alley led he could hear the laughter and calls of children playing some game out of doors. He wondered how he could have been so nervous and for an instant he thought of going back into the house to wait quietly for Else. But instantly he felt that nervous fright of something stealing over him again. In any case it was better to walk up to Cranston House and ask the servants about the child. One of the women had perhaps taken a fancy to her, and was even now giving her tea and cake.

He walked quickly to Belgrave Square, and then up the broad streets, listening as he went, whenever there was no other sound, for the tiny footsteps. But he heard nothing and was laughing at himself when he rang the servants' bell at the big house. Of course, the child must be there.

The person who opened the door was quite an inferior person, for it was a back door, but affected the manners of the front, and stared at Mr. Puckler superciliously under the strong light.

No little girl had been seen, and he knew "nothing about no dolls."

"She is my little girl," said Mr. Puckler tremulously, for all his anxiety was returning tenfold, "and I am afraid something has happened."

The inferior person said rudely that "nothing could have happened to her in that house, because she had not been there, which was a jolly god reason why;" and Mr. Puckler was obliged to admit that the man ought to know, as it was his business to keep the door and let people in. He wished to be allowed to speak to the under nurse who knew him; but the man was ruder than ever, and finally shut the door in his face.

When the doll doctor was alone in the street, he steadied himself by the railing, for he felt as though he were breaking in two, just as some dolls break, in the middle of the backbone.

Presently he knew that he must be doing something to find Else, and that gave him strength. He began to walk as quickly as he could through the streets, following every highway and byway which his little girl might have taken on her errand. He also asked several policemen in vain if they had seen her, and most of them answered him kindly, for they saw that he was a sober man and in his right senses, and some of them had little girls of their own.

It was one o'clock in the morning when he went up to his own door again, worn out and hopeless and broken-hearted. As he turned the key in the lock, his heart stood still, for he knew that he was awake and had not been dreaming, and that he had really heard those tiny footsteps pattering to meet him inside the house along the passage.

But he was too unhappy to be much frightened any more, and his heart was a dull regular pain, that found its way all through him with every pulse. So he went in, and hung up his hat in the dark, and found the matches in the cupboard and the candlestick in its place in the corner.

Mr. Puckler was so overcome and so completely worn out that he sat down in his chair before the work-table and almost fainted, as his face dropped forward upon his folded hands. Beside him the solitary candle burned steadily with a low flame in the still warm air.

"Else! Else!" he moaned against his yellow knuckles. And that was all he could say, and it was no relief to him. On the contrary, the very sound of the name was a new and sharp pain that pierced his ears and his head and his very soul. For every time he repeated her name it meant that little Else was dead, somewhere out in the streets of London in the dark.

He was so terribly hurt that he did not even feel something pulling gently at the skirt of his old coat, so gently that it was like the nibbling of a tiny mouse. He might have thought that it was really a mouse if he had noticed it.

"Else! Else!" he groaned against his hands.

Then a cool breath stirred his thin hair, and the low flame of the one candle dropped down almost to a mere spark, not flickering as though a draught were going to blow it out, but just dropping down as if it were tired out. Mr. Puckler felt his hands stiffening with fright under his face; and there was a faint rustling sound, like some small silk thing blown in a gentle breeze. He sat up straight, stark and scared, as a small wooden voice spoke in the stillness.

"Pa-pa," it said, with a break between the syllables.

Mr. Puckler stood up in a single jump, and his chair fell over backwards with a smashing noise upon the wooden floor. The candle had almost gone out.

It was Nina's doll voice that had spoken, and he should have known it among the voices of a hundred other dolls. And yet there was something more in it, a little human ring, with a pitiful cry and a call for help, and the wail of a hurt child. Mr. Puckler stood up, stark and stiff, and tried to look round, but at first he could not, for he seemed to be frozen from head to foot.

Then he made a great effort, and he raised one hand to each of his temples, and pressed his own head round as he would have turned a doll's. The candle was burning so low that it might as well have been out altogether, for any light it gave, and the room seemed quite dark at first. Then he saw something. He would not have believed that he could be more frightened than he had been just before that. But he was, and his knees shook, for he saw the doll standing in the middle of the floor, shining with a faint and ghostly radiance, her beautiful glassy brown eyes fixed on his. And across her face the very thin line of the break he had mended shone as though it were drawn in light with a fine point of white flame.

Yet there was something more in the eyes, too; there was something human, like Else's own, but as if only the doll saw him through them, and not Else. And there was enough of Else to bring back all his pain and to make him forget his fear.

"Else! my little Else!" he cried aloud.

The small ghost moved, and its doll arm slowly rose and fell with a stiff, mechanical motion. "Pa-pa," it said.

It seemed this time that there was even more of Else's tone echoing somewhere between the wooden notes that reached his ears so distinctly, and yet so far away. Else was calling him, he was sure.

His face was perfectly white in the gloom, but his knees did not shake any more, and he felt that he was less frightened.

"Yes, child! But where? Where?" he asked. "Where are you, Else?"

"Pa-pa!"

The syllables died away in the quiet room. There was a low rustling of silk, the glassy brown eyes turned slowly away, and Mr. Puckler heard the pitter-patter of the small feet in the bronze kid slippers as the figure ran straight to the door. Then the candle burned high again, the room was full of light, and he was alone.

Mr. Puckler passed his hand over his eyes and looked about him. He could see everything quite clearly, and he felt that he must have been dreaming, though he was standing instead of sitting down, as he should have been if he had just woken up. The candle burned brightly now. There were the dolls to be mended, lying in a row with their toes up. The third one had lost her right shoe, and Else had been making one. He knew that, and he certainly was not dreaming now. He had not been dreaming when he had come in from his fruitless search and had heard the doll's footsteps running to the door. He had not fallen asleep in his chair. How could he possibly have fallen asleep when his heart was breaking? He had been awake all the time.

He steadied himself, set the fallen chair upon its legs, and said to himself again very emphatically, that he was a foolish old man. He ought to be out in the streets looking for his child, asking questions, and enquiring at the police stations, where all accidents were reported as soon as they were known, or at the hospitals.

"Pa-pa!"

The longing, wailing, pitiful little wooden cry rang from the passage, outside the door, and Mr. Puckler stood for an instant with his white face, transfixed and rooted to the spot. A moment later his hand was on the latch. Then he was in the passage, with the light streaming from the open door behind him.

Quite at the other end he saw the little phantom shining clearly in the shadow, and the right hand seemed to beckon to him as the arm rose and fell once more. He knew all at once that it had not come to frighten him but to lead him, and when it disappeared, and he walked boldly towards the door, he knew that it was in the street outside, waiting for him. He forgot that he was tired and had eaten no supper, and had walked many miles, for a sudden hope ran through and through him, like a golden stream of life.

And sure enough, at the corner of the alley, at the corner of the street, and out in Belgrave Square, he saw the small ghost flitting before him. Sometimes it was only a shadow, where there was other light, but then the glare of the lamps made a pale green sheen on its little Mother Hubbard frock of silk; and sometimes, where the streets were dark and silent, the whole figure shone out brightly, with its yellow curls and rosy neck. It seemed to trot along like a tiny child, and Mr. Puckler could almost hear the pattering of the bronze kid slippers on the pavement as it ran. But it went so very fast, and he could only just keep up with it, tearing along with his hat on the back of his head and his thin hair blown by the night breeze, and his horn-rimmed spectacles firmly set upon his broad nose.

On and on he went, and he had no idea where he was. He did not even care, for he knew certainly that he was going the right way.

Then at last, in a wide, quiet street, he was standing before a big, sober-looking door that had two lamps on each side of it, and a polished brass bell-handle, which he pulled.

And just inside, when the door was opened, in the bright light, there was a little shadow, and the pale green sheen of the little silk dress, and once more the small cry came to his ears, less pitiful, more longing.

"Pa-pa!"

The shadow turned suddenly bright, and out of the brightness the beautiful brown glass eyes were turned up happily to his, while the rosy mouth smiled so divinely that the phantom doll looked almost like a little angel just then.

"A little girl was brought in soon after ten o'clock," said the quiet voice of the hospital doorkeeper. "I think they thought she was only stunned. She was holding a big brown-paper box against her, and they could not get it out of her arms. She had a long plait of brown hair that hung down as they carried her."

"She is my little girl," said Mr. Puckler, but he hardly heard his own voice.

He leaned over Else's face in the gentle light of the children's ward, and when he had stood there a minute the beautiful brown eyes opened and looked up to his.

"Pa-pa!" cried Else, softly, "I knew you would come!"

Then Mr. Puckler did not know what he did or said for a moment, and what he felt was worth all the fear and terror and despair that had almost killed him that night. But by and by Else was telling her story, and the nurse let her speak, for there were only two other children in the room, who were getting well and were sound asleep.

"They were big boys with bad faces," said Else, "and they tried to get Nina away from me, but I held on and fought as well as I could till one of them hit me with something, and I don't remember any more, for I tumbled down, and I suppose the boys ran away, and somebody found me there. But I'm afraid Nina is all smashed."

"Here is the box," said the nurse. "We could not take it out of her arms till she came to herself. Would you like to see if the doll is broken?"

And she undid the string cleverly, but Nina was all smashed to pieces. Only the gentle light of the children's ward made a pale green sheen in the folds of her little Mother Hubbard frock.

Stories by
H. B. Marriott Watson

THE THING IN THE COPSE

A melancholy silence held the nether wastes as I came down upon the back of the village. I had no thought of horror or remorse; no revulsion turned me from the sober contemplation of that still, stiff figure in the copse, its eyes open upon the dusk unmeaningly.

It was true the thing bobbed in and out of my mind persistently, as though that fell moment of fury had stamped an indelible picture on my brain; but its motions had come to be well-nigh mechanical, and it was only at intervals I was aware that it was dancing there. Flitting as a speck in the eyesight, it was no distress to me; I had no care lest it should come a permanent visual sensation. Of the dead itself I recked nothing; there was no relic of hatred in me for the strewn and helpless body, nor any fear of its particular vengeance. I had put from her for ever (it seemed to me) the material object of her shame and madness; and though my soul now should keep the earth until the crack of doom, it should have the solace of her desolate company. In vain, after all, had she turned from me; the empty world gaped for her now as it had done for me since that terrible hour two nights gone. The horrid glee of this reflection ran through my veins, but no malignity for the dead or for the living had part in my peculiar joy. Indeed, now he had withdrawn from the possibility of her touch, and there was no longer the mocking picture of her delicate caress, I seemed to myself clean rid of animosity against him; and that last thought of admiration which had flashed so strangely upon me at the supreme moment of his fall recurred to my newly dispassionate mind. I would not deny

191

him a fine courage and a rude air of distinction; he had made no craven struggle in his end, but dropped softly in the long ferns without a word, gone to his shameful account unwincingly.

The steep thin track, banked and overarched with the gloom of deep thickets, widened upon a sudden in a place of heaving yews. The winds brushing round a corner in the downs swept past me upon the deep valley, raising a dismal singing in the pines. Against the low lights of heaven the still, black body with its open eyes tossed and swayed, and low noises were growing in the long corn, when from the darkness of the lower reaches she fluttered into my sight. She came as a white shadow of skirts out of the heart of the rustling thicket, but I knew her on the instant in that blackness, as I have ever known her by her mere proximity. I was acquainted with her errand, too; for he had thrust a gibe at my frenzy; and where he had waited for the tryst, there had he perished. Standing in the centre of the way, I watched her draw near; she came with a start and a slight cry; shrank into the shadows; moved as to pass me swiftly; then, pausing, she raised one arm across her face and bowed her head upon her moving bosom. I could not discern her features; but the lithe grace of her familiar body leapt into possession of my soul. The black Thing dangled in my eyes upon the trees—I took a step to her and saw her face, the face that had touched mine so often, aghast with fear and shame. Could sorrow turn that laughing face to this pallid spectre of loveliness? I had not seen her since that hour when I had all but thrown her from the Hall into the howling night.

"You!" said I tensely. "You!"

She put out her hands, as it were in a gesture of despair, still bowed and mute. I looked upon her in the falling dusk as mute as she, and the memory of her invisible beauty made a chasm in my thoughts.

"It is no use to speak of pardon," she whispered at last, the dear, tremulous whisper that had been wont to murmur at my ears; "I have come too low for pardon. It is only pity that I ask."

"Pity!" I echoed, blinking at the black Thing that tossed about her head.

"There were some excuses for me had I the shamelessness to name them. I was mistaken in myself. My mother—I had seen little of you, save that you were great and noble. A girl's fancy—a girl's blunder—and my mother—"

"Twelve months married," I murmured; "but twelve months."

"I fought for you against myself and him," she said. "God knows I fought—but in a little—"

"Twelve months," I murmured; "but twelve months."

"I was too weak for my own passions. God knows, who made us, why such passions are poured into weak vessels."

"Some for dishonour," I said: "some for dishonour."

"You were too high for me. I never knew you. You had stern moods. I could not reach them. Love turned to fear of you. I was afraid, and betrayed you in my fear. Yours was not the heart of a lover."

"Your breath was the spirit of my body," I murmured. "Your trembling heart was my life. Fire ran in my veins at the touch of your soft fingers. Your eyes mirrored my heaven. Soul and body, body and soul, you stood between me and the night." My voice sank smothered between my lips, and I knew I muttered to myself. It seemed as if I watched her pale, pitiful face and slight body from a great distance. Her soft tones ran murmurously on; but now the trees buzzed in my ears, and the air, thick with flitting Things, shut out the sight of her. The narrow way fled reeling from my vision into the deep valley below.

"I ask no pardon," I heard her cry, "but one thing only."

She lifted her head, and her white face fronted mine with a wild entreaty.

"I have dishonoured you and yours," she said. "I have no hope or future in this world. There is one thing only left me. Give me that," she said, raising her clasped hands to me. "Give me that, you who are so strong and merciful."

"Is it pity?" I asked, staring at her beseeching eyes.

"Yes, pity," she implored. "Give me pity and all that flows from pity. Stand to me now in the place of God, who has forsaken me, and give me this one thing. They said you were taken with the fury

of devils; they said you were relentless, mad with hate and the desire of vengeance. But you are not. They have spoken false of you,"
she cried. "You are calm and still. You look down upon this thing
and despise it—you are so far above it—but you have no grudge
against it. You will deal nobly by it. There are no petty passions in
your nature. They told me you were sworn to withhold from me
freedom, to keep me in the dust. But you will not refuse this thing.
I have put away from life all that is best and wisest, all that is most
gracious and worthiest; I have thrown immortality to the winds. I
am shipwrecked of all save this one thing—the piteous pleasure of
a wretched crawling worm. Give me this out of your nobility. I pray
to you as to God, come not between us: give me my freedom, and
let me take up my miserable life with *him*."

"You put me in God's place," I said.

"Yes, yes," she said eagerly, "in God's place. You shall dispense
mercy. You shall pity. I want no pardon. I am in the mire before
you; let me live my lowly life. I have but one passion, but one
thought, but one desire, but one hope, and that is in him. Do not
keep me in chains. Set me free that I may go to my bonds with him
and keep my paltry happiness secure. See, I tell you this, because
you are my God. You are not upon my world; you breathe a loftier
air. You have never loved me, a creature of such vain clay. Nothing
could re-unite us two; you have no need of a dog at your heels to
kick. Let me go out of your life. You have no need of me. Even had
you loved me, you would not, you dare not, have me back."

She gasped her wild sentences in my ears, a figure of forlorn
entreaty; and her face of beauty, shining into mine, drove the black
flecks from my sight, so that I beheld her suddenly the one being
my of constant thoughts and prayers this twelvemonth.

"As God is my witness," I cried to Heaven, "I would take you
out of Hell, though your soul were in black ashes."

Her outstretched hands dropped a little; her wide eyes lowered;
and she shrank and shuddered from me in her fear. And by her
drifted that Thing in the waving ferns. She fell upon her knees in
the rough pathway and clasped my hand.

"You are my God," she whispered. "Give me this man."

I shook her from me, and turned down the slope toward the black thicket.

"Vengeance," said I, "belongeth unto God." I laughed. "Go," said I, "I will give you this man."

I could see her eyes gleam for a moment, as with a vivid joy; she made as though to follow me, but I moved to the very portals of the dark yews, and in a little she turned and went up the track. Pausing on the threshold of my downward way, I watched her white skirts creeping into the gloom; and then I too turned and climbed down upon the village, leaving her to mount upwards to the downs, where lay that dread Thing waiting for her in the copse.

THE BRAZEN CROSS

I laughed at her vivacious display of fear, and went a space further into the wood. I called to her, but she stood irresponsive on the white road. I retraced my way to the verge of the open, and took hold of her hand.

"Come," I said, "this superstition is ridiculous. You have gone this path many a time; it is the shortest track to the village."

"It is Christmas Eve," she returned with a nervous shiver.

"What of that?" I answered lightly. "A wood is all one at Christmas or midsummer."

She shook her head, but I could see she was plainly yielding to my persuasion.

"It was an ancient place of burial," she said, "where are still the disfigured bones of those that lived before Christ."

"Every foot of green earth covers some decay," I said. "Come; the white road takes a tedious circuit into the valley."

"They say," she went on, and a thin tremble ran in her voice—"they say that evil spirits take possession of this place on this night. They must vanish with the midnight bells for a twelvemonth; on Christmas Eve alone are they abroad."

"I see," I answered, laughing; "it is their protest against a Saviour. But come; for the wind is rising, and a gale is growing on the moor."

Her eyes shifted fearfully as she regarded me, and her skirts were fluttering in the fern. As she stood thus silent, there entered into my heart that fierce desire of her which had so long been beating about my soul. I snatched her hand, and, bending to her, held that wondering gaze with mine. A still peace stole into her face; the warm blood trembled in her fingers; I knew her for my captive, as she knew me for hers. We were thus for some short seconds, and then a sigh, as it were the distant voice of some encaged spirit, escaped her lips; and my own mind followed the course of her thoughts. I loosened my grasp of her hand, but ere it fell from me a thrill started through her body, and the fingers closed upon mine with a little convulsive catch. In an instant an ecstasy had taken me, and she was swaying in my arms, passive and unafraid. The supreme delight of that moment touches me even now to the very quick of my being. I strained her to me, my voice murmuring words of endearment. She withdrew herself from me, watching my eyes with a troubled gaze.

"You will marry in this New Year," she said earnestly. "It is laid upon you. What would she think? You have your honour. You have been mad, and you have infected me with madness. It is the evil spirits of this field;" and she shuddered.

"I will be no slave to a preposterous notion of honour," I cried. "Is a man bound from his childhood? What our fathers have declared to us—shall we take that upon the mere statement? I have lived as a fool—"

"But you shall die as a man of honour," she broke in upon my fervour.

"Rather," said I, "as a man of taste." I took her into my arms again, and her reluctant body yielded to my strenuous passion.

"Remember," she murmured. "Ah, remember."

"There is nothing irreparable," I answered. "All will wear a gay face in a week. She cares nothing for me; and I, even at this hour, have seen the folly of obedience. Your love has turned the stream of my life from a smooth and narrow channel. That is all. Better the contentment of two hearts than of a very giddy vanity."

She made no sign, but it seemed to me that she surrendered herself to my pleading.

"We will take the track through the wood?" I said, caressing her.

"Yes," she whispered faintly.

The grey clouds were flying in troops over the moon, and the wind clapped boisterously about our ears as we passed into the shelter of the pines. Over the moor, which stretched solitary to the black hills, it scudded and romped towards the back parts of the valley; and as I turned upon the very threshold of the wood it seemed as though the plain was in the possession of many roystering tenants—so much of stir and motion was visible among the bracken and the gorse. On the outset of the forest the straight columns of the firs were creaking, but the inner recesses lay hushed and dark, secluded in a shelving bottom. I think that the noises of the fierce wind, which blew with an icy breath, had restored to her a sense of security; for though we might not now be heard without shouting, she clung restfully to my arm, and the short snatches of light that blinked through the flying clouds revealed a soft and happy smile moving on her face. As for myself, I had now my world, and was become its veritable captain. The wood roared in our ears; we slipped from the embrace of the gale, and dropped down into the silent close which had been the ancient sepulchre of ancient peoples. And here a great change befell. In the quiet of that place I could hear the wind howling on the moor, and the sound of our footsteps struck harshly on the stillness. I had scant room but for the one burning thought; yet for a moment the strangeness of this unspeakable stillness flashed through my mind, and I perceived with an ignoble joy that her old fears were recurring to her. She will press closer to me, I thought; and was filled with an extravagant delight of her touch. Suddenly, and when we were about the heart of the thicket, little noises got up among the dead leaves, and a thin whistling in the skeleton branches. She clutched me in a quick terror, and I soothed her gently.

"It is nothing, my love," I said; "the wind has broken into the valley."

"It is the graves," she gasped. "The spirits are come out."

She turned her face aslant towards the growing noises, which appeared to creep along the ground; the dead leaves hissed and slithered. Her body bent across me, and her arms went round my neck; but she held her eyes towards that crawling noise.

"Sweetheart," I said, "be brave."

But on that instant a rushing fury filled the air, and a great wind tore through the trees; vacancy shrieked and moaned at us; and the gabble of a thousand voices mocked us in the branches. In my sight was nothing save the stirless wood and the empty sky; in my ears were outrageous sounds innumerable. At the first outset of these strange presences she gave a low cry and tightened upon me; and then a flash swept over my eyes, and in that second her arms were ript from my neck, and with a long wail of fear she fled down the deep paths and vanished with the noises into the wood.

When I returned to the full possession of my wits I drew myself together and sped after her. The way she had taken led over a heavy slope, down which I was plunged into an infernal blackness where the underwood rose thick and sheer upon all sides. Informed with a pricking dread I called to her at the top of my voice, and clamours awoke in the gully; but I could see no sign of her, and the copse was now as empty and as silent as a churchyard under the moon. In this desperate mood I ran along the track, crying to the night without response, and presently burst out upon the meadows that lay at the back of the village. Here, too, all was silent, though the wrack was racing in the sky, and the frosty lights twinkled in the distant cottages. I had stood irresolute and fearful for some minutes, the subject of a rising horror, when there was a sudden crackle of branches, and I saw her fleeting upon me out of the dense brushwood. The apparition was so abrupt that I momentarily started aback, but, as quickly recovering, rushed to meet her with a thrill of gladness. She made a weird figure in her flight; her hair streaming at her back, her dress disordered on her bosom, her hands clenching in the air. She would have swung by me in her panic, had I not arrested her with my arm. She stayed, panting and wide-orbed, gazing at me with a distraught look, as it were of exultation.

"Sweetheart," I said, "you have been very foolish to allow this terror," and made to take her in my arms.

She broke into laughter, murmurous and sweet, staring at me still from between her unblinking lids. The thought that came to me then was fraught with unspeakable horror, and I watched her in awe. The eyes shone spectrally on mine; the lips parted, as it seemed, in a mocking smile; and the dishevelled hair was curving and heaving in ragged waves on her head. Her face was the face of a maenad aflame. "My heart," I said, all agitation, "be mine, be mine again. In the name of God," I cried, "close those eyes and come to me! Remember, we have been in love's land this night."

"I remember," she answered, and her voice rang shrilly in the air, "that this night we have been with the dead."

She threw herself back, and laughed, and I saw the tresses jigging on her head, screwing and whirling like the snakes in the head of a Medusa. Her laughter shook her, and, breaking from me she danced over the meadows into the night. And then I knew that the vulgar superstition of this place was true, and that the devils of the immemorial graveyard had crept into her hair and were gnawing at her brain.

That Christmas Day was a time of doubt and agony to me. I had no word of her whom I loved, and from her who was to be my wife came many weary messages. Impatiently between the thought of both I stood in the balance, unable to resolve my mind. My course had seemed plain before—plain and troublesome; to disengage myself from an arduous contract was clearer wisdom than to go shuffling through an unlovely marriage.

But now I could be sure of nothing, for she that had divorced me from my duty was in the possession of an Evil so gross as to withhold her humanity from her. And as the week wore on towards the New Year I was in no better case. Everywhere I heard of the visitation that had fallen upon her family, and all the countryside had pity on her. All day, I heard, she would keep the house, singing (they whispered) profane and hideous catches, the anxious care of her parents; but at nights, when the stars were full, she was abroad, riotous and mad, in the copses. The thought was too grievous for me, and I haunted the park at moonrise to get some more certain knowledge of her. On these excursions I saw her once, and the sight was pitiful and abhorrent. It was not that her awful tenants had robbed her of her beauty; that was unchanged—nay, rather raised to an unnatural glory by her madness. But to see her flying wildly through the trees, her large and mocking eyes sparkling under the stars, and the devils jigging in her hair, took me with such a sense of horror that I fled, ashamed and sick. She dangled an arm to me as she flashed past, tossing up her face and screaming at the sky. Thereafter I had no hope of her, but, schooling myself to the straight lines of duty, began with a poor heart to prepare against my wedding.

It was on the first day of the New Year that I was finally to resign from my dearest hope and open a fresh and uninspiring life with my cold bride. The thing had got thus far, and must reach the end. It was a bright, white morning (for the snow had fallen betimes) when I entered the little church, dumb to the fate arranged for me. As the service proceeded, the pitiable pretence, both of her and of myself, grew well-nigh intolerable, and I think never marriage has been imposed upon such indifferent auditors. But within a little of the end, and while we were yet upon the precincts of the altar, there came a sharp sound from the lower part of the church, and turning swiftly I perceived *her* coming up the aisle. She moved slowly, as though each step were made against an invisible resistance; her hair was twisting and coiling on her bare head; her wintry eyes were fastened upon me. I gave a short cry, but she took no notice, merely gazing from her wild and struggling eyes as she dragged herself towards the chancel. The church rose in a mutter of fear. I made a step to her. But at the chancel rails, and where the great Brazen Cross uplifts itself below the oriel windows, she fell suddenly to her knees. I watched her face. The devils jigged in her hair; it stirred gently, and then flowed soft and rich about her neck; a shudder rushed through her; she hid her face in her hands. And when she raised it again, and her eyes sought mine, they were filled with a quiet smile of love, dewy with tears, and desolate with a sad and hopeless pain.

The Devil of the Marsh

It was nigh upon dusk when I drew close to the Great Marsh, and already the white vapours were about, riding across the sunken levels like ghosts in a churchyard. Though I had set forth in a mood of wild delight, I had sobered in the lonely ride across the moor and was now uneasily alert. As my horse jerked down the grassy slopes that fell away to the jaws of the swamp I could see thin streams of mist rise slowly, hover like wraiths above the long rushes, and then, turning gradually more material, go blowing heavily away across the flat. The appearance of the place at this desolate hour, so remote from human society and so darkly significant of evil presences, struck me with a certain wonder that she should have chosen this spot for our meeting. She was a familiar of the moors, where I had invariably encountered her; but it was like her arrogant caprice to test my devotion by some such dreary assignation. The wide and horrid prospect depressed me beyond reason, but the fact of her neighbourhood drew me on, and my spirits mounted at the thought that at last she was to put me in possession of herself. Tethering my horse upon the verge of the swamp, I soon discovered the path that crossed it, and entering struck out boldly for the heart. The track could have been little used, for the reeds, which stood high above the level of my eyes upon either side, straggled everywhere across in low arches, through which I dodged, and broke my way with some inconvenience and much impatience. A full half hour I was solitary in that wilderness, and when at last a sound other than my own footsteps broke the silence the dusk had fallen.

I was moving very slowly at the time, with a mind half disposed to turn from the melancholy expedition, which it seemed to me now must surely be a cruel jest she had played upon me. While some such reluctance held me, I was suddenly arrested by a hoarse croaking which broke out upon my left, sounding somewhere from the reeds in the black mire. A little further it came again from close at hand, and when I had passed on a few more steps in wonder and perplexity, I heard it for the third time. I stopped and listened, but the marsh was as a grave, and so taking the noise for the signal of some raucous frog, I resumed my way. But in a little the croaking was repeated, and coming quickly to a stand I pushed the reeds aside and peered into the darkness. I could see nothing, but at the immediate moment of my pause I thought I detected the sound of some body trailing through the rushes. My distaste for the adventure grew with this suspicion, and had it not been for my delirious infatuation I had assuredly turned back and ridden home. The ghastly sound pursued me at intervals along the track, until at last, irritated beyond endurance by the sense of this persistent and invisible company, I broke into a sort of run. This, it seemed, the creature (whatever it was) could not achieve, for I heard no more of it, and continued my way in peace. My path at length ran out from among the reeds upon the smooth flat of which she had spoken, and here my heart quickened, and the gloom of the dreadful place lifted. The flat lay in the very centre of the marsh, and here and there in it a gaunt bush or withered tree rose like a spectre against the white mists. At the further end I fancied some kind of building loomed up; but the fog which had been gathering ever since my entrance upon the passage sailed down upon me at that moment and the prospect went out with suddenness. As I stood waiting for the clouds to pass, a voice cried to me out of its centre, and I saw her next second with bands of mist swirling about her body, come rushing to me from the darkness. She put her long arms about me, and, drawing her close, I looked into her deep eyes. Far down in them, it seemed to me, I could discern a mystic laughter dancing in the wells of light, and I had that ecstatic sense of nearness to some spirit of fire which was wont to possess me at her contact.

"At last," she said, "at last, my beloved!" I caressed her.

"Why," said I, tingling at the nerves, "why have you put this dolorous journey between us? And what mad freak is your presence in this swamp?" She uttered her silver laugh, and nestled to me again.

"I am the creature of this place," she answered. "This is my home. I have sworn you should behold me in my native sin ere you ravished me away."

"Come, then," said I; "I have seen; let there be an end of this. I know you, what you are. This marsh chokes up my heart. God forbid you should spend more of your days here. Come."

"You are in haste," she cried. "There is yet much to learn. Look, my friend," she said, "you who know me, what I am. This is my prison, and I have inherited its properties. Have you no fear?"

For answer I pulled her to me, and her warm lips drove out the horrid humours of the night; but the swift passage of a flickering mockery over her eyes struck me as a flash of lightning, and I grew chill again.

"I have the marsh in my blood," she whispered: "the marsh and the fog of it. Think ere you vow to me, for I am the cloud in a starry night."

A lithe and lovely creature, palpable of warm flesh, she lifted her magic face to mine and besought me plaintively with these words. The dews of the nightfall hung on her lashes, and seemed to plead with me for her forlorn and solitary plight.

"Behold!" I cried, "witch or devil of the marsh, you shall come with me! I have known you on the moors, a roving apparition of beauty; nothing more I know, nothing more I ask. I care not what this dismal haunt means; not what these strange and mystic eyes. You have powers and senses above me; your sphere and habits are as mysterious and incomprehensible as your beauty. But that," I said, "is mine, and the world that is mine shall be yours also."

She moved her head nearer to me with an antic gesture, and her gleaming eyes glanced up at me with a sudden flash, the similitude (great heavens!) of a hooded snake. Starting, I fell away, but at that moment she turned her face and set it fast towards the fog that came rolling in thick volumes over the flat. Noiselessly the great cloud crept down upon us, and all dazed and troubled I watched her watching it in silence. It was as if she awaited some omen of horror, and I too trembled in the fear of its coming.

Then suddenly out of the night issued the hoarse and hideous croaking I had heard upon my passage. I reached out my arm to take her hand, but in an instant the mists broke over us, and I was groping in the vacancy. Something like panic took hold of me, and, beating through the blind obscurity, I rushed over the flat, calling upon her. In a little the swirl went by, and I perceived her upon the margin of the swamp, her arm raised as in imperious command. I ran to her, but stopped, amazed and shaken by a fearful sight. Low by the dripping reeds crouched a small squat thing, in the likeness of a monstrous frog, coughing and choking in its throat. As I stared, the creature rose upon its legs and disclosed a horrid human resemblance. Its face was white and thin, with long black hair; its body gnarled and twisted as with the ague of a thousand years. Shaking, it whined in a breathless voice, pointing a skeleton finger at the woman by my side.

"Your eyes were my guide," it quavered. "Do you think that after all these years I have no knowledge of your eyes? Lo, is there aught of evil in you I am not instructed in? This is the Hell you designed for me, and now you would leave me to a greater."

The wretch paused, and panting leaned upon a bush, while she stood silent, mocking him with her eyes, and soothing my terror with her soft touch.

"Hear!" he cried, turning to me, "hear the tale of this woman that you may know her as she is. She is the Presence of the marshes. Woman or Devil I know not, but only that the accursed marsh has crept into her soul and she herself is become its Evil Spirit; she herself, that lives and grows young and beautiful by it, has its full power to blight and chill and slay. I, who was once as you are, have this knowledge. What bones lie deep in this black swamp who can say but she? She has drained of health, she has drained of mind and of soul; what is between her and her desire that she should not drain also of life? She has made me a devil in her Hell, and now she would leave me to my solitary pain, and go search for another victim. But she shall not!" he screamed through his chattering teeth; "she shall not! My Hell is also hers! She shall not!"

Her smiling untroubled eyes left his face and turned to me: she put out her arms, swaying towards me, and so fervid and so great a light glowed in her face that, as one distraught of superhuman means, I took her into my embrace. And then the madness seized me.

"Woman or devil," I said, "I will go with you! Of what account this pitiful past? Blight me even as that wretch, so be only you are with me."

She laughed, and, disengaging herself, leaned, half-clinging to me, towards the coughing creature by the mire.

"Come," I cried, catching her by the waist. "Come!" She laughed again a silver-ringing laugh. She moved with me slowly across the flat to where the track started for the portals of the marsh. She laughed and clung to me.

But at the edge of the track I was startled by a shrill, hoarse screaming; and behold, from my very feet, that loathsome creature rose up and wound his long black arms about her shrieking and crying in his pain. Stooping I pushed him from her skirts, and with one sweep of my arm drew her across the pathway; as her face passed mine her eyes were wide and smiling. Then of a sudden the still mist enveloped us once more; but ere it descended I had a glimpse of that contorted figure trembling on the margin, the white face drawn and full of desolate pain. At the sight an icy shiver ran through me. And then through the yellow gloom the shadow of her darted past me to the further side. I heard the hoarse cough, the dim noise of a struggle, a swishing sound, a thin cry, and then the sucking of the slime over something in the rushes. I leapt forward: and once again the fog thinned, and I beheld her, woman or devil, standing upon the verge, and peering with smiling eyes into the foul and sickly bog. With a sharp cry wrung from my nerveless soul, I turned and fled down the narrow way from that accursed spot; and as I ran the thickening fog closed round me, and I heard far off and lessening still the silver sound of her mocking laughter.

THE STONE CHAMBER

It was not until early summer that Warrington took possession of Marvyn Abbey. He had bought the property in the preceding autumn, but the place had so fallen into decay through the disorders of time that more than six months elapsed ere it was inhabitable. The delay, however, fell out conveniently for Warrington; for the Bosanquets spent the winter abroad, and nothing must suit but he must spend it with them. There was never a man who pursued his passion with such ardour. He was ever at Miss Bosanquet's skirts, and bade fair to make her as steadfast a husband as he was attached a lover. Thus it was not until after his return from that prolonged exile that he had the opportunity of inspecting the repairs discharged by his architect. He was nothing out of the common in character, but was full of kindly impulses and a fellow of impetuous blood. When he called upon me in my chambers he spoke with some excitement of his Abbey, as also of his approaching marriage; and finally, breaking into an exhibition of genuine affection, declared that we had been so long and so continuously intimate that I, and none other, must help him warm his house and marry his bride. It had indeed been always understood between us that I should serve him at the ceremony, but now it appeared that I must start my duties even earlier. The prospect of a summer holiday in Utterbourne pleased me. It was a charming village, set upon the slope of a wooded hill and within call of the sea. I had a slight knowledge of the district from a riding excursion taken

through that part of Devonshire; and years before, and ere
Warrington had come into his money, had viewed the Abbey ruins
from a distance with the polite curiosity of a passing tourist.

I examined them now with new eyes as we drove up the avenue. The face which the ancient building presented to the valley
was of magnificent design, but now much worn and battered.

Part of it, the right wing, I judged to be long past the uses of a
dwelling, for the walls had crumbled away, huge gaps opened in
the foundations, and the roof was quite dismantled.

Warrington had very wisely left this portion to its own sinister
decay; it was the left wing which had been restored, and which we
were to inhabit. The entrance, I will confess, was a little mean, for
the large doorway had been bricked up and an ordinary modern
door gave upon the spacious terrace and the winding gardens. But
apart from this, the work of restoration had been undertaken with
skill and piety, and the interior had retained its native dignity,
while resuming an air of proper comfort. The old oak had been
repaired congruous with the original designs, and the great rooms
had been as little altered as was requisite to adapt them for daily use.

Warrington passed quickly from chamber to chamber in evident delight, directing my attention upon this and upon that, and
eagerly requiring my congratulations and approval. My comments
must have satisfied him, for the place attracted me vastly. The only
criticism I ventured was to remark upon the size of the rooms and
to question if they might dwarf the insignificant human figures they
were to entertain.

He laughed. "Not a bit," said he. "Roaring fires in winter in
those fine old fireplaces; and as for summer, the more space the
better. We shall be jolly."

I followed him along the noble hall, and we stopped before a
small door of very black oak.

"The bedrooms," he explained, as he turned the key, "are all
upstairs, but mine is not ready yet.

"And besides, I am reserving it; I won't sleep in it till—you understand," he concluded, with a smiling suggestion of embarrassment.

I understood very well. He threw the door open.

"I am going to use this in the meantime," he continued. "Queer little room, isn't it? It used to be a sort of library. How do you think it looks?"

We had entered as he spoke, and stood, distributing our glances in that vague and general way in which a room is surveyed. It was a chamber of much smaller proportions than the rest, and was dimly lighted by two long narrow windows sunk in the great walls. The bed and the modern fittings looked strangely out of keeping with its ancient privacy. The walls were rudely distempered with barbaric frescos, dating, I conjectured, from the fourteenth century; and the floor was of stone, worn into grooves and hollows with the feet of many generations. As I was taking in these facts, there came over me a sudden curiosity as to those dead Marvyns who had held the Abbey for so long. This silent chamber seemed to suggest questions of their history; it spoke eloquently of past ages and past deeds, fallen now into oblivion. Here, within these thick walls, no echo from the outer world might carry, no sound would ring within its solitary seclusion. Even the silence seemed to confer with one upon the ancient transactions of that extinct House.

Warrington stirred, and turned suddenly to me. "I hope it's not damp," said he, with a slight shiver. "It looks rather solemn. I thought furniture would brighten it up."

"I should think it would be very comfortable," said I. "You will never be disturbed by any sounds at any rate."

"No," he answered, hesitatingly; and then, quickly, on one of his impulses: "Hang it, Heywood, there's too much silence here for me." Then he laughed. "Oh, I shall do very well for a month or two." And with that appeared to return to his former placid cheerfulness.

The train of thought started in that sombre chamber served to entertain me several times that day. I questioned Warrington at dinner, which we took in one of the smaller rooms, commanding a lovely prospect of dale and sea. He shook his head. Archæological lore, as indeed anything else out of the borders of actual life, held very little interest for him.

"The Marvyns died out in 1714, I believe," he said, indifferently; "someone told me that—the man I bought it from, I think. They might just as well have kept the place up since; but I think it has been only occupied twice between then and now, and the last time was forty years ago. It would have rotted to pieces if I hadn't taken it. Perhaps Mrs. Batty could tell you. She's lived in these parts almost all her life."

To humour me, and affected, I doubt not, by a certain pride in his new possession, he put the query to his housekeeper upon her appearance subsequently; but it seemed that her knowledge was little fuller than his own, though she had gathered some vague traditions of the countryside.

The Marvyns had not left a reputable name, if rumour spoke truly; theirs was a family to which black deeds had been credited. They were ill-starred also in their fortunes, and had become extinct suddenly; but for the rest, the events had fallen too many generations ago to be current now between the memories of the village.

Warrington, who was more eager to discuss the future than to recall the past, was vastly excited by his anticipations. St. Pharamond, Sir William Bosanquet's house, lay across the valley, barely five miles away; and as the family had now returned, it was easy to forgive Warrington's elation.

"What do you think?" he said, late that evening; and clapping me upon the shoulder, "You have seen Marion; here is the house. Am I not lucky? Damn it, Heywood, I'm not pious, but I am disposed to thank God! I'm not a bad fellow, but I'm no saint; it's fortunate that it's not only the virtuous that are rewarded. In fact, it's usually contrariwise. I owe this to—Lord, I don't know what I owe it to. Is it my money? Of course, Marion doesn't care a rap for that; but then, you see, I mightn't have known her without it. Of course, there's the house, too. I'm thankful I have money. At any rate, here's my new life. Just look about and take it in, old fellow.

If you knew how a man may be ashamed of himself! But there, I've done. You know I'm decent at heart—you must count my life from today." And with this outbreak he lifted the glass between fingers that trembled with the warmth of his emotions, and tossed off his wine.

He did himself but justice when he claimed to be a good fellow; and, in truth, I was myself somewhat moved by his obvious feeling. I remember that we shook hands very affectionately, and my sympathy was the prelude to a long and confidential talk, which lasted until quite a late hour.

At the foot of the staircase, where we parted, he detained me.

"This is the last of my wayward days," he said, with a smile. "Late hours—liquor—all go. You shall see. Goodnight. You know your room. I shall be up long before you." And with that he vanished briskly into the darkness that hung about the lower parts of the passage.

I watched him go, and it struck me quite vaguely what a slight impression his candle made upon that channel of opaque gloom. It seemed merely as a thread of light that illumined nothing.

Warrington himself was rapt into the prevalent blackness; but long afterwards, and even when his footsteps had died away upon the heavy carpet, the tiny beam was visible, advancing and flickering in the distance.

My window, which was modern, opened upon a little balcony, where, as the night was warm and I was indisposed for sleep, I spent half an hour enjoying the air. I was in a sentimental mood, and my thoughts turned upon the suggestions which Warrington's conversation had induced. It was not until I was in bed, and had blown out the light, that they settled upon the square, dark chamber in which my host was to pass the night. As I have said, I was wakeful, owing, no doubt, to the high pitch of the emotions which we had encouraged; but presently my fancies became inarticulate and incoherent, and then I was overtaken by profound sleep.

Warrington was up before me, as he had predicted, and met me in the breakfast-room.

"What a beggar you are to sleep!" he said, with a smile. "I've hammered at your door for half an hour."

I apologized for myself, alleging the rich country air in my defence, and mentioned that I had had some difficulty in getting to sleep.

"So had I," he remarked, as we sat down to the table. "We got very excited, I suppose. Just see what you have there, Heywood. Eggs? Oh, damn it, one can have too much of eggs!" He frowned, and lifted a third cover. "Why in the name of common sense can't Mrs. Batty give us more variety?" he asked, impatiently.

I deprecated his displeasure, suggesting that we should do very well; indeed, his discontent seemed to me quite unnecessary. But I supposed Warrington had been rather spoiled by many years of club life.

He settled himself without replying, and began to pick over his plate in a gingerly manner.

"There's one thing I will have here, Heywood," he observed. "I will have things well appointed."

"I'm not going to let life in the country mean an uncomfortable life. A man can't change the habits of a lifetime."

In contrast with his exhilarated professions of the previous evening, this struck me with a sense of amusement at the moment; and the incongruity may have occurred to him, for he went on:

"Marion's not over strong, you know, and must have things *comme il faut*. She shan't decline upon a lower level. The worst of these rustics is that they have no imagination." He held up a piece of bacon on his fork, and surveyed it with disgust. "Now, look at that! Why the devil don't they take tips from civilized people like the French?"

It was so unlike him to exhibit this petulance that I put it down to a bad night, and without discovering the connection of my thoughts, asked him how he liked his bedroom.

"Oh, pretty well, pretty well," he said, indifferently. "It's not so cold as I thought. But I slept badly. I always do in a strange bed;" and pushing aside his plate, he lit a cigarette. "When you've finished that garbage, Heywood, we'll have a stroll round the Abbey," he said.

His good temper returned during our walk, and he indicated to me various improvements which he contemplated, with something

of his old ardour. The left wing of the house, as I have said, was
entire, but a little apart were the ruins of a chapel. Surrounded by
a low moss-grown wall, it was full of picturesque charm; the
roofless chancel was spread with ivy, but the aisles were intact.
Grass grew between the stones and the floor, and many creepers
had strayed through chinks in the wall into those sacred precincts.
The solemn quietude of the ruin, maintained under the spell of
death, awed me a little, but upon Warrington apparently it made
no impression. He was only zealous that I should properly appreciate the distinction of such a property. I stooped and drew the
weeds away from one of the slabs in the aisle, and was able to trace
upon it the relics of lettering, well-nigh obliterated under the cor-
rosion of time.

"There are tombs," said I.

"Oh, yes," he answered, with a certain relish. "I understand the
Marvyns used it as a mausoleum. They are all buried here. Some
good brasses, I am told."

The associations of the place engaged me; the aspect of the
Abbey faced the past; it seemed to refuse communion with the
present; and somehow the thought of those two decent humdrum
lives which should be spent within its shelter savoured of the in-
congruous. The white-capped maids and the emblazoned butlers
that should tread these halls offered a ridiculous appearance beside my fancies of the ancient building. For all that, I envied
Warrington his home, and so I told him, with a humorous hint that
I was fitter to appreciate its glories than himself.

He laughed. "Oh, I don't know," said he. "I like the old-world
look as much as you do. I have always had a notion of something
venerable. It seems to serve you for ancestors." And he was undoubtedly delighted with my enthusiasm.

But at lunch again he chopped round to his previous irritation,
only now quite another matter provoked his anger. He had received
a letter by the second post from Miss Bosanquet, which, if I may
judge from his perplexity, must have been unusually confused. He
read and re-read it, his brow lowering.

"What the deuce does she mean?" he asked, testily. "She first makes an arrangement for us to ride over today, and now I can't make out whether we are to go to St. Pharamond, or they are coming to us. Just look at it, will you, Heywood?"

I glanced through the note, but could offer no final solution, whereupon he broke out again:

"That's just like women—they never can say anything straightforwardly. Why, in the name of goodness, couldn't she leave things as they were? You see," he observed, rather in answer, as I fancied, to my silence, "we don't know what to do now; if we stay here they mayn't come, and if we go probably we shall cross them." And he snapped his fingers in annoyance.

I was cheerful enough, perhaps because the responsibility was not mine, and ventured to suggest that we might ride over, and return if we missed them. But he dismissed the subject sharply by saying:

"No, I'll stay. I'm not going on a fool's errand," and drew my attention to some point in the decoration of the room.

The Bosanquets did not arrive during the afternoon, and Warrington's ill-humour increased.

His love-sick state pleaded in excuse of him, but he was certainly not a pleasant companion. He was sour and snappish, and one could introduce no statement to which he would not find a contradiction. So unamiable did he grow that at last I discovered a pretext to leave him, and rambled to the back of the Abbey into the precincts of the old chapel. The day was falling, and the summer sun flared through the western windows upon the bare aisle. The creepers rustled upon the gaping walls, and the tall grasses waved in shadows over the bodies of the forgotten dead. As I stood contemplating the effect, and meditating greatly upon the anterior fortunes of the Abbey, my attention fell upon a huge slab of marble, upon which the yellow light struck sharply. The faded lettering rose into greater definition before my eyes and I read slowly:

"Here lyeth the body of Sir Rupert Marvyn."

Beyond a date, very difficult to decipher, there was nothing more; of eulogy, of style, of record, of pious considerations such as were usual to the period, not a word. I read the numerals variously as 1723 and 1745; but however they ran it was probable that the stone covered the resting-place of the last Marvyn. The history of this futile house interested me not a little, partly for Warrington's sake, and in part from a natural bent towards ancient records; and I made a mental note of the name and date.

When I returned Warrington's surliness had entirely vanished, and had given place to an effusion of boisterous spirits. He apologized jovially for his bad temper.

"It was the disappointment of not seeing Marion," he said. "You will understand that some day, old fellow. But, anyhow, we'll go over tomorrow," and forthwith proceeded to enliven the dinner with an ostentation of good-fellowship I had seldom witnessed in him. I began to suspect that he had heard again from St. Pharamond, though he chose to conceal the fact from me. The wine was admirable; though Warrington himself was no great judge, he had entrusted the selection to a good palate. We had a merry meal, drank a little more than was prudent, and smoked our cigars upon the terrace in the fresh air. Warrington was restless. He pushed his glass from him. "I'll tell you what, old chap," he broke out, "I'll give you a game of billiards. I've got a decent table."

I demurred. The air was too delicious, and I was in no humour for a sharp use of my wits. He laughed, though he seemed rather disappointed.

"It's almost sacrilege to play billiards in an Abbey," I said, whimsically. "What would the ghosts of the old Marvyns think?"

"Oh, hang the Marvyns!" he rejoined, crossly. "You're always talking of them."

He rose and entered the house, returning presently with a flagon of whisky and some glasses.

"Try this," he said. "We've had no liqueurs," and pouring out some spirit he swallowed it raw.

I stared, for Warrington rarely took spirits, being more of a wine drinker; moreover, he must have taken nearly the quarter of a tumbler. But he did not notice my surprise, and, seating himself, lit another cigar.

"I don't mean to have things quiet here," he observed, reflectively. "I don't believe in your stagnant rustic life. What I intend to do is to keep the place warm—plenty of house parties, things going on all the year. I shall expect you down for the shooting, Ned. The coverts promise well this year."

I assented willingly enough, and he rambled on again.

"I don't know that I shall use the Abbey so much. I think I'll live in town a good deal. It's brighter there. I don't know though. I like the place. Hang it, it's a rattling good shop, there's no mistake about it. Look here," he broke off, abruptly, "bring your glass in, and I'll show you something."

I was little inclined to move, but he was so peremptory that I followed him with a sigh. We entered one of the smaller rooms which overlooked the terrace, and had been diverted into a comfortable library. He flung back the windows.

"There's air for you," he cried. "Now, sit down," and walking to a cupboard produced a second flagon of whisky. "Irish!" he ejaculated, clumping it on the table. "Take your choice," and turning again to the cupboard, presently sat down with his hands under the table. "Now, then, Ned," he said, with a short laugh. "Fill up, and we'll have some fun," with which he suddenly threw a pack of cards upon the board.

I opened my eyes, for I do not suppose Warrington had touched cards since his college days; but, interpreting my look in his own way, he cried:

"Oh, I'm not married yet. Warrington's his own man still. Poker? Eh?"

"Anything you like," said I, with resignation.

A peculiar expression of delight gleamed in his eyes, and he shuffled the cards feverishly.

"Cut," said he, and helped himself to more whisky.

It was shameful to be playing there with that beautiful night without, but there seemed no help for it. Warrington had a run of luck, though he played with little skill; and his excitement grew as he won.

"Let us make it ten shillings," he suggested.

I shook my head. "You forget I'm not a millionaire," I replied. "Bah!" he cried. "I like a game worth the victory. Well, fire away." His eyes gloated upon the cards, and he fingered them with unctuous affection. The behaviour of the man amazed me. I began to win.

Warrington's face slowly assumed a dull, lowering expression; he played eagerly, avariciously; he disputed my points, and was querulous.

"Oh, we've had enough!" I cried in distaste.

"By Jove, you don't!" he exclaimed, jumping to his feet. "You're the winner, Heywood, and I'll see you damned before I let you off my revenge!"

The words startled me no less than the fury which rang in his accents. I gazed at him in stupefaction. The whites of his eyes showed wildly, and a sullen, angry look determined his face.

Suddenly I was arrested by the suspicion of something upon his neck.

"What's that?" I asked. "You've cut yourself."

He put his hand to his face. "Nonsense," he replied, in a surly fashion.

I looked closer, and then I saw my mistake. It was a round, faint red mark, the size of a florin, upon the column of his throat, and I set it down to the accidental pressure of some button.

"Come on!" he insisted, impatiently.

"Bah! Warrington," I said, for I imagined that he had been over-excited by the whisky he had taken. "It's only a matter of a few pounds. Why make a fuss? Tomorrow will serve."

After a moment his eyes fell, and he gave an awkward laugh. "Oh, well, that'll do," said he.

"But I got so infernally excited."

"Whisky," said I, sententiously.

He glanced at the bottle. "How many glasses have I had?" and he whistled. "By Jove, Ned, this won't do! I must turn over a new leaf. Come on; let's look at the night."

I was only too glad to get away from the table, and we were soon upon the terrace again.

Warrington was silent, and his gaze went constantly across the valley, where the moon was rising, and in the direction in which, as he had indicated to me, St. Pharamond lay. When he said goodnight he was still pre-occupied.

"I hope you will sleep better," he said.

"And you, too," I added.

He smiled. "I don't suppose I shall wake the whole night through," he said; and then, as I was turning to go, he caught me quickly by the arm.

"Ned," he said, impulsively and very earnestly, "don't let me make a fool of myself again. I know it's the excitement of everything. But I want to be as good as I can for her."

I pressed his hand. "All right, old fellow," I said; and we parted.

I think I have never enjoyed sounder slumber than that night. The first thing I was aware of was the singing of thrushes outside my window. I rose and looked forth, and the sun was hanging high in the eastern sky, the grass and the young green of the trees were shining with dew. With an uncomfortable feeling that I was very late I hastily dressed and went downstairs. Warrington was waiting for me in the breakfast-room, as upon the previous morning, and when he turned from the window at my approach, the sight of his face startled me. It was drawn and haggard, and his eyes were shot with blood; it was a face broken and savage with dissipation. He made no answer to my questioning, but seated himself with a morose air.

"Now you have come," he said, sullenly, "we may as well begin. But it's not my fault if the coffee's cold."

I examined him critically, and passed some comment upon his appearance.

"You don't look up to much," I said. "Another bad night?"

"No; I slept well enough," he responded, ungraciously; and then, after a pause: "I'll tell you what, Heywood. You shall give me my revenge after breakfast."

"Nonsense," I said, after a momentary silence. "You're going over to St. Pharamond."

"Hang it!" was his retort, "one can't be always bothering about women. You seem mightily indisposed to meet me again."

"I certainly won't this morning," I answered, rather sharply, for the man's manner grated upon me. "This evening, if you like; and then the silly business shall end."

He said something in an undertone of grumble, and the rest of the meal passed in silence. But I entertained an uneasy suspicion of him, and after all he was my friend, with whom I was under obligations not to quarrel; and so when we rose, I approached him.

"Look here, Warrington," I said. "What's the matter with you? Have you been drinking?

"Remember what you asked me last night."

"Hold your damned row!" was all the answer he vouchsafed, as he whirled away from me, but with an embarrassed display of shame.

But I was not to be put off in that way, and I spoke somewhat more sharply.

"We're going to have this out, Warrington," I said. "If you are ill, let us understand that; but I'm not going to stay here with you in this cantankerous spirit."

"I'm not ill," he replied testily.

"Look at yourself," I cried, and turned him about to the mirror over the mantelpiece.

He started a little, and a frown of perplexity gathered on his forehead.

"Good Lord! I'm not like that, Ned," he said, in a different voice. "I must have been drunk last night." And with a sort of groan, he directed a piteous look at me.

"Come," I was constrained to answer, "pull yourself together. The ride will do you good. And no more whisky."

"No, by Heaven, no!" he cried vehemently, and seemed to shiver; but then, suddenly taking my arm, he walked out of the room.

The morning lay still and golden. Warrington's eyes went forth across the valley.

"Come round to the stables, Ned," he said, impulsively. "You shall choose you own nag."

I shook my head. "I'll choose yours," said I, "but I am not going with you." He looked surprised.

"No, ride by yourself. You don't want a companion on such an errand. I'll stay here, and pursue my investigations into the Marvyns."

A scowl crossed his face, but only for an instant, and then he answered: "All right, old chap; do as you like. Anyway, I'm off at once." And presently, when his horse was brought, he was laughing merrily.

"You'll have a dull day, Ned; but it's your own fault, you duffer. You'll have to lunch by yourself, as I shan't be back till late." And, gaily flourishing his whip, he trotted down the drive.

It was some relief to me to be rid of him, for, in truth, his moods had worn my nerves, and I had not looked for a holiday of this disquieting nature. When he returned, I had no doubt it would be with quite another face, and meanwhile I was excellent company for myself. After lunch I amused myself for half an hour with idle tricks upon the billiard-table, and, tiring of my pastime, fell upon the housekeeper as I returned along the corridor. She was a woman nearer to sixty than fifty, with a comfortable, portly figure, and an amiable expression. Her eyes invited me ever so respectfully to conversation, and stopping, I entered into talk. She inquired if I liked my room and how I slept.

"'Tis a nice look-out you have, Sir," said she. "That was where old Lady Martin slept."

It appeared that she had served as kitchen-maid to the previous tenants of the Abbey, nearly fifty years before.

"Oh, I know the old house in and out," she asserted; "and I arranged the rooms with Mr. Warrington."

We were standing opposite the low doorway which gave entrance to Warrington's bedroom, and my eyes unconsciously shot in that direction. Mrs. Batty followed my glance.

"I didn't want him to have that," she said; "but he was set upon it. It's smallish for a bedroom, and in my opinion isn't fit for more than a lumber-room. That's what Sir William used it for."

I pushed open the door and stepped over the threshold, and the housekeeper followed me.

"No," she said, glancing round; "and it's in my mind that it's damp, Sir."

Again I had a curious feeling that the silence was speaking in my ear; the atmosphere was thick and heavy, and a musty smell, as of faded draperies, penetrated my nostrils. The whole room looked indescribably dingy, despite the new hangings. I went over to the narrow window and peered through the diamond panes. Outside, but seen dimly through that ancient and discoloured glass, the ruins of the chapel confronted me, bare and stark, in the yellow sunlight. I turned.

"There are no ghosts in the Abbey, I suppose, Mrs. Batty?" I asked, whimsically.

But she took my inquiry very gravely. "I have never heard tell of one, Sir," she protested; "and if there was such a thing I should have known it."

As I was rejoining her a strange low whirring was audible, and looking up I saw in a corner of the high-arched roof a horrible face watching me out of black narrow eyes. I confess that I was very much startled at the apparition, but the next moment realized what it was. The creature hung with its ugly fleshy wings extended over a grotesque stone head that leered down upon me, its evil-looking snout projecting into the room; it lay perfectly still, returning me glance for glance, until moved by the repulsion of its presence I clapped my hands, and cried loudly; then, slowly flitting in a circle round the roof, it vanished with a flapping of wings into some darker corner of the rafters. Mrs. Batty was astounded, and expressed surprise that it had managed to conceal itself for so long.

"Oh, bats live in holes," I answered. "Probably there is some small access through the masonry." But the incident had sent an uncomfortable shiver through me all the same.

Later that day I began to recognize that, short of an abrupt return to town, my time was not likely to be spent very pleasantly. But it was the personal problem so far as it concerned Warrington himself that distressed me even more. He came back from St.

Pharamond in a morose and ugly temper, quite alien to his kindly nature. It seems that he had quarrelled bitterly with Miss Bosanquet, but upon what I could not determine, nor did I press him for an explanation. But the fumes of his anger were still rising when we met, and our dinner was a most depressing meal.

He was in a degree of irritation which rendered it impossible to address him, and I soon withdrew into my thoughts. I saw, however, that he was drinking far too much, as, indeed, was plain subsequently when he invited me into the library. Once more he produced the hateful cards, and I was compelled to play, as he reminded me somewhat churlishly that I had promised him his revenge.

"Understand, Warrington," I said, firmly, "I play tonight, but never again, whatever the result In fact, I am in half the mind to return to town tomorrow."

He gave me a look as he sat down, but said nothing, and the game began. He lost heavily from the first, and as nothing would content him but we must constantly raise the stakes, in a shore time I had won several hundred pounds. He bore the reverses very ill, breaking out from time to time into some angry exclamation, now petulantly questioning my playing, and muttering oaths under his breath. But I was resolved that he should have no cause of complaint against me for this one night, and disregarding his insane fits of temper, I played steadily and silently. As the tally of my gains mounted he changed colour slowly, his face assuming a ghastly expression, and his eyes suspiciously denoting my actions. At length he rose, and throwing himself quickly across the table, seized my hand ferociously as I dealt a couple of cards.

"Damn you! I see your tricks," he cried, in frenzied passion. "Drop that hand, do you hear?"

"Drop that hand, or by—"

But he got no further, for, rising myself, I wrenched my hand from his grasp, and turned upon him, in almost as great a passion as himself. But suddenly, and even as I opened my mouth to speak, I stopped short with a cry of horror. His face was livid to the lips, his eyes were cast with blood, and upon the dirty white of his flesh, right in the centre of his throat, the round red scar, flaming and ugly as a wound, stared upon me.

"Warrington" I cried, "what is this? What have you?—" And I pointed in alarm to the spot.

"Mind your own business," he said, with a sneer. "It is well to try and draw off attention from your knavery. But that trick won't answer with me."

Without another word I flung the IOU's upon the table, and turning on my heel, left the room. I was furious with him, and fully resolved to leave the Abbey in the morning. I made my way up-stairs to my room, and then, seating myself upon the balcony, en-deavoured to recover my self- possession.

The more I considered, the more unaccountable was Warrington's behaviour. He had always been a perfectly courte-ous man, with a great lump of kindness in his nature; whereas these last few days he had been nothing other than a savage. It seemed certain that he must be ill or going mad; and as I reflected upon this the conjecture struck me with a sense of pity. If it was that he was losing his senses, how horrible was the tragedy in face of the new and lovely prospects opening in his life. Stimulated by this growing conviction, I resolved to go down and see him, more par-ticularly as I now recalled his pleading voice that I should help him, on the previous evening. Was it not possible that this pathetic appeal derived from the instinct of the insane to protect them-selves?

I found him still in the library; his head had fallen upon the table, and the state of the whisky bottle by his arm showed only too clearly his condition. I shook him vigorously, and he opened his eyes.

"Warrington, you must go to bed," I said.

He smiled, and greeted me quite affectionately. Obviously he was not so drunk as I had supposed.

"What is the time, Ned?" he asked.

I told him it was one o'clock, at which he rose briskly.

"Lord, I've been asleep," he said. "Help me, Ned. I don't think I'm sober. Where have you been?"

I assisted him to his room, and he undressed slowly, and with an effort. Somehow, as I stood watching him, I yielded to an unknown impulse and said, suddenly:

"Warrington, don't sleep here. Come and share my room."

"My dear fellow," he replied, with a foolish laugh, "yours is not the only room in the house. I can use half-a-dozen if I like."

"Well, use one of them," I answered.

He shook his head. "I'm going to sleep here," he returned, obstinately.

I made no further effort to influence him, for, after all, now that the words were out, I had absolutely no reason to give him or myself for my proposition. And so I left him. When I had closed the door, and was turning to go along the passage, I heard very clearly, as it seemed to me, a plaintive cry, muffled and faint, but very disturbing, which sounded from the room.

Instantly I opened the door again. Warrington was in bed, and the heavy sound of his breathing told me that he was asleep. It was impossible that he could have uttered the cry. A night-light was burning by his bedside, shedding a strong illumination over the immediate vicinity, and throwing antic shadows on the walls. As I turned to go, there was a whirring of wings, a brief flap behind me, and the room was plunged in darkness. The obscene creature that lived in the recesses of the roof must have knocked out the tiny light with its wings. Then Warrington's breathing ceased, and there was no sound at all. And then once more the silence seemed to gather round me slowly and heavily, and whisper to me. I had a vague sense of being prevailed upon, of being enticed and lured by something in the surrounding air; a sort of horror circumscribed me, and I broke from the invisible ring and rushed from the room. The door clanged behind me, and as I hastened along the hail, once more there seemed to ring in my ears the faint and melancholy cry.

I awoke, in the sombre twilight that precedes the dawn, from a sleep troubled and encumbered with evil dreams. The birds had not yet begun their day, and a vast silence brooded over the Abbey gardens. Looking out of my window, I caught sight of a dark figure

stealing cautiously round the corner of the ruined chapel. The fur-
tive gait, as well as the appearance of a man at that early hour,
struck me with surprise; and hastily throwing on some clothes, I
ran downstairs, and, opening the hall-door, went out. When I
reached the porch which gave entrance to the aisle I stopped suddenly, for there before me, with his head to the ground, and peering among the tall grasses, was the object of my pursuit. Then I
stepped quickly forward and laid a hand upon his shoulder. It was
Warrington.

"What are you doing here?" I asked.

He turned and looked at me in bewilderment. His eyes wore a
dazed expression, and he blinked in perplexity before he replied.

"It's you, is it?" he said weakly. "I thought—" and then paused.
"What is it?" he asked.

"I followed you here," I explained. "I only saw your figure, and
thought it might be some intruder."

He avoided my eyes. "I thought I heard a cry out here," he answered.

"Warrington," I said, with some earnestness, "come back to
bed."

He made no answer, and slipping my arm in his, I led him away.
On the doorstep he stopped, and lifted his face to me.

"Do you think it's possible—" he began, as if to inquire of me,
and then again paused. With a slight shiver he proceeded to his
room, while I followed him. He sat down upon his bed, and his
eyes strayed to the barred window absently. The black shadow of
the chapel was visible through the panes.

"Don't say anything about this," he said, suddenly. "Don't let
Marion know."

I laughed, but it was an awkward laugh.

"Why, that you were alarmed by a cry for help, and went in
search like a gentleman?" I asked, jestingly.

"You heard it, then?" he said, eagerly.

I shook my head, for I was not going to encourage his fancies.
"You had better go to sleep," I replied, "and get rid of these night-
mares."

He sighed and lay back upon his pillow, dressed as he was. Ere I left him he had fallen into a profound slumber.

If I had expected a surly mood in him at breakfast I was much mistaken. There was not a trace of his nocturnal dissipations; he did not seem even to remember them, and he made no allusion whatever to our adventure in the dawn. He perused a letter carefully, and threw it over to me with a grin.

"Lor, what queer sheep women are!" he exclaimed, with rather a coarse laugh.

I glanced at the letter without thinking, but ere I had read half of it I put it aside. It was certainly not meant for my eyes, and I marvelled at Warrington's indelicacy in making public, as it were, that very private matter. The note was from Miss Bosanquet, and was clearly designed for his own heart, couched as it was in the terms of warm and fond affection. No man should see such letters save he for whom they are written.

"You see, they're coming over to dine," he remarked, carelessly. "Trust a girl to make it up if you let her alone long enough."

I made no answer; but though Warrington's grossness irritated me, I reflected with satisfaction upon his return to good humour, which I attributed to the reconciliation.

When I moved out upon the terrace the maid had entered to remove the breakfast things. I was conscious of a slight exclamation behind me, and Warrington joined me presently, with a loud guffaw.

"That's a damned pretty girl!" he said, with unction. "I'm glad Mrs. Batty got her. I like to have good-looking servants."

I suddenly interpreted the incident, and shrugged my shoulders.

"You're a perfect boor this morning, Warrington," I exclaimed, irritably.

He only laughed. "You're a dull dog of a saint, Heywood," he retorted. "Come along," and dragged me out in no amiable spirit.

I had forgotten how perfect a host Warrington could be, but that evening he was displayed at his best. The Bosanquets arrived early. Sir William was an easy-going man, fond of books and of

wine, and I now guessed at the taste which had decided Warrington's cellar. Miss Bosanquet was as charming as I remembered her
to be; and if any objection might be taken to Warrington himself
by my anxious eyes it was merely that he seemed a trifle excited, a
fault which, in the circumstances, I was able to condone. Sir William hung about the table, sipping his wine.

Warrington, who had been very abstemious, grew restless, and,
finally apologizing in his graceful way, left me to keep the baronet
company. I was the less disinclined to do so as I was anxious not
to intrude upon the lovers, and Sir William was discussing the history of the Abbey.

He had an old volume somewhere in his library which related
to it, and, seeing that I was interested, invited me to look it up.

We sat long, and it was not until later that the horrible affair
which I must narrate occurred.

The evening was close and oppressive, owing to the thunder,
which already rumbled far away in the south. When we rose we
found that Warrington and Miss Bosanquet were in the garden,
and thither we followed. As at first we did not find them, Sir William, who had noted the approaching storm with some uneasiness,
left me to make arrangements for his return; and I strolled along
the paths by myself, enjoying a cigarette. I had reached the shrub-
bery upon the further side of the chapel, when I heard the sound
of voices—a man's rough and rasping, a woman's pleading and informed with fear. A sharp cry ensued, and without hesitation I
plunged through the thicket in the direction of the speakers. The
sight that met me appalled me for the moment. Darkness was falling, lit with ominous flashes; and the two figures stood out distinctly in the bushes, in an attitude of struggle. I could not mistake the voices now. I heard Warrington's, brusque with anger, and
almost savage in its tones, crying, "You shall!" and there followed
a murmur from the girl, a little sob, and then a piercing cry. I
sprang forward and seized Warrington by the arm; when, to my
horror, I perceived that he had taken her wrist in both hands
and was roughly twisting it, after the cruel habit of schoolboys.
The malevolent cruelty of the action so astounded me that for an

instant I remained motionless; I almost heard the bones in the frail wrist cracking; and then, in a second, I had seized Warrington's hands in a grip of iron, and flung him violently to the ground. The girl fell with him, and as I picked her up he rose too, and, clenching his fists, made as though to come at me, but instead turned and went sullenly, and with a ferocious look of hate upon his face, out of the thicket.

Miss Bosanquet came to very shortly, and though the agony of the pain must have been considerable to a delicate girl, I believe it was rather the incredible horror of the act under which she swooned. For my part I had nothing to say: not one word relative to the incident dared pass my lips. I inquired if she was better, and then, putting her arm in mine, led her gently towards the house. Her heart beat hard against me, and she breathed heavily, leaning on me for support. At the chapel I stopped, feeling suddenly that I dare not let her be seen in this condition, and bewildered greatly by the whole atrocious business.

"Come and rest in here," I suggested, and we entered the chapel.

I set her on a slab of marble, and stood waiting by her side. I talked fluently about anything; for lack of a subject, upon the state of the chapel and the curious tomb I had discovered. Recovering a little, she joined presently in my remarks. It was plain that she was putting a severe restraint upon herself. I moved aside the grasses, and read aloud the inscription on Sir Rupert's grave-piece, and turning to the next, which was rankly overgrown, feigned to search further. As I was bending there, suddenly, and by what thread of thought I know not, I identified the spot with that upon which I had found Warrington stooping that morning. With a sweep of my hand I brushed back the weeds, uprooting some with my fingers, and kneeling in the twilight, pored over the monument. Suddenly a wild flare of light streamed down the sky, and a great crash of thunder followed. Miss Bosanquet started to her feet and I to mine. The heaven was lit up, as it were, with sunlight, and, as I turned, my eyes fell upon the now uncovered stone. Plainly the lettering flashed in my eyes:

"Priscilla, Lady Marvyn."

Then the clouds opened, and the rain fell in spouts, shouting and dancing upon the ancient roof overhead.

We were under a very precarious shelter, and I was uneasy that Miss Bosanquet should run the risk of that flimsy, ravaged edifice; and so in a momentary lull I managed to get her to the house.

I found Sir William in a restless state of nerves. He was a timorous man, and the thunder had upset him, more particularly as he and his daughter were now storm-bound for some time. There was no possibility of venturing into those rude elements for an hour or more. Warrington was not inside, and no one had seen him. In the light Miss Bosanquet's face frightened me; her eyes were large and scared, and her colour very dead white. Clearly she was very near a breakdown. I found Mrs. Batty, and told her that the young lady had been severely shaken by the storm, suggesting that she had better lie down for a little. Returning with me, the housekeeper led off the unfortunate girl, and Sir William and I were left together. He paced the room impatiently, and constantly inquired if there were any signs of improvement in the weather. He also asked for Warrington, irritably. The burden of the whole dreadful night seemed fallen upon me. Passing through the hall I met Mrs. Batty again. Her usually placid features were disturbed and aghast.

"What is the matter?" I asked. "Is Miss Bosanquet—"

"No, Sir; I think she's sleeping," she replied. "She's in—she is in Mr. Warrington's room."

I started. "Are there no other rooms?" I asked, abruptly.

"There are none ready, Sir, except yours," she answered, "and I thought—"

"You should have taken her there," I said, sharply. The woman looked at me and opened her mouth. "Good heavens!" I said, irritably, "what is the matter? Everyone is mad tonight."

"Alice is gone, Sir," she blurted forth.

Alice, I remembered, was the name of one of her maids.

"What do you mean?" I asked, for her air of panic betokened something graver than her words.

The thunder broke over the house and drowned her voice.

"She can't be out in this storm—she must have taken refuge somewhere," I said.

At that the strings of her tongue loosened, and she burst forth with her tale. It was an abominable narrative.

"Where is Mr. Warrington?" I asked; but she shook her head.

There was a moment's silence between us, and we eyed each other aghast. "She will be all right," I said at last, as if dismissing the subject.

The housekeeper wrung her hands. "I never would have thought it!" she repeated, dismally. "I never would have thought it!"

"There is some mistake," I said; but, somehow, I knew better. Indeed, I felt now that I had almost been prepared for it.

"She ran towards the village," whispered Mrs. Batty. "God knows where she was going! The river lies that way."

"Pooh!" I exclaimed. "Don't talk nonsense. It is all a mistake. Come, have you any brandy?" Brought back to the material round of her duties she bustled away with a sort of briskness, and returned with a flagon and glasses. I took a strong nip, and went back to Sir William. He was feverish, and declaimed against the weather unceasingly. I had to listen to the string of misfortunes which he recounted in the season's crops. It seemed all so futile, with his daughter involved in her horrid tragedy in a neighbouring room. He was better after some brandy, and grew more cheerful, but assiduously wondered about Warrington.

"Oh, he's been caught in the storm and taken refuge somewhere," I explained, vainly. I wondered if the next day would ever dawn.

By degrees that thunder rolled slowly into the northern parts of the sky, and only fitful flashes seamed the heavens. It had lasted now more than two hours. Sir William declared his intention of starting, and asked for his daughter. I rang for Mrs. Batty, and sent her to rouse Miss Bosanquet.

Almost immediately there was a knock upon the door, and the housekeeper was in the doorway, with an agitated expression, demanding to see me. Sir William was looking out of the window, and fortunately did not see her.

"Please come to Miss Bosanquet, Sir," she cried, very scared. "Please come at once."

In alarm I hastily ran down the corridor and entered Warrington's room. The girl was lying upon the bed, her hair flowing upon the pillow; her eyes, wide open and filled with terror, stared at the ceiling, and her hands clutched and twined in the coverlet as if in an agony of pain. A gasping sound issued from her, as though she were struggling for breath under suffocation. Her whole appearance was as of one in the murderous grasp of an assailant.

I bent over. "Throw the light, quick," I called to Mrs. Batty; and as I put my hand on her shoulder to lift her, the creature that lived in the chamber rose suddenly from the shadow upon the further side of the bed, and sailed with a flapping noise up to the cornice. With an exclamation of horror I pulled the girl's head forward, and the candle-light glowed on her pallid face. Upon the soft flesh of the slender throat was a round red mark, the size of a florin.

At the sight I almost let her fall upon the pillow again; but, commanding my nerves, I put my arms round her, and, lifting her bodily from the bed, carried her from the room. Mrs. Batty followed.

"What shall we do?" she asked, in a low voice.

"Take her away from this damned chamber!" I cried. "Anywhere—the hall, the kitchen rather."

I laid my burden upon a sofa in the dining-room, and despatching Mrs. Batty for the brandy, gave Miss Bosanquet a draught. Slowly the horror faded from her eyes; they closed, and then she looked at me.

"What have you?—where am I?" she asked.

"You have been unwell," I said. "Pray don't disturb yourself yet."

She shuddered, and closed her eyes again.

Very little more was said. Sir William pressed for his horses, and as the sky was clearing I made no attempt to detain him, more particularly as the sooner Miss Bosanquet left the Abbey the better for herself. In half an hour she recovered sufficiently to go, and I helped her into the carriage. She never referred to her seizure, but thanked me for my kindness. That was all. No one asked after

Warrington—not even Sir William. He had forgotten everything, save his anxiety to get back. As the carriage turned from the steps I saw the mark upon the girl's throat, now grown fainter.

I waited up till late into the morning, but there was no sign of Warrington when I went to bed.

Nor had he made his appearance when I descended to breakfast. A letter in his handwriting, however, and with the London postmark, awaited me. It was a pitiful scrawl, in the very penmanship of which one might trace the desperate emotions by which he was torn. He implored my forgiveness. "Am I a devil?" he asked. "Am I mad? It was not I! It was not I!" he repeated, underlining the sentence with impetuous dashes. "You know," he wrote; "and you know, therefore, that everything is at an end for me. I am going abroad today. I shall never see the Abbey again."

It was well that he had gone, as I hardly think that I could have faced him; and yet I was loth myself to leave the matter in this horrible tangle. I felt that it was enjoined upon me to meet the problems, and I endeavoured to do so as best I might. Mrs. Batty gave me news of the girl Alice.

It was bad enough, though not so bad as both of us had feared. I was able to make arrangements on the instant, which I hoped might bury that lamentable affair for the time. There remained Miss Bosanquet; but that difficulty seemed beyond me. I could see no avenue out of the tragedy. I heard nothing save that she was ill— an illness attributed upon all hands to the shock of exposure to the thunderstorm. Only I knew better, and a vague disinclination to fly from the responsibilities of the position kept me hanging on at Utterbourne.

It was in those days before my visit to St. Pharamond that I turned my attention more particularly to the thing which had forced itself relentlessly upon me. I was never a superstitious man; the gossip of old wives interested me merely as a curious and unsympathetic observer. And yet I was vaguely discomfited by the transaction in the Abbey, and it was with some reluctance that I decided to make a further test of Warrington's bedroom. Mrs. Batty received my determination to change my room easily enough, but with a protest as to the dampness of the Stone Chamber. It was plain that her suspicions had not marched with mine. On the second night after Warrington's departure I occupied the room for the first time.

I lay awake for a couple of hours, with a reading lamp by my bed, and a volume of travels in my hand, and then, feeling very tired, put out the light and went to sleep. Nothing distracted me that night; indeed, I slept more soundly and peaceably than before in that house. I rose, too, experiencing quite an exhilaration, and it was not until I was dressing before the glass that I remembered the circumstances of my mission; but then I was at once pulled up, startled swiftly out of my cheerful temper. Faintly visible upon my throat was the same round mark which I had already seen stamped upon Warrington and Miss Bosanquet. With that, all my former doubts returned in force, augmented and militant. My mind recurred to the bat, and tales of bloodsucking by those evil creatures revived in my memory. But when I had remembered that these were of foreign beasts, and that I was in England, I dismissed them lightly enough. Still, the impress of that mark remained, and alarmed me. It could not come by accident; to suppose so manifold a coincidence was absurd. The puzzle dwelt with me, unsolved, and the fingers of dread slowly crept over me.

Yet I slept again in the room. Having but myself for company, and being somewhat bored and dull, I fear I took more spirit than was my custom, and the result was that I again slept profoundly. I awoke about three in the morning, and was surprised to find the lamp still burning.

I had forgotten it in my stupid state of somnolence. As I turned to put it out, the bat swept by me and circled for an instant above my head. So overpowered with torpor was I that I scarcely noticed it, and my head was no sooner at rest than I was once more unconscious. The red mark was stronger next morning, though, as on the previous day, it wore off with the fall of evening.

But I merely observed the fact without any concern; indeed, now the matter of my investigation seemed to have drawn very remote. I was growing indifferent, I supposed, through familiarity.

But the solitude was palling upon me, and I spent a very restless day. A sharp ride I took in the afternoon was the one agreeable experience of the day. I reflected that if this burden were to continue I must hasten up to town. I had no desire to tie myself to Warrington's apron, in his interest. So dreary was the evening, that after I had strolled round the grounds and into the chapel by moonlight, I returned to the library and endeavoured to pass the time with Warrington's cards.

But it was poor fun with no antagonist to pit myself against; and I was throwing down the pack in disgust when one of the manservants entered with the whisky.

It was not until long afterwards that I fully realized the course of my action; but even at the time I was aware of a curious subfeeling of shamefacedness. I am sure that the thing fell naturally, and that there was no awkwardness in my approaching him. Nor, after the first surprise, did he offer any objection. Later he was hardly expected to do so, seeing that he was winning very quickly. The reason of that I guessed afterwards, but during the play I was amazed to note at intervals how strangely my irritation was aroused. Finally, I swept the cards to the floor, and rose, the man, with a smile in which triumph blended with uneasiness, rose also.

"Damn you, get away!" I said, angrily.

True to his traditions to the close, he answered me with respect, and obeyed; and I sat staring at the table. With a sudden flush, the grotesque folly of the night's business came to me, and my eyes fell on the whisky bottle. It was nearly empty. Then I went to bed.

Voices cried all night in that chamber—soft, pleading voices. There was nothing to alarm in them; they seemed in a manner to coo me to sleep. But presently a sharper cry roused me from my semi-slumber; and getting up, I flung open the window. The wind rushed round the Abbey, sweeping with noises against the corners and gables. The black chapel lay still in the moonlight, and drew my eyes. But, resisting a strange, unaccountable impulse to go further, I went back to bed.

The events of the following day are better related without comment.

At breakfast I found a letter from Sir William Bosanquet, inviting me to come over to St. Pharamond. I was at once conscious of an eager desire to do so: it seemed somehow as though I had been waiting for this. The visit assumed preposterous proportions, and I was impatient for the afternoon.

Sir William was polite, but not, as I thought, cordial. He never alluded to Warrington, from which I guessed that he had been informed of the breach, and I conjectured also that the invitation extended to me was rather an act of courtesy to a solitary stranger than due to a desire for my company. Nevertheless, when he presently suggested that I should stay to dinner, I accepted promptly. For, to say the truth, I had not yet seen Miss Bosanquet, and I experienced a strange curiosity to do so. When at last she made her appearance, I was struck, almost for the first time, by her beauty. She was certainly a handsome girl, though she had a delicate air of ill-health.

After dinner Sir William remembered by accident the book on the Abbey which he had promised to show me, and after a brief hunt in the library we found it. Shortly afterwards he was called away, and with an apology left me. With a curious eagerness I turned the pages of the volume and settled down to read.

It was published early in the century, and purported to relate the history of the Abbey and its owners. But it was one chapter which specially drew my interest—that which recounted the fate of the last Marvyn. The family had become extinct through a bloody tragedy; that fact held me.

The bare narrative, long since passed from the memory of tradition, was here set forth in the baldest statements. The names of Sir Rupert Marvyn and Priscilla, Lady Marvyn, shook me strangely, but particularly the latter. Some links of connection with those gravestones lying in the Abbey chapel constrained me intimately. The history of that evil race was stained and discoloured with blood, and the end was in fitting harmony—a lurid holocaust of crime. There had been two brothers, but it was hard to choose between the foulness of their lives. If either, the younger, William, was the worse; so at least the narrative would have it. The details of his excesses had not survived, but it was abundantly plain that they were both notorious gamblers.

The story of their deaths was wrapt in doubt, the theme of conjecture only, and probability; for none was by to observe save the three veritable actors—who were at once involved together in a bloody dissolution. Priscilla, the wife of Sir Rupert, was suspected of an intrigue with her brother-in-law. She would seem to have been tainted with the corruption of the family into which she had married. But according to a second rumour, chronicled by the author, there was some doubt if the woman were not the worst of the three. Nothing was known of her parentage; she had returned with the passionate Sir Rupert to the Abbey after one of his prolonged absences, and was accepted as his legal wife. This was the woman whose infamous beauty had brought a terrible sin between the brothers.

Upon the night which witnessed the extinction of this miserable family, the two brothers had been gambling together. It was known from the high voices that they had quarrelled, and it is supposed that, heated with wine and with the lust of play, the younger had thrown some taunt at Sir Rupert in respect to his wife. Whereupon—but this is all conjecture—the elder stabbed him to death. At least, it was understood that at this point the sounds of a struggle were heard, and a bitter cry. The report of the servants ran that upon this noise Lady Marvyn rushed into the room and locked the door behind her. Fright was busy with those servants, long used to the savage manners of the house. According to witnesses, no further sound was heard subsequently to Lady Marvyn's entrance; yet when the doors were at last broken open by the authorities, the three bodies were discovered upon the floor.

How Sir Rupert and his wife met their deaths there was no record. "This tragedy," proceeded the scribe, "took place in the Stone Chamber underneath the stairway."

I had got so far when the entrance of Miss Bosanquet disturbed me. I remember rising in a dazed condition—the room swung about me. A conviction, hitherto resisted and stealthily entertained upon compulsion, now overpowered me.

"I thought my father was here," explained Miss Bosanquet, with a quick glance round the room.

I explained the circumstances, and she hesitated in my neighbourhood with a slight air of embarrassment.

"I have not thanked you properly, Mr. Heywood," she said presently, in a low voice, scarcely articulate. "You have been very considerate and kind. Let me thank you now." And ended with a tiny spasmodic sob.

Somehow, an impulse overmastered my tongue. Fresh from the perusal of that chapter, queer possibilities crowded in my mind, odd considerations urged me.

"Miss Bosanquet," said I, abruptly, "let me speak of that a little. I will not touch on details."

"Please," she cried, with a shrinking notion as of one that would retreat in very alarm.

"Nay," said I, eagerly; "hear me. It is no wantonness that would press the memory upon you."

"You have been a witness to distressful acts; you have seen a man under the influence of temporary madness. Nay, even yourself, you have been a victim to the same unaccountable phenomena."

"What do you mean?" she cried, tensely.

"I will say no more," said I. "I should incur your laughter. No, you would not laugh, but my dim suspicions would leave you still incredulous. But if this were so, and if these were the phenomena of a brief madness, surely you would make your memory a grave to bury the past."

"I cannot do that," said she, in low tones.

"What!" I asked. "Would you turn from your lover, aye, even from a friend, because he was smitten with disease? Consider; if your dearest upon earth tossed in a fever upon his bed, and denied you in his ravings, using you despitefully, it would not be he that entreated you so. When he was quit of his madness and returned to his proper person, would you not forget—would you not rather recall his insanity with the pity of affection?"

"I do not understand you," she whispered.

"You read your Bible," said I. "You have wondered at the evil spirits that possessed poor victims. Why should you decide that these things have ceased? We are too dogmatic in our modern world. Who can say under what malign influence a soul may pass, and out of its own custody?"

She looked at me earnestly, searching my eyes.

"You hint at strange things," said she, very low.

But somehow, even as I met her eyes, the spirit of my mission failed me. My gaze, I felt, devoured her ruthlessly. The light shone on her pale and comely features; they burned me with an irresistible attraction. I put forth my hand and took hers gently. It was passive to my touch, as though in acknowledgment of my kindly offices. All the while I experienced a sense of fierce elation. In my blood ran, as it had been fire, a horrible incentive, and I knew that I was holding her hand very tightly. She herself seemed to grow conscious of this, for she made an effort to withdraw her fingers, at which, the passion rushing through my body, I clutched them closer, laughing aloud. I saw a wondering look dawn in her eyes, and her bosom thinly veiled, heaved with a tiny tremor. I was aware that I was drawing her steadily to me. Suddenly her bewildered eyes, dropping from my face, lit with a flare of terror, and, wrenching her hand away, she fell back with a cry, her gaze riveted upon my throat.

"That accursed mark! What is it? What is it?—" she cried, shivering from head to foot.

In an instant, the wild blood singing in my head, I sprang towards her. What would have followed I know not, but at that moment the door opened and Sir William returned. He regarded us with consternation; but Miss Bosanquet had fainted, and the next moment he was at her side. I stood near, watching her come to with a certain nameless fury, as of a beast cheated of its prey.

Sir William turned to me, and in his most courteous manner begged me to excuse the untoward scene. His daughter, he said, was not at all strong, and he ended by suggesting that I should leave them for a time.

Reluctantly I obeyed, but when I was out of the house, I took a sudden panic. The demoniac possession lifted, and in a craven state of trembling I saddled my horse, and rode for the Abbey as if my life depended upon my speed.

I arrived at about ten o'clock, and immediately gave orders to have my bed prepared in my old room. In my shaken condition the sinister influences of that stone chamber terrified me; and it was not until I had drunk deeply that I regained my composure.

But I was destined to get little sleep. I had steadily resolved to keep my thoughts off the matter until the morning, but the spell of the chamber was strong upon me. I awoke after midnight with an irresistible feeling drawing me to the room. I was conscious of the impulse, and combated it, but in the end succumbed; and throwing on my clothes, took a light and went downstairs. I flung wide the door of the room and peered in, listening, as though for some voice of welcome. It was as silent as a sepulchre; but directly I crossed the threshold voices seemed to surround and coax me. I stood wavering, with a curious fascination upon me. I knew I could not return to my own room, and I now had no desire to do so. As I stood, my candle flaring solemnly against the darkness, I noticed upon the floor in an alcove bare of carpet, a large black mark, which appeared to be a stain. Bending down, I examined it, passing my fingers over the stone. It moved to my touch. Setting the candle upon the floor, I put my fingertips to the edges, and pulled hard. As I did so the sounds that were ringing in my ears died instantaneously; the next moment the slab turned with a crash, and discovered a gaping hole of impenetrable blackness.

The patch of chasm thus opened to my eyes was near a yard square. The candle held to it shed a dim light upon a stone step a foot or two below, and it was clear to me that a stairway communicated with the depths. Whether it had been used as a cellar in times gone by I could not divine, but I was soon to determine this doubt; for, stirred by a strange eagerness, I slipped my legs through the hole, and let myself cautiously down with the light in my hand. There were a dozen steps to descend ere I reached the floor and what turned out to be a narrow passage. The vault ran forward straight as an arrow before my eyes, and slowly I moved on. Dank and chill was the air in those close confines, and the sound of my feet returned from those walls dull and sullen. But I kept on, and, with infinite care, must have penetrated quite a hundred yards along that musty corridor ere I came out upon an ampler chamber. Here the air was freer, and I could perceive with the aid of my light that the dimensions of the place were lofty. Above, a solitary ray of moonlight, sliding through a crack, informed me that I was not far from the level of the earth. It fell upon a block of stone, which rose in the middle of the vault, and which I now inspected with interest. As the candle threw its flickering beams upon this I realized where I was.

I scarcely needed the rude lettering upon the coffins to acquaint me that here was the family vault of the Marvyns. And now I began to perceive upon all sides whereon my feeble light fell the crumbling relics of the forgotten dead—coffins fallen into decay, bones and grinning skulls resting in corners, disposed by the hand of chance and time. This formidable array of the mortal remains of that poor family moved me to a shudder. I turned from those ugly memorials once more to the central altar where the two coffins rested in this sombre silence. The lid had fallen from the one, disclosing to my sight the grisly skeleton of a man, that mocked and leered at me.

It seemed in a manner to my fascinated eyes to challenge my mortality, inviting me too to the rude and grotesque sleep of death. I knew, as by an instinct, that I was standing by the bones of Sir Rupert Marvyn, the protagonist in that terrible crime which had locked three souls in eternal ruin. The consideration of this miserable spectacle held me motionless for some moments, and then I moved a step closer and cast my light upon the second coffin.

As I did so I was aware of a change within myself. The grave and melancholy thoughts which I had entertained, the sober bent of my solemn reflections, gave place instantly to a strange exultation, an unholy sense of elation. My pulse swung feverishly, and, while my eyes were riveted upon the tarnished silver of the plate, I stretched forth a tremulously eager hand and touched the lid. It rattled gently under my fingers. Disturbed by the noise, I hastily withdrew them; but whether it was the impetus offered by my touch, or through some horrible and nameless circumstance—God knows—slowly and softly a gap opened between the lid and the body of the coffin! Before my startled eyes the awful thing happened, and yet I was conscious of no terror, merely of surprise and—it seems terrible to admit—of a feeling of eager expectancy.

The lid rose slowly on the one side, and as it lifted the dark space between it and the coffin grew gently charged with light. At that moment my feeble candle, which had been gradually diminishing, guttered and flickered. I seemed to catch a glimpse of something, as it were, of white and shining raiment inside the coffin; and then came a rush of wings and a whirring sound within the vault. I gave a cry, and stepping back missed my foothold; the guttering candle was jerked from my grasp, and I fell prone to the floor in darkness. The next moment a sheet of flame flashed in the chamber and lit up the grotesque skeletons about me; and at the same time a piercing cry rang forth. Jumping to my feet, I gave a dazed glance at the conflagration. The whole vault was in flames. Dazed and horror-struck, I rushed blindly to the entrance; but as I did so the horrible cry pierced my ears again, and I saw the bat swoop round and circle swiftly into the flames. Then, finding the exit, I dashed with all the speed of terror down the passage, groping my way along the walls, and striking myself a dozen times in my terrified flight.

Arrived in my room, I pushed over the stone and listened. Not a sound was audible. With a white face and a body torn and bleeding I rushed from the room, and locking the door behind me, made my way upstairs to my bedroom. Here I poured myself out a stiff glass of brandy.

It was six months later ere Warrington returned. In the meantime he had sold the Abbey. It was inevitable that he should do so; and yet the new owner, I believe, has found no drawback in his property, and the Stone Chamber is still used for a bedroom upon occasions, being considered very old-fashioned. But there are some facts against which no appeal is possible, and so it was in his case. In my relation of the tragedy I have made no attempt at explanation, hardly even to myself; and it appears now for the first time in print, of course with suppositious names.

COACHWHIP PUBLICATIONS

COACHWHIPBOOKS.COM

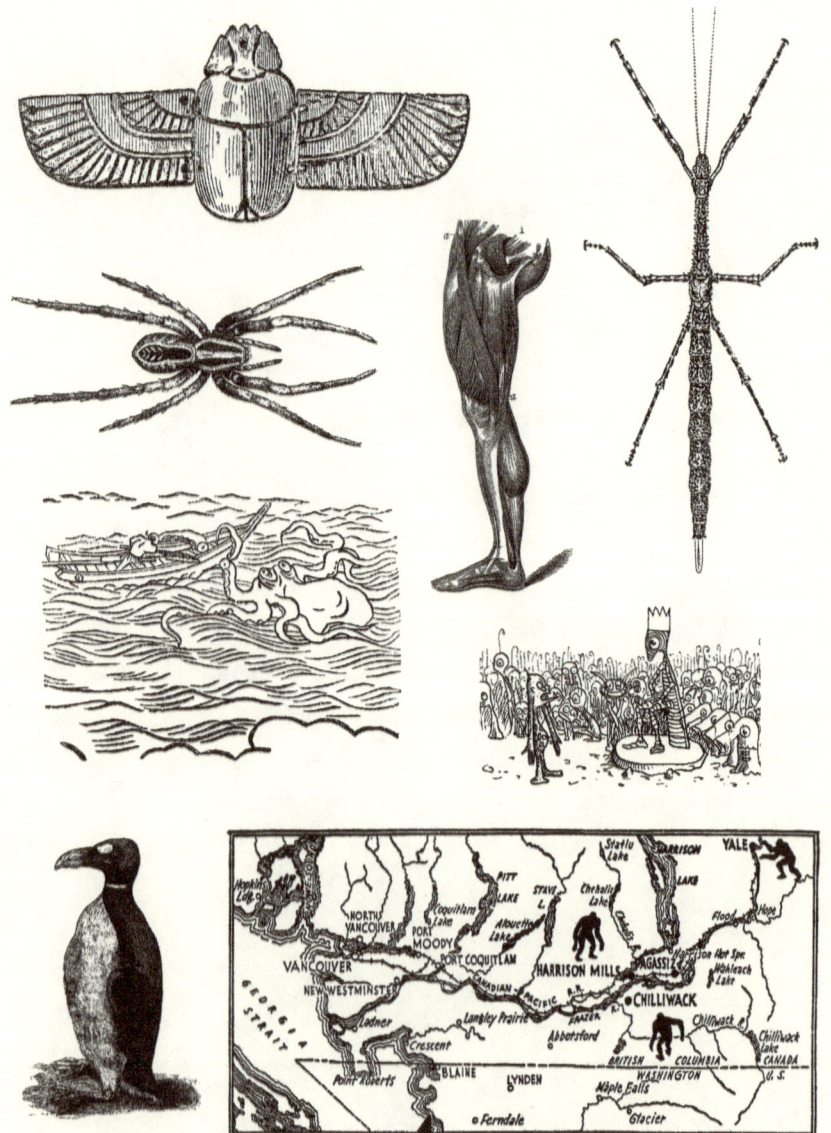

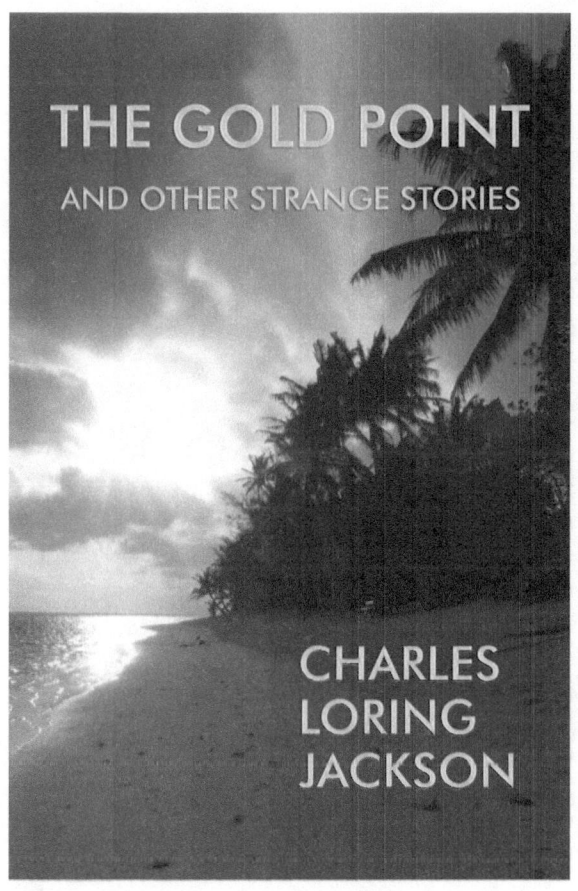

The Gold Point and Other Strange Stories
ISBN 1-61646-085-7

COACHWHIP PUBLICATIONS

COACHWHIPBOOKS.COM

BLACK SPIRITS
AND WHITE
RALPH ADAMS CRAM

TALES OF THE
SUPERNATURAL
JAMES PLATT

SHADOWS GOTHIC
AND GROTESQUE

Shadows Gothic and Grotesque
ISBN 1-61646-059-8

Coachwhip Publications

Also Available

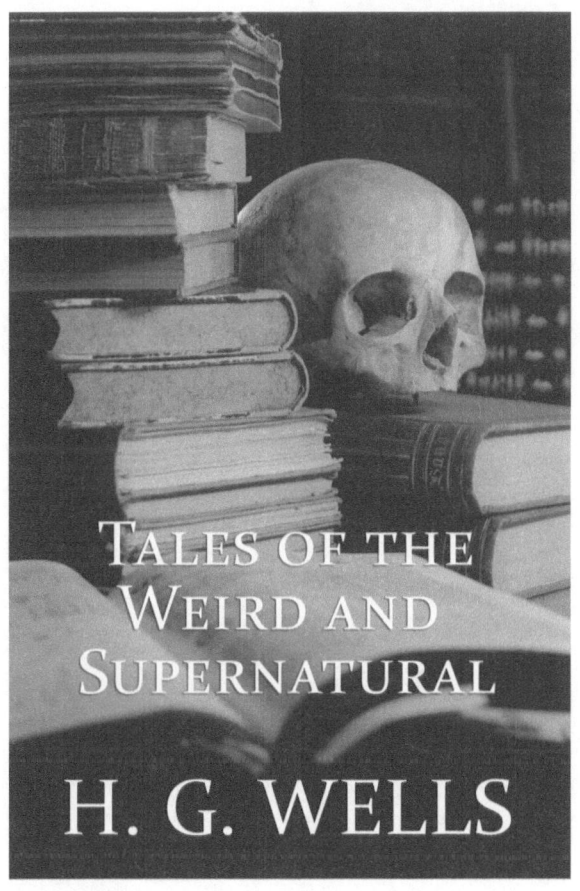

H. G. Wells:
Tales of the Weird and Supernatural
ISBN 1-61646-072-5

www.ingramcontent.com/pod-product-compliance
Lightning Source LLC
Chambersburg PA
CBHW020638260626
47157CB00008B/2799